# WOMEN OF Fire AND Snow

SHORT STORIES

NATI DEL PASO

Para mis mujeres de fuego, de nieve y de sangre: Pia, Gigi, Sophia, Regina, y Raphaella.

ISBN: 978-1-66780-063-9
eBook ISBN: 978-1-66780-064-6

# CONTENTS

# Illegal Matters

**ANTONIA RODE THE BUS** to work while trying to do her chemistry homework on her phone. When her phone buzzed for the third time, she glanced at the texts from her mother: "*La migra tiene a papá.*"

Her throat tightened; fear gripped her gut. What would her father do? Who would take care of her mother, brothers, and little sister? She debated getting off the bus and making her way home instead of going to work. Her family lived in Ocean Shores, Washington, three hours from Seattle where she attended university. She called her mother, but it went to voicemail.

Antonia shoved the phone into her bag, first checking to see if Ethan, her boyfriend, had texted her. Nothing. She rushed to JennyPho, the Vietnamese restaurant where she worked since her freshman year. The September rains had people craving hot soup, and the place was busy even though it was not yet 6:00 p.m.

Antonia hung her backpack and jacket in the back room and pulled on an apron over her black jeans and T-shirt, cinching it tight across her tiny waist. Braiding her chocolate-colored hair, she blinked away the tears from her brown eyes and practiced smiling.

Ngoc walked in and asked, "What's wrong?" as she piled her backpack on top of Antonia's and reached for an identical apron. Ngoc was the same height as Antonia, barely over five feet tall, slight, and sylphlike with dark brown eyes. Although Ngoc was born in the US, they shared a bond as daughters of immigrants.

"How do you know?" asked Antonia.

Ngoc shrugged, then flipped her bangs that kept getting into her eyes, making her ponytail bounce.

"My father was detained by ICE."

Ngoc hugged her tightly. "I'm sorry. Are you alright?"

Antonia shook her head. "I don't know what to do."

"What happens if they send him back?"

"I don't know. Most of the family is here." Antonia sighed and squeezed Ngoc's arm. "Let's get to work. There is nothing I can do right now."

For the next four hours, they stuffed spring rolls, chopped jalapeños, and carried trays of steaming bowls of *pho* to hungry patrons. When Joe, the owner, came in to close at eight thirty, Antonia asked to speak privately. Slender and agile, the middle-aged man was kind and supportive.

Leading her to his back office that also doubled as the supply closet, he offered her one of the two folding chairs.

"How's school?" asked Joe, smiling. "Are you a doctor now? Are you going to quit?"

Antonia shook her head and swallowed. "I'm not in med school yet; I have two years before I apply. I need your advice."

"Of course!" said Joe. Antonia trusted him. An immigrant from Vietnam after the fall of Saigon, who was barely making it with his restaurant, Joe was fair and flexible when they were in exams. "How can I help?"

She told him what she knew.

"You need a lawyer for your father."

"We don't have money. Can we get a public defender?"

Joe shook his head. "There are no public defenders for the undocumented in immigration court. You will have to pay for a lawyer. Does your mother have papers?"

Antonia shook her head. "Only twin brothers were born here." Antonia slumped in her chair. This was hopeless. "Do you know any lawyers?"

Joe reached into his back pocket and pulled out a business card from his wallet. "The lawyer that helped me get my papers retired, but a lawyer who was here for lunch gave me his card. I'll also give you a couple months' advance."

Antonia thanked Joe and went to get her backpack. Ngoc was waiting for her. Antonia sat on a chair in the utility room with her head in her hands; Ngoc put her hand on her back.

"I need to get a lawyer, and I don't know how I am going to pay for it."

"We'll figure it out together. We'll rob a bank!"

Antonia smiled. She thought Ngoc would probably help her rob a bank if she asked. She supported her mother, working two jobs with no benefits while going to school, completing her prerequisite classes one at a time so she could apply to a nursing program.

"It might be the only way," said Antonia. "Let's go. I need to call my mom and find out exactly what happened."

Antonia checked her phone during the twenty-minute ride home, but Ethan had still not replied to any of her texts. As she approached her stop, she fished out the can of pepper spray she carried everywhere. Then, jumping over puddles, she ran through the light rain to the narrow two-story house where she rented a tiny room in the basement, cheaper than the dorms. She peered at the entrance, calling:

"Mr. John?"

"What's the password?" a raspy voice came from the dark stairwell under the front steps.

"Taco Tuesday."

"Good evening, m'lady."

Antonia sighed in relief. Mr. John was an elderly homeless man that slept at the bottom of the stairs to her room. The owner of the house made sure he had food, blankets, and even medicine, and in return, he watched their home. They'd tried getting him services, but Mr. John refused, claiming the system always screwed the black man.

After locking herself in, she flopped on the bed and dialed her mother, who answered at the first ring.

"*Mami, que pasó?*"

"I'm so worried *m'hija*. Two officers who always sit in their car outside the oyster farm and watch the employees—"

"What officers?"

"The *migra*! They sit in their car and watch the employees of the oyster farm. Once, they took four workers. This time they took your father. We had just dropped the twins with Nora, the babysitter. Her husband is the one in jail for hitting her, remember?"

"Mami, please! Just tell me what happened."

"*Uf!* You're always in a bad mood! They stopped us; the officers knew our names. After letting Papi park the truck in a safe place, they handcuffed him and took him away. Mimi and I walked home."

"Where did they take him? Why now?"

"I don't know, but they're taking workers who never break the law. *Que vamos a hacer?*"

"Don't worry, Mami. Joe recommended a lawyer and will give me an advance. Text me if you hear from Papi. I need to study."

Antonia took out a yogurt from the mini fridge, which together with a hotplate on top of a file cabinet and a microwave made up her kitchen. She sat eating at the card table against the wall piled with books and her laptop. It was tiny but she had her own bathroom.

Antonia reheated black coffee and sat at the kitchen table to study, pushing away the worry for her father. There was nothing she could do for him at the moment, so she immersed herself in her work. Time flew as she fell into a flow when the buzz of her phone interrupted her; it was a text from Ethan. "Sent you my essay. Let me know what you think."

"Shit!" she thought, "I don't have time." She fought a pang of annoyance. Ethan hadn't answered her texts all day, and now he expected her to help with his homework? She sighed, I'm lucky he's with me. Wasn't love about being there for one another? Exhausted, she reviewed the essay, making corrections as she went. She emailed him the edits, proud about editing a native speaker's paper. Ethan needed her.

Antonia fell asleep at the kitchen table doing chemistry problems. She awoke at 5:00 a.m. and was out the door by 5:30. The warmth of the taco truck welcomed her as she rushed into the small space where the owners, Mr. and Mrs. Sanchez, greeted her like always with a hot mug of coffee and a black bean burrito.

"Stayed up late again?" asked Mrs. Sanchez, peering at the deep bags underneath Antonia's eyes.

"Chemistry test," she answered, not wanting to worry them with her problems. They were also undocumented.

"One day, you'll be getting up late and going to play golf before you go see your patients," Mrs. Sanchez chuckled, giving Antonia a one-armed hug. Antonia grinned in return and went to work preparing the breakfast burritos.

"Morning," she said to Mr. Sanchez, the burly man cooking bacon and eggs on the grill.

"*Buenos días,* Antonia. I know you have class, but we need you to stay just five minutes after we close."

Antonia nodded, pursing her lips. Damn it! She wouldn't have time to review her notes before class. For the next two hours, she steamed burritos and poured coffee and orange juice for construction workers, baggy-eyed medical personnel, and early-bird students.

A woman in scrubs returned her burrito to Antonia complaining.

"I asked without hot sauce; it's too spicy."

"No, you said mild salsa. It has mild salsa."

"Well, this isn't mild. I can't eat this."

Antonia took the paper plate, burrito and all, and threw it in the trash. She called out to Mr. Sanchez.

"Veggie burrito NO salsa, not even mild!"

"Forget it!" the woman huffed as she walked away.

"What's the matter?" asked Mrs. Sanchez.

Antonia's face burned. This was the third time Sra. Sanchez asked. I could've handled that client better. She forced herself to smile and be polite for the rest of her shift.

By eight fifteen, when the food ran out, Mr. Sanchez closed the windows of the taco truck, fished something out of his pocket, and handed it to Antonia.

"What's this?" she asked.

"We want to help you apply for DACA."

"But this is too much!" said Antonia, holding up the roll of twenty-dollar bills.

"One thousand," specified Mrs. Sanchez.

"There's enough for you and your sister Lily," explained Mr. Sanchez.

"Mimi!" corrected Mrs. Sanchez.

"Thank you so much, but I can't accept this," Antonia said, trying to return the money.

"Nonsense!" he said, shooing her away. "Now go to school so you can cure me of my gout."

Antonia hugged them both, her heart bursting. She stuffed the large cash roll in her jeans' pocket, and left the truck. Tilting her head, she breathed in the cool morning air scented with pine and seawater and swore she would never be cranky at work again. The bright blue of the sky contrasted with the green of the pines and the bright yellows and reds of the maples, offering respite from the stream of eternal Seattle gray rainy days. Mid-breath, she remembered her father, and the light feeling vanished, replaced by a heaviness in her heart. She rushed into chemistry class, catching Ethan leaning over the desk and talking to a blond girl who had been flirting with him since the quarter started. A blush spread across her cheeks and she forced a smile as she approached.

"Hi," she said.

Ethan quickly stood up straight. "Hi," he answered, kissing her on the cheek. A handsome young man with curly brown hair, fine features, and blue eyes, he was different from the other young men. Ethan was a self-proclaimed artist who wrote poetry and short stories, rejecting pop culture and anything commercial or made for the masses. She felt special when he included her among his small circle of confidants. When they'd met, he was fascinated with her undocumented status, but Antonia worried he would realize how ordinary she was and would dump her.

The blond girl looked Antonia up and down before turning to the person behind her. Ethan and Antonia took the seats next to her.

"How was the test?" Antonia asked.

"Shhhh!" Ethan looked around to see if anyone had heard her. "I don't want anyone to know I am repeating calculus."

Especially the girl next to you. Antonia assessed the blond girl's looks from the corner of her eye, she was very pretty.

"I have bad news about my dad. They stopped him for a traffic stop, and immigration has him," maybe he'll feel guilty for flirting.

"Antonia, I am sorry about your dad. It sucks!" he squeezed her arm. "Maybe I can come over after work tonight?"

Antonia nodded, touched that he cared for her. Everyone flirts, she told herself, but he cares about me and my problems; that's what counts. She took out her notebook and silenced her phone. Ethan leaned over and whispered in her ear:

"I know you have a lot on your plate right now, but did you review my paper?"

"Yes, I did. I sent it to you at 1:00 a.m."

"Thanks. I haven't had time to check my email."

The professor started the class.

As she walked to her psychology class, Antonia saw a missed call from a number she did not recognize. She checked her voicemail—it was her dad.

"You need to get a lawyer, *hija*. Can you bring your mami to see me in Portland?"

Antonia swallowed the lump in her throat that threatened to cut off her breath. With a three-and-a-half-hour bus ride each way, there was no way she would make it back in time for her shift at JennyPho. A nagging fear settled among her thoughts, where was she going to get the money if she didn't work?

By midafternoon, Antonia and her mother arrived at the detention center. The trip cost $100.

Antonia was surprised to see protesters surrounding the ICE building.

"Look!" She elbowed her mother and pointed at the signs that read, "Abolish ICE."

Her mother peered at her, perplexed. "Why are they here?"

"They are here for us, Mami! They're protesting ICE." Suddenly, Antonia did not feel so alone.

"I'm sorry we brought you here."

"I'm not! I'm glad I am here and not back with *Abuela*. There are no schools there, no work either."

Mother sighed. "What if they put us in prison? At least your brothers were born here. If you marry Ethan, he can make you a citizen."

"We'll get married; I'll be a doctor and take care of you and the family." Antonia tried to sound more confident than she felt, for Mami but also for herself.

Her mother sighed and squeezed her arm. "Sometimes, I don't know who you are anymore."

"I'm still me, Mami!" Antonia stopped, searching her mother's face.

"You have your own home, your ideas. You're more a *gringa* every day."

"I wish I was! Then they wouldn't deport us."

Her mother gripped her arm and muttered, "*Tu hija, ni de aquí, ni de allá.*"

They walked into the building, Antonia shaking with every step as sweat pearled on her forehead, her mother looking around like a scared mouse. After going through a metal detector and leaving their bags in a locker, they huddled together in the stark, cold visiting room, metal tables and chairs reminding them where they were. Spotting her father coming through the door, Antonia waved. Dark circles shadowed his eyes. Rushing into his arms, she clung to him; her mother did the same on the other side. All three of them were blinking furiously, trying to hold back their tears.

"We don't have much time," Antonia said, dabbing at her eyes as she sat back on the bench. Her mother patted her hand gently.

"*Como estás*?" asked Antonia's mother.

"I'm ok. *Ustedes*?" father said.

"We're fine. Antonia's working to get a lawyer."

Her mother caressed her father's arm, looking him over. He turned to Antonia, "Gracias, *hija*. When you talk to the lawyer, tell him they caught me trying to come in with a fake green card before we brought you here. Also, they will transfer me to Tacoma soon."

Antonia nodded. If only she had her cell phone to write notes.

"Are they feeding you?" asked her mother, touching his cheek.

"*Si.* How will you get to work?"

They both turned to Antonia.

"I can take you, Mami," she said. "I'll drop out."

"Wait! I can get a ride from Juan Martinez. Stay in school until we know what happens."

"You mean if they deport me?" asked her father.

"It won't happen, Papi; I have the name of a lawyer. You've never broken the law. It can't happen, right?"

"And the twins were born here!" added her mother.

He nodded without meeting their eyes. A loud buzzer sounded overhead making them jump.

Father rose and took Antonia's hands. "Take care of your mother and your brothers and sister. If I get deported, sell the truck and use the money. Do not come to Mexico! *Me oyes?* It is too dangerous for girls there."

"Yes, Papi, I'll take care of everything."

Antonia looked down, blinking away tears as her parents held each other and said goodbye.

Back on the bus, Antonia smiled as she listened to a message from Ethan saying how he supported her and all undocumented people. She texted an update to Ngoc, who had been sending Antonia encouraging emojis throughout the day and tried to study by reading her phone.

The next day, Antonia skipped anthropology class to meet with the lawyer before work. She checked in with a receptionist and waited in a small reception area until a balding, redheaded man came out and extended a small hand in greeting.

"Ms. Cardenas? I am Lee Welch."

Antonia shook the outstretched hand as he looked her up and down. Did he hold my hand a little longer than normal? She shrugged it off. He was smiling at her kindly. He probably didn't expect someone so young. Welch was in his early sixties, with a bald crown surrounded by thin, wispy hair stretched in a semicircle from one ear to the other. Freckles covered his face and forehead. He limped a little as he led her into his office, where boxes overflowing with files lined a corner and a film of plastic still covered the file cabinet. The walls were empty of pictures and decorations, and only a computer adorned the large desk. She slid into a chair in front of his desk, and he sat across from her. Music played from his computer, a man with a deep raspy voice sang "Hallelujah."

Welch silenced the music and smiled. "How can I help, Ms. Cardenas?"

Antonia told Welch about her dad. He listened attentively, asking questions and taking notes on a large yellow pad.

"Your father was caught with a fake green card?"

Antonia blushed and nodded. "He said to tell you he was stopped at the border and sent back. He returned six months later."

Welch frowned. "I can take a look at his case, but if ICE detained him before, there might not be anything I can do. Can you pay my retainer?"

"How much is it?"

"I will need ten thousand dollars up front plus costs after that. I know it's a lot of money, but these things are expensive."

Antonia bit her lower lip. Where would she get that kind of money? "Can we make a payment plan?"

Welch laughed and stared at her with interest. "What do you do?"

"I am a full-time student at UW, and I have two jobs."

"Whoa! Two jobs? And you go to school full-time?"

"Yes, I am majoring in biology, pre-med. I work as a server at a Vietnamese restaurant, and in the morning, I work at a burrito and *tamal* truck."

"What kind of tamales? I love Mexican food."

"They're not your usual tamales. These are Oaxaca style. They're wrapped in banana leaves with mole sauce, stuffed with pork or chicken."

"Well, Antonia, let's meet back here on Friday at four. Bring me a couple of those tamales, and I will see what we can do."

Antonia asked Ngoc to accompany her to the appointment on Friday so they could go from there to a party, but secretly she wanted company, unsure about the lawyer. Welch showed them into his office, and Antonia caught him looking them up and down as they shook off their jackets. She tugged on her short dress, wishing they hadn't come dressed up for the party.

"We're going to a party on campus," volunteered Antonia, letting him know they weren't dressed up for him.

"I thought it would cheer her up," added Ngoc.

Welch brought out another chair for Ngoc and sat behind his desk. He took out a manila folder and tapped it with his fingers. "I won't sugarcoat anything; this is a complicated case."

Antonia swallowed.

"But I think I can help. If I'm going to do this, I will need your help. You and I will be meeting a lot."

"Of course!" said Antonia. "I'll do whatever it takes. I'm thinking of taking the quarter off so I can have more time to work."

"You can't do that!" said Ngoc. She turned to Welch. "She's the top student in her class. She's going to med school." Looking at Antonia, she said, "If you leave now, you will lose your financial aid!"

"No one is dropping out of school," said Welch. "I'm sure we can work something out. Antonia, at what time do you finish at the restaurant?"

"Around ten or ten thirty."

"Mmmmm—" he said, biting on a pencil's eraser, "I'm here nine to five, seven, if I have a lot of work. Could you meet at eight thirty in the morning?"

Antonia shook her head, chewing on her nails. "I work at the truck, and my first class is at 9:30 a.m."

"Well, I have a meeting on Tuesdays downtown that ends around nine—"

"She can be here at 9:00 p.m.," said Ngoc.

"I can't—"

"Yes, you can. On Tuesdays, I'll clean up the restaurant until your father is free. That way, you'll have time to come here and then get home to study."

"Ok, then!" exclaimed Welch enthusiastically, "We have a plan. We will need documents, and I'll need to talk to your mother."

Antonia left the office full of hope. She took out her phone to order an Uber and swore, "Fuck!"

"What?"

"Ethan wants us to go to a poetry reading instead. I guess he forgot about the party. Do you mind?"

Ngoc shrugged. "We promised a lot of people we would be there."

"I know! I'm sorry. Just this time." Antonia batted her eyes and pouted. "Please?"

Ngoc laughed. "Fine," she said, "but this is the last time. He always does this to you!"

"Not always! I thought you liked him?"

"I did at the beginning when he'd give us rides home after work, but—"

"But what?"

"You always do what he wants."

"Come on! Just this last time, I promise. He has been weird, so this way, I'll get to talk to him."

"Ok," Ngoc said, giving in.

Exhausted and nervous, Tuesday evening, Antonia followed the lawyer through an empty building to his office and sat by his desk. Instead of sitting behind his desk, Welch sat in the chair next to hers.

"How are you doing?" asked Welch. "How is school?"

"School's ok."

"Just ok? Your friend implied you were doing great."

Antonia shrugged; the quiet building was unnerving. "I study hard, but I'm a little behind with all that's happening."

He nodded. "So, after talking to your mother on the phone and reviewing your father's case, it will be difficult and a lot of hard work on my part, but I think I can help you."

"Really?"

Welch took her hand. Antonia stiffened but didn't pull it away. "I want to help you, but this is not going to be cheap."

Antonia pulled her hand away and pushed her chair back. “I have three thousand for your retainer but—”

“I want to help you and your family, Antonia, but you know better than anyone that a person needs to make a living. If I take on the case, I will be giving up paying clients. Now, if you come after work and help me out here, then I could take on your case and will only charge you the $3000.”

“Help you out? Like file or clean the office?”

“Yeah, something like that,” Welch said, putting his hand on her knee.

Antonia’s face flushed. Welch’s slender, delicate fingers, which had never known manual labor, nauseated her. She froze.

Welch leaned in to kiss her on the mouth, but she turned her head, and he kissed her neck. His lips were dry and hot. He snaked his hand up her thigh; she pushed it away and stood up.

“Stop!” she said.

His eyes flashed in anger.

“I have my period, sorry.” She crossed her arms around her chest. Her heart beating furiously, avoiding his eyes.

His eyes softened. “OK. You know who doesn’t have a period?” He smiled, unzipping his pants. “Come here, you funny little thing.”

Antonia rode the bus with her arms wrapped around her and the hoody of her jacket hiding her face. Every time Welch intruded on her thoughts, she visualized the human body and named each bone until she jumped from the bus and marched home, forgetting to take out her pepper spray. She called out for Mr. John but Ethan answered instead.

“Hey!”

"Hi," she answered, her face growing hot, grateful for the dark.

"I've missed you," he said, hugging her as she unlocked the door, then kissing her neck and touching her breast.

She pushed his hand away. "I'm so tired. I've hardly slept since my dad's arrest."

But Ethan was already inside. Antonia bolted to the bathroom without turning on the light.

Ethan followed her. "How is he? Did you find a lawyer?"

Antonia locked the bathroom door and leaned against it. "I'll be right out."

She washed her face and brushed her teeth followed by mouthwash. He can never find out. No one can.

When she came out, Ethan put his arms around her and ground his hips into her. "Don't you want me anymore? Haven't you missed me?" His hands wandered over her back.

She wanted to hide her face in his chest and cry, but he'd ask her what was wrong. "I have missed you, but you never reply to my texts."

"But I'm always thinking about you." He looked her in the eye. "You're the only one that can get me to sleep." He kissed her on the mouth. "I know you are tired, so just help me out. I'll come quick, I promise." He was already zipping down his pants and unbuckling his belt. Antonia knelt in front of him, taking him in her mouth. At least he loves me.

The next day, Antonia glanced around the bookstore when they denied her card. Blushing, she scurried away. Head bowed. Eyes glued to the floor. I need that psychology textbook! Her hand shook as she called her mother.

"*Que pasó?*" answered her mother. "Any news from the lawyer?"

"Nothing yet, Mami. Did you take money from my account?"

"I used the card to buy soccer uniforms for your brothers. It was only eighty-five dollars."

"I was going to buy my textbook with that money, but now I don't have enough."

"Just go to the library, *m'hija*."

Antonia bit her tongue. Her mother didn't understand that you couldn't check out textbooks. "Mami, do you have enough now that Papi can't work?"

"We've never had enough! But we'll get by."

"I'll deposit some money tomorrow, Mami, so you buy groceries and pay the bills, ok?" Antonia touched the roll of bills Mr. and Mrs. Sanchez had given her.

"*Bueno.* Be safe and call me if you hear anything from the lawyer."

Antonia sighed and said good night.

For the first time, Antonia overslept, after tossing and turning most of the night. Late to the food truck, she noticed *señora* Sanchez glancing at her every few minutes, trying to guess what was wrong. Determined to keep her secret, she left before she could ask, then slept through psychology.

Ethan waited for her at the door of their chemistry class. "Antonia, I think we should open our relationship."

Antonia looked around the busy hallway, someone jostled her with their backpack. "Can we talk about this later?"

"You never have time to talk; you're always working or studying. I'm just tired of this."

"What do you mean?"

"When you're not working, you're doing homework or going to see your family. I just need to be able to hang out with other people."

Heat spread up from her neck to her face. She crossed her arms, hating him, smug and full of himself. "You mean other girls?"

"What's wrong with that? I just don't want us to be exclusive, but we'd still be together."

Antonia blinked back the tears; I won't let him see me cry! He wants me for sex but wants to date the blond. She tried to say something hurtful, clever but could only think of things in Spanish Ethan couldn't understand. Her body buzzed, and her stomach tightened. Gritting her teeth, she sat next to him as the professor started the test.

As always, Ethan positioned himself to copy her answers and she let him cheat as usual. After he turned in his test and strutted out of the classroom, she quickly changed her answers.

"Thanks!" Ethan said when she met him outside. "Can I come over tonight so we can finish talking?"

Before she could reply, the blond rushed over and kissed Ethan on the cheek, "Thanks for letting me copy your test. You're a genius!"

"Yeah, you bet he is," replied Antonia, walking away. Ethan watched her leave, a puzzled look on his face.

The following Tuesday, Antonia waited for her friend Anahi outside Welch's office. She had asked her to go with her, ostensibly because Anahi also needed immigration advice. After thirty minutes had passed with no sign of her friend and no return texts, Antonia debated what to do when Welch opened the door of the building. She pretended to be late.

He smiled back and stepped aside to let her in. They went to his office and locked the door.

Antonia stared at his beer belly in disgust. He immediately pushed her against his office door and put his hand on her breast. She shoved his hand away.

"Wait! Before you do anything, tell me what you have done about my father's case."

"Come on, show me some appreciation first." He tried to hug her, but Antonia ducked and moved farther away from him. She needed time.

"Before I do anything, tell me about my father's case."

"You're feisty today. Well, your father has a hearing next Tuesday afternoon at the Tacoma Detention Center. Do you still want me to be there as his lawyer?"

"Really? This coming Tuesday? Is that good or bad?"

"If he has a lawyer at the hearing, there is a good chance he can get out, but if you no longer need my help…"

"What do I need to do?"

"We need to go to the next level. This is a complicated case. I want to make love to you. Are you committed to seeing this through?"

He licked his lips, and her flesh crawled. I need to buy some time. "I'll do what you want but not here."

Welch smiled. "I know the perfect place! I'll get us a cabin in Snoqualmie for the weekend."

"I work on Saturdays—"

"Your father's hearing is the following Tuesday. One night is not that much to ask, is it?"

Later that night, Antonia researched a free legal agency Anahi recommended, but the application for services took a month. Closing her laptop, she put her face in her hands. If they deport my father, we're all screwed! Even working full-time there wouldn't be enough to support the family, not as long as she didn't have a degree. She'd have to go through with it. Her stomach rolled. Sighing, she opened the laptop and searched for Snoqualmie. The city was thirty miles east of Seattle, nestled in the Cascades. It sat between three forks of the Snoqualmie River and was famous for its waterfalls and being haunted.

As Antonia read that Snoqualmie was a known dumping ground for organized crime and the Green River Killer himself buried five bodies there, an alarm rang in her mind. What if Welch didn't want only sex? She shook her head, smothering the warning blasting inside her. Murders only happened in the movies. I should tell someone just in case, but who? No one could ever know about what Welch made her do.

Antonia clicked on a link to a site called Snoqualmie Strange. The website declared Snoqualmie was a mystical place where magical creatures roamed the woods traveling through portals to other dimensions. Jim Saint James, the author of the site, explained he was the last in a succession of eight wardens who protected Snoqualmie territory and the portals to other worlds. There were tabs for reporting strange events, photos of tools the wardens used, and a list of dates when the portals opened, warning visitors to stay away.

That's silly! The internet was full of made-up stuff. She closed the website. She looked in the mirror at the dark circles under her eyes and her features, sharper from weight loss. I can do this. I will have sex with that creep and get my father out and never see him again. She opened her psychology book and struggled to read while images of dead bodies distracted her.

After work on Wednesday, Antonia and Ngoc sat drinking bubble tea after cleaning up the restaurant. Making sure Joe and the cook weren't near, Antonia leaned in and whispered. "I'm calling in sick on Saturday."

"Why?"

"Family drama; I'll be sleeping at my mom's."

"What's wrong?" asked Ngoc.

"Nothing, why?" asked Antonia.

"I know you!"

She told Ngoc about Ethan. But she didn't care about him anymore, or the blond or school. She couldn't tell Ngoc about the lawyer. No one can ever know! Swallowing bile as she chewed on her bottom lip.

"He deserved it."

"What?" asked Antonia, puzzled.

"Ethan! That asshole deserves it."

Antonia pushed the intruding images of the lawyer away. "I never wanted him to be expelled, just to fail the test."

"Then why did you write the correct answers off by one? You could have made up random answers, and he wouldn't have been caught."

Antonia turned scarlet. "Oh my God, I feel terrible."

"Don't! Ethan's a jerk."

The restaurant's cook approached grinning and placed a large tray of sizzling pot stickers in front of them. Ngoc thanked him in Vietnamese as he went back to the kitchen.

"I will never get tired of these," said Ngoc, pouring sriracha sauce on one of the treats and shoving the whole thing into her mouth.

Antonia nodded as she forced one in her mouth and struggled to swallow.

"I'm sorry you broke up, but you deserve someone better."

Antonia didn't answer. I don't deserve anyone! Maybe I'm only good for sex.

Ngoc squeezed her hand and made a paste with soy sauce and chilis to dunk the remaining pot stickers. "It's a good thing UW expelled him, so you don't have to do all his homework."

"I didn't do all his homework!" protested Antonia weakly. When had she turned into a pushover? What had happened to her?

"Did you talk to your parents about nursing school?" she asked, steering the conversation away from her.

"Yeah." Ngoc sighed and pushed the plate away. "They said there's no way they're letting me move to Spokane to do the program. I'm going to reapply in Seattle."

"I am so sorry, Ngoc; it sounded like it was a perfect opportunity."

Ngoc picked up the plates, and before taking them to the kitchen, said, "Sometimes I wish I was like the white girls who can do whatever they want."

Antonia sighed in agreement as she wiped down the table.

The next day, Antonia was headed into her chemistry class when the blond girl that had copied Ethan's quiz stopped her at the door.

"Antonia, can I talk to you for a minute?"

Antonia stopped and stared at the blond, "I don't want any drama."

"I just want to know the truth. Did you fail on purpose?"

"No, I passed. After Ethan turned his test in, I corrected my answers. Ethan has always copied my tests. He had just dumped me, apparently for you, and I wanted to get back at him. I didn't know you were copying him until after the test."

"I knew it! He told me how he was always helping you, how you would cheat off his tests, and how he was always saving you. I guess it was the other way around."

"Yup. Were you also suspended?"

"Yeah, but just for this quarter. I think I'll transfer to another school. Is it also a lie that Ethan hid you from ICE?"

Antonia rolled her eyes. "That is so fucking typical, always pretending to be the hero. Or the misunderstood person too fucking sensitive for this world."

"Or how he can't stay too long with someone because he's fire and darkness?"

"I kept telling him to pick one, darkness or fire."

The blond laughed. They stood in awkward silence until Antonia said, "At least we are rid of him. I need to go to class."

"Sure," said the blond.

As Antonia headed into the classroom, the blond called out, "Hey! Just a heads-up. Ethan said he was going to call ICE on you."

Antonia shook her head, just what I need.

Saturday afternoon, Antonia glared out of the window of Welch's Toyota as he drove east through rain slapping the windshield so hard that it appeared to be rising from the ground. Dark gray clouds hung low on the freeway snaking through the central Cascade forest. The radio blasted Leonard Cohen, his growling basso voice triggering shivers down her spine.

"Fuck! First day of fall and it won't stop raining," Lee said, as the wipers frantically flew over the windshield, squeaking with each back and forth. "It's a good thing the cabin has a fireplace, so we'll be nice and cozy."

Antonia bit her lower lip, staring at the road ahead, wishing for an accident to send them flying off the road.

Welch put his hand on her knee. "The cabin is by the river, and there are no homes in a two-mile radius."

"I told my mother I was going with a friend to a cabin; she always tracks my phone."

Welch seized her phone and threw it out the window where it smashed into bits and pieces. "I don't want your mother ruining our weekend. I'll get you a new one on Sunday." He put his hand on her thigh.

Antonia swallowed and fought the urge to swat his hand away as he caressed her thigh every time higher. By the time they reached the cabin, he was stroking her crotch. She scrambled out of the car in front of a wood cottage surrounded by brush and cedars so tall she couldn't see their tops. The river roared nearby. Welch fidgeted with the lockbox and finally flung open the front door. The house was dark and dank. A spider dangled from a web that covered one corner of the room.

Welch dropped his bag on the full-sized bed against the wall and pulled out a black, see-through bodysuit. "Put this on."

"But it's freezing," said Antonia, holding up the lacy thing with two fingers.

"I'll get a fire going and get us some drinks."

Antonia locked herself in the bathroom, searching for a way to escape. But the window was too small. Her heart pounded. Things were going too fast. She needed to think, but Lee knocked on the door. "Can't wait to see you in that thing!"

Slowly, Antonia took off her clothes and folded them, leaving them in a pile on a stool. After a few tries, she fit into the lingerie, grateful the mirror above the sink was too small to see herself. She opened the door and peeked out. Lee was leaning over the table, his finger inside a glass, stirring. He jumped when she closed the bathroom door.

"Look at you!" he said, smiling. "You look like a Victoria's Secret model."

He rushed over and gave her one of the glasses. "Here, it's malbec."

Antonia held the glass, looking for somewhere to place it, but Lee grabbed her hand and pushed the glass to her lips. "Don't waste it; it's a forty-dollar bottle."

Antonia took a sip of the sour beverage as her stomach contracted.

"More," he said as she swallowed a big gulp.

He turned to the fireplace, and Antonia sat in a chair by the table. "My feet are freezing," she said as she massaged them, trying to peek into the leather pouch next to the wine. While Welch stoked the fire, she lifted a medicine bottle from the bag. Trazodone. Was this his medication? Had he put it in her wine?

The fire crackled. Welch took a rope from his bag. "Come here, beautiful."

Antonia's heart pounded so hard she prayed for a heart attack, anything to get her out of this. She froze.

Welch advanced on her. "I just want to play. I'm not going to hurt you."

Antonia's eyes watered, and she coughed. Smoke poured from the fireplace engulfing the small cottage.

Welch opened a window. "Fuck! The fireplace is plugged," he said as he grabbed a towel and waved it at the smoke. "Open the door!"

Antonia dashed to the door pulling on the handle, but it wouldn't open. Lee drew a key from his pocket and unlocked it, letting the cold air rush into the room as Antonia stood at the door, gasping. A voice screamed inside her, get out! Lee coughed, holding on to the frame. Suddenly, Antonia bolted toward the river. The soles of her bare feet stung as they trampled over twigs, stones, and pine needles.

"Stop!" cried Lee, "Let the smoke dissipate, and we can go back inside."

But Antonia dashed through the woods, even though the ground shifted and moved like waves. A hammer pounded on her brain, and her legs were slow to respond. She stumbled but grasped the trunk of a maple to keep from falling.

Lee shuffled toward her, favoring his right leg. Antonia tottered. Her legs were stiff, refusing to obey her. I should give up, lay down to sleep. I want it to be over. Her vision doubled as images of her mother and father floated in her mind's eye. What would they do when she was dead? She'd never felt so tired. Trying to push away the wet hair from her eyes, she struggled to raise her hand which seemed to have weights attached to it. A sharp rock sent shooting pain from her foot up to her hip, dissipating the drowsiness. Her sister's face popped into her mind.

"Stop!" said Welch, gasping for breath, "There's nowhere to go."

Antonia was almost at the bank, the river's roar like a beacon; its icy waters promised safety if she could reach it in time. But Lee charged, pushing her forward; she fell on her face, her hand touching the bank.

Welch yanked her by the hair. "You're coming back to the cabin now!"

Antonia grasped Lee's hands as he dragged her by the hair five feet away from the bank, then flung her to the ground, his hands on his knees breathing hard. Scrambling to her feet, she lowered her shoulder and pushed with her legs, crashing into him. He plunged into the raging river that swallowed him whole.

Spots floated across Antonia's eyes then, everything went black.

"Wake up! You need to find shelter, or you'll freeze."

Antonia opened her eyes. A male figure towered above her, a shadow in the dark; she could only make out his cape. Cowering, she raised her arm to shield her face. "Please, don't!"

"I am not here to hurt you. I'm the warden."

His voice had an unearthly quality, as if he was speaking to her behind an invisible barrier. Every part of Antonia's body screamed in pain, but the loudest protests came from her foot and scalp. She sat up, and the man took a step back, receding into the shadows. He must be a park ranger, she thought.

"You should know better than to be out during the equinox when all forces have equal power."

Antonia shook her head. I don't have time for this, she thought, listening for any sound from Welch. Blushing, she crossed her arms, only dressed in the tattered remains of the body suit.

The warden draped his cape around Antonia's shoulders, it reeked of wood smoke. A cape? Maybe he's into role playing, she thought.

"During the equinox, the portals open so I roam to keep the evil and dangerous creatures from crossing over. You need to find shelter."

Antonia stood up, but her legs gave out and she fell to her knees. "Is he gone?" she asked, peering into the dark woods as the memories flooded back.

"The man you pushed into the river?"

A feline-shaped shadow, three times the size of a golden retriever, strolled to the river and growled deeply. Antonia squeezed her eyes and opened them, but the cat-like creature was still there.

"That is the phantom cougar; she was ready to attack the man when you shoved him."

"Is he dead?"

"I don't know. He may have been swept through a portal or could be caught between worlds."

Antonia shook her head. "I don't understand. What worlds?"

"There are millions of parallel worlds in the forbidden forest; this forest has one of many portals which open during sacred times. During the autumn equinox, when all forces are equal, the gateways open."

"Are you here to help me?"

"I don't help people. Humans are the reason lower, primitive forces, destructive elements manifest more frequently and powerfully. Pollution and the destruction of nature have weakened the elemental spirits: the river, the trees, the mountains that guard our world. I'm too busy protecting the valley and the portal."

"But she did!" she said, pointing at the cougar by the bank.

"The phantom cougar protects those pure of heart, but tonight, she returns to her world. We will accompany you back to the cabin, but do not venture into the forest until the morning when the portals close."

She limped back to the cabin, the cougar and warden always a few steps behind, melting into the shadows whenever she glanced at them. A wave of nausea overcame her, and she hurled red fluid that left a sour taste in her mouth. Arriving at the cabin, the warden and cougar disappeared. They must've been hallucinations from the drug Welch gave me. The door stood open allowing the light from inside to spill onto the path.

She stopped at the entrance. Frozen. What if Welch was inside, waiting for her? He could lock her in again. She pulled out the key from the lock and rushed to the kitchen sink, where she drank from the faucet, the water so cold her teeth ached.

Looking around the room, she searched for a way home, cursing because Welch's car keys were in his pocket. His phone was on the table so she dialed one of the few numbers she knew from memory.

"Antonia?" answered Ngoc.

While waiting for Ngoc, Antonia picked up every trace she'd left in the cabin and gathered it in a plastic bag, including the torn fragments of the body suit. Emptying Lee's bag, three knives, still encased in their protective clear shield, fell on the bed, followed by rolls of duct tape and a small saw. A sobbing fit convulsed her body as she fell to her knees. Gasping she shifted her weight onto her wounded foot, the searing jolt slapped her back to reality. "Get a grip!" she said out loud, then took a dish rag and cleaned every surface twice until Ngoc's headlights shone through the blinds' slats.

Once on the road, Antonia told Ngoc everything that happened with the lawyer except the part about the warden and the cougar, convinced it was a side effect of the drug. Ngoc wiped a tear, her eyes fixed on the road ahead, nodding her head.

"Why didn't you tell me anything?"

"You know why."

Ngoc nodded. "He looked so normal, you know?"

Ngoc's phone buzzed. "Fuck! It's my parents. I took the van while they were sleeping; they must be furious."

"I'm sorry I got you into trouble."

Ngoc squeezed Antonia's hand. "I'm not. I'll make something up."

At Antonia's house, Ngoc rolled down the window. "It's not your fault. What he did was wrong, and I swear to never say a word."

Antonia opened her eyes. Welch was on top of her. She tried to move but she was bound to the bed. He held up a knife so sharp it sliced the light. "This knife is for Mimi. I'll buy new ones for Mami and Papi. He took out a serrated dagger the size of his forearm. "This one is for you."

Antonia awoke screaming. Too shaken to go back to sleep, she paced the kitchen. The next day was her father's hearing and she'd failed him. She grabbed her new phone to call her mother with the bad news and saw twenty missed texts from Ngoc.

"Call me. My parents called their immigration lawyer and she will help your father tomorrow for free. Call me so I can give her all the information."

Tuesday morning, Antonia and her mother arrived at the Tacoma Detention Center and waited for the lawyer. A few minutes before the hearing, a very slender young woman wearing a skirt and jacket ran into the facility. She yelled out, "Antonia?" and ran to them as they waved at her.

"So sorry I'm late. So much traffic. I'm Julie French; it's nice to meet you in person." She shook their hands, then opened her briefcase and removed some documents. "This should be pretty simple. I'm going to go see him and we'll talk after the hearing."

As the attorney hurried away, Antonia and her mother looked at each other.

"Do you think she can help us?" asked Mami.

"God, I hope so," said Antonia, as her stomach churned with hope and worry.

A group of detainees dressed in bright orange—women, men, teens—entered and sat in the front row. It was hard to follow what was happening. There were no witnesses, no jury, just burly guards and the judge. The courtroom was packed, and though the judge kept calling "order," there was a constant hum of human voices and fussy babies.

When it was her father's turn, Antonia held her breath and clasped her mother's cold and clammy hand. They strained to make out the words but couldn't. After a few minutes, Antonia's father returned to his place.

At the end of the hearing, Antonia rushed out to find the lawyer, who was smiling.

"The judge dismissed the charges," said the lawyer.

Antonia took her hand and thanked her. Her mother hugged the lawyer, who laughed. She shook their hands and said she was going to go see her next client. They yelled thanks at her as she left the building.

"*Ahora que?*" Antonia's mother asked.

"Let me see."

The clerk at the information desk told them to wait until her father was released, warning that it would take some time. Antonia and her mother sat on a hard, wooden bench and watched people come and go. Cell phones were not permitted in the center, so they talked about school and work. Maybe things would work out, thought Antonia. Lee's knives flashed before her eyes, and she shuddered.

At 5:00 p.m. an officer asked them to leave because they were closing the courtroom.

"But we are waiting for my father," said Antonia.

Her mother grabbed on tight to her arm. "My husband is coming. We wait, yes?"

"Sorry, ma'am, but there's no one left. You have to leave the building; we're closing."

"But the judge dismissed the charges," said Antonia. "They let him go. They said to wait for him."

"Listen, I'm sorry, but you need to leave."

"*Vámonos!*" said her mother, pulling her toward the exit.

"No! I am not leaving without my father."

The guard hesitated. "Wait here. Let me see what I can find out. Write your father's name on this pad."

Antonia wrote her father's name in a shaky scrawl and then put her arm around her mother as the guard walked away. He came back a few minutes later, a somber look on his face.

"Miss, I am very sorry, but your father has been removed. The judge dismissed the charges, but he has been or is being deported as we speak. He was taken away in an ICE van."

Antonia's mother groaned and fell to the floor, wailing. It took all Antonia's strength to remain on her feet. Numb, she mumbled thanks to the guard and helped her mother up, guiding her to the exit. Without her father, it was up to Antonia to care for her family.

"Let's go home, Mami. I'm going to teach you how to drive."

Antonia spent the night with her family, and before she left for school, slipped her father's obsidian dagger into her backpack. She was sure Welch had drowned in the river but the ceremonial dagger, once used for human sacrifices in pre-Columbian Mexico, made her feel safe. Like a talisman, she thought.

The next afternoon, Antonia piled bowls and plates onto her tray when a blond woman walked into the restaurant, searching the tables.

"Can I get you a table?" she asked.

The woman shook her head and zeroed in on the wound on her forehead. "I'm Detective Twyla Brown, Seattle Police. Is Ngoc Nguyen here?"

The glasses on the tray clashed when Antonia's hands shook. "I'll fetch her from the kitchen."

Ngoc was chopping jalapeños when Antonia rushed in and almost dropped the tray. "There's a detective here, and she wants to talk to you!"

"Now?"

Antonia gulped, nodding.

Ngoc washed her hands at the sink. "Don't worry. I'm not going to let them deport you."

"What are you going to say?"

But Ngoc was already closing the kitchen door. Antonia hovered by it, straining to hear what they were saying, catching only phrases and words: "Welch, missing, cell phone, lawyer."

Ngoc opened the door and took her bag and jacket from the utility room. "I told her how the lawyer Lee Welch invited me to his cabin and tried to rape me, so I pushed him into the river. I have to go with her to the station."

"You can't do that! I'm telling her the truth," Antonia said, pushing the swinging kitchen door. But Ngoc held her in a hug.

"No, they'll deport you. Please," she whispered.

A few hours later, Antonia paced her room, staring at her phone, waiting for texts from Ngoc. Her stomach grumbled and contracted painfully. When someone knocked, she rushed to open, expecting Ngoc.

It was Ngoc and the female detective. "May we come in?" she asked.

Antonia opened the door, and they crowded into the room, standing around the bed.

"I told her I pushed Welch into the river, but she insisted on talking to you," Ngoc said, giving Antonia warning glances.

"Antonia," said Detective Brown, her eyes roaming around the room and staring again at the scar on her forehead. "What happened?"

Antonia touched the scrape. "I fell on the stairs."

"Nasty, your hands too?"

Antonia glanced at her palms, scratched and raw.

"Where were you Saturday afternoon?" asked the detective.

"I was home, sick." Antonia forced herself to look at the detective so she would believe the lie.

"Did you know Lee Welch?"

Antonia and Ngoc looked at each other. "Who?"

"Don't bullshit me! We searched Welch's office today. Anything you want to tell me?"

The detective knows we're lying; our story has too many holes. Antonia sighed, "He was my lawyer. I'm the one that pushed him into the river; Ngoc was trying to protect me."

The detective sat on the bed. "I'm glad you told me. Why did Welch call your cell phone?" she asked, looking at Ngoc.

"I used it to call her to pick me up." Antonia recounted her experiences with Welch while Ngoc grasped her hand. "I didn't want to hurt him, but he forced me to have sex." Even though it meant deportation, a burden lifted from her shoulders as she let go of her secret. Turning to hug Ngoc, she said,

"Thank you, but I can't let you go to jail for me."

"No one's going to jail, ladies."

"But I killed Welch, and I don't have papers!"

"I'm not here to deport you; you have my word. The owner of the cabin reported Welch's car and stuff still there, his phone showed a call to Ngoc."

A crash of metal outside the basement window made them jump, startled. "It's Mr. John," said Antonia.

The pretty detective continued. "The Miami public defender's office fired Welch twelve years ago. He then practiced law in Tennessee where several sexual harassment complaints were filed against him. My guess is he resigned quietly in exchange. That was just a few months before you met him."

"See? He was a perv!" said Ngoc.

"This man," Detective Twyla shook her head grimacing, "he had knives, rope, and narcotics in his car. I think he planned more than a weekend with you."

"Trazadone. I think he put it in my wine."

"Yup. Everywhere he's lived, I found an increase of missing undocumented women. The women he represented tended to jump bail and disappear without a trace. At least that is what he would tell the immigration court."

"And because they were undocumented, no one looked for them," said Antonia, shuddering. I could've been one more.

Twyla put her hand on the door. "Let's go down to the station to get your statements."

Before Welch busted down the door, the smell smacked Antonia; a mixture of moldy oranges, spoiled fish, and rotten egg that exploded into her room. She stood up as he struck the detective on the head with a bat making her crumple to the floor.

"I'm here!" said Welch in a hollow voice that reminded Antonia of the Hallelujah song he would play in his office.

Ngoc grasped Antonia, shrieking.

Covered in the tattered remains of a shirt and filling the doorway, Welch glared at them. He grinned, sending a shiver down Antonia's spine. "I was mad when you pushed me in the river. That wasn't very nice. I could've drowned!"

Dropping the bat, he leaned over the detective and grabbed her gun, pointing it at them. "And after all I did for your family."

Ngoc held on so tightly Antonia struggled to breathe.

He advanced. The hair on the back of Antonia's neck rose. "To think I tried to help you people! You are all a bunch of illegal cockroaches. All I asked for was a little attention; it's not as if you little whores don't enjoy it. But instead, you shoved me into the river. You're coming with me."

"You can't take her!" Ngoc said, standing in front of Antonia.

But Antonia stepped around Ngoc. "I'll go with you if you let Ngoc go."

"Antonia, no!" Ngoc cried, tears falling down her cheek.

"We can't beat him; he's got a gun."

Suddenly, Mr. John appeared behind Welch; he grasped him in a chokehold. They wrestled. Antonia lunged for her backpack. A gunshot exploded in the room making her ears ring.

Mr. John fell on the floor. A red stain spread across his lower stomach as he groaned.

"Mr. John!" yelled Antonia.

Welch pointed the gun at Antonia. "Come here!"

Antonia approached Welch, her hand in the backpack. He wasn't human anymore. Evil oozed from him. Her fingers grasped the obsidian dagger in her bag. In a swift movement, she yanked it out and plunged it into his heart; black blood flowed over her hand as she pulled it out, plunging and slicing him again. "Die, you fucking freak! Die!"

He shuddered and fell, convulsing. Antonia knelt next to Mr. John. "Ngoc! Call 911!"

Two months later, Antonia placed a box on the bed of her dorm room. "This is the last one."

Ngoc opened the blinds. "I'm glad you don't have a roommate; I plan on staying over. I always wanted to live in the dorms."

Antonia shook out a bedsheet, taking stock of the last month. Detective Twyla Brown had arranged U visas for Antonia, her mother, and sister, affording them legal status. Mr. John was still recuperating in the VA. Determined to help her father return, she was saving for his coyote. The university took over her cost of attendance and even offered Ngoc a place in the nursing program, but Ngoc declined, applying to the police force instead.

"What's wrong?" asked Ngoc, sitting on the bed hugging a pillow.

"Nothing."

"Antonia, I know you! Tell me!"

Antonia sat next to Ngoc, staring out the window while twisting a strand of hair between her fingers. "I don't think I'll ever be normal again."

Ngoc put her arm around her shoulders. "I'm glad we're not normal."

Antonia shook her head. "What he did to me, what he made me do, it's like he ruined me!"

Ngoc kneeled in front of her friend and grasped her hands. "No one can ruin you! You're too strong for that. You protected your family and killed a monster twice! Don't become what he wanted."

Antonia wiped a tear away with the back of her hand, then hugged her friend. She was right; it was time to move on, but she would keep the obsidian knife under her pillow.

Detective Brown knocked on the open door. "Thought I'd check out your new digs."

"Come in!" said Antonia, taking a box off her desk chair and offering it to her.

Twyla placed a pack of forty-eight noodle cups in her arms. "Here, I survived college on these." She walked around the room and leaned to look out the window.

"Thanks," said Antonia, searching for a place to put it.

"I just needed to ask you a quick question from the night at the cabin."

Ngoc grimaced and Antonia nodded.

"Was anybody else there in the cabin or in the forest that day?"

"No. Just Welch and me. Why?"

Twyla turned to walk away. "Nothing important. When I went back to the cabin, I found a weird cape behind the sofa. Must've been left there by the owner. Take care."

Antonia shivered and looked east through her window toward the forests of Snoqualmie and beyond.

# The Devil You Know

## Sunday

**EMILIANA MANEUVERED A POT** of dried black beans under the flowing faucet. A skull materialized on the surface of the water making her drop the pot clattering in the sink. The skull disappeared. She shut off the faucet and listened to see if the noise had awoken Estela, but there was nothing. Estela was so medicated, she could sleep through a mariachi band playing full blast.

It was Sunday afternoon. Luis, her grandson, was working, and his wife Estela was taking a nap.

I must have imagined it, thought Emiliana, setting the pot on the counter. The skull looked like Tzitzimitl. That old demon hadn't bothered her in years. Just thinking about her sent a shudder down Emiliana's spine.

Emiliana put on her raincoat and went on her mile-long afternoon walk in Seward Park in South Seattle. Her hips, knees, and hands blasted with pain, but she forced herself into the pouring rain, wading through puddles in her child-sized boots, the cold drops kissing her cheeks.

I'm too old for this! I should be spending my last days in the sun, slowing down into the rhythms of nature. Instead, I'm in this dark place, still caring for the family. I don't know how long I can keep doing it.

She crossed from Luis's low-income neighborhood into the more expensive blocks encircling the park. As she approached, the trees, lots, and homes became larger. She entered the park and stood on the bank of Lake Washington. In the distance, Mount Rainier loomed, a curtain of clouds partially drawn across its profile. Emiliana removed her boots and socks, gracefully balancing on each ancient foot in turn, despite her arthritis. The shock of the cold, wet grass ignited a longing for Mexico.

Something darted in the periphery, catching her eye. She searched the shadows of the cedars, where tree trunks and hawthorns took on menacing forms. Blinking, she bent to study the mycelium, which extended to the soles of her weathered feet. "Thank you, Mother Earth," she prayed, "please give me energy."

Eyes closed, Emiliana hummed an ancient song. With each exhalation, she blew away every thought … every sensation. Her mind quiet, she opened another sense, one with no name, and fear gripped her heart. Tatiana was in danger! She inhaled and opened her mind's eye. Her great-granddaughter struggled in a pool of black sludge; a fiend hovered over her.

Emiliana visualized Tatiana. Average height, toned, strong limbs covered with lean muscle from swimming and running. Brown hair fell heavily below her shoulders to frame a heart-shaped face, with large almond eyes and caramel skin. Smart, kind, respectful. Never a problem until six months ago, when she'd invited them to dinner to introduce them to a new husband and house. Emiliana's pulse quickened. She put on her boots and hurried home. The urgency made the uphill walk back more strenuous than usual. Gasping for breath, she stood at the corner as the cold night air stung her cheeks. The lights from homes in the valley spread out like so many earth-bound stars.

"He's coming for her," a low guttural voice said. The words were *Zapotec*, of the ancient valley peoples.

She turned, expecting a man, but the street was empty.

## Monday

Luis drove Emiliana past Snoqualmie Ridge, a bedroom city forty miles east of Seattle, then wound down the country road, over a one-lane bridge, past manicured horse ranches, small farms, and large estates. He stopped at the beginning of a dirt driveway framed by giant evergreens that obscured the house at the end. The large, modern, cabin-style house nestled against a stark escarpment that shot into the sky. Mount Si was the western boundary of the Cascades, dividing rain-soaked Western Washington from its drier eastern sister. Its face, sprinkled with dark green pines and golden-leaved maples, glowed in the afternoon light.

"You see, Emiliana?" he asked in a conspiratorial tone, playing with his mustache. "Why does he bring her so far away out here? No neighbors and far from us."

In the passenger seat, Emiliana sat up straight, clutching a large canvas bag to her chest. Her thin, gray braid stretched down her back, reaching beyond her small waist. If she pointed her toes, her child-sized boots would barely reach the floorboard.

"*M'hijo*, maybe he loves nature, like me? It's beautiful!" She lowered the window and breathed in the pine-scented air. "It smells good. Seattle smells of cars."

"Wait until it's dark and raining all day,"

"It's dark and rainy in Seattle too, but all I hear is traffic. Listen! I hear water, the river!"

"Yeah, it's the north fork of the river right behind the house. It's so isolated."

"You're a city boy. You don't appreciate nature. That's why you are bitter."

"You know that's not why I'm worried."

"I know, I worry too."

"I just want to know why!" Luis pounded the steering wheel. "She had a job, an apartment, then gets married to this English guy we know nothing about!"

Emiliana nodded. "Maybe she fell in love. The heart doesn't follow rules, you know." She was relieved Tatiana was safe after the accident. Her visions were seldom wrong, but thankfully this was one of those times.

"Keep an eye on Liam, Emiliana. I don't trust him. He only let you come because he thinks you are a dumb, old Mexican woman. Don't let him know who you really are." He took her left hand and squeezed it gently. "I failed Nico, I can't fail my daughter too."

Emiliana returned the gentle pressure on Luis's hand. He'd never forgiven himself for Nico's death; it was normal for him to be worried. "Nico had so many demons."

Abruptly, Luis turned away and looked at the house. He put the car in gear and drove slowly up the lane. He parked and helped Emiliana out.

When Emiliana planted her feet on the gravel drive, an uneasiness stirred in her belly. She zipped her jacket and slung her canvas bag over her shoulder while Luis hauled her suitcase to the foot of the porch stairs. The door swung open, and Liam stood waiting for them with his boyish smile. Fit and lean, with steel-blue eyes, he exuded confidence.

Emiliana looked up at Liam and was startled to see spirits encircling him. The tall man was completely oblivious to them as they passed through him, shock and confusion distorting their ghostly faces. Luis gently nudged her forward. She shook her head and gripped the railing as she climbed the porch stairs.

"Thank you for helping us out, Emiliana," Liam said as he leaned in to kiss the old woman's wrinkled cheek. His unshaven chin scratched her face as heaviness settled over her heart. Liam nodded at Luis and tried to take Emiliana's bag from him, but Luis held onto it as his daughter's husband showed them into the house.

Emiliana's eyes widened at the contrast between the natural exterior and stuffy, oppressive indoors. She took in the flared-armed couch and matching loveseat upholstered in brown velvet, with matching damask drapes. As they weaved around antique mahogany tables, credenzas, and armoires, she struggled to imagine Tatiana there.

"Where's my girl?" asked Luis, looking around the living room.

"She's sleeping," answered Liam. "She took a nap after lunch. Is her mother coming?"

"She doesn't want to drive so far out here, but she says hello," said Luis, shaking his head with a look of impatience.

"It's only forty-five minutes from Seattle," replied Liam.

Emiliana took off her boots and set them by the door underneath a mirror framed in gold antique leaf. "You're becoming a grumpy old man!" she said to Luis.

"Old man? I'm only nine years older than Liam. Anyway, it's forty-five minutes without traffic. But when is there no traffic?"

"You need to stop making excuses for her," muttered Liam.

"For *whom*?" Luis clenched his jaw, his face red.

"We all know she needs professional help. She can't even show up when her daughter is in an accident."

"Her migraines paralyze her."

"Enough. This is not the time," said Emiliana, in her broken English. "Show me my room. You go see Tatiana."

"Thank you for intervening," said Liam as he took Emiliana's bag and showed her to the guest room on the first floor. "What they did to Tatiana is inexcusable."

"We all have our struggles," she answered, reluctant to discuss family matters with a stranger.

Emiliana's room had a full-sized bed with a carved mahogany headboard covered in a forest green and gold damask bedspread. Next to the bed an ornate night table held an antique glass lamp that cast a glow against the afternoon gloom.

"I hope you are comfortable here. Our floors are heated so that should help your arthritis," said Liam, putting the bag on the bed.

Emiliana nodded and looked out the window. The yard stretched out to the border of maples and pines by the river.

"That mountain is Mount Si. It's beautiful but it shields us from the sun! It can get pretty gloomy in the mornings and late afternoons."

Emiliana stood in front of a gold-leaf framed picture of a vase of roses.

"Aren't they lovely? I collect antique furniture. I brought almost everything from England."

A large golden retriever bounded into the room, jumping from Liam to Emiliana, excitedly wagging its tail.

"Down, Luna! Down!" commanded Liam. Luna sat on her hind legs and looked up, panting.

"I am glad you're here, Emiliana. I'm afraid to leave Tatiana alone."

"How are *you*?" asked Emiliana, petting the dog while trying to ignore the spirits that encircled Liam.

Liam looked up, caught off guard. "Me? I'm fine. Just a few cuts and bruises. We're so lucky to be alive!"

"And you're not sad?"

Liam turned away from Emiliana to look out the window, as if to hide his tears.

"I keep thinking about the night of the accident. If only I had been driving …" He paused, then sighed and continued, "I'm glad she can't remember much, but I think she blames herself."

"What happened?"

"A bull elk jumped in front of the car. Tatiana was distracted, and it was raining so hard. She swerved to avoid the elk, and we drove into a ditch and just kept flipping over and over. It was horrible …"

*"Ay m'hijo!"* said Emiliana with concern. "That's bad. You all need healing, body and spirit." No wonder his energy was dark.

"We were lucky, really. We could have died. We're just banged up."

"I am here for both of you."

Liam gave her a strained smile. "Please let me know if I can get you anything to make your stay more comfortable. I will leave you to unpack. Tatiana should be joining us for dinner."

After Luis left, Emiliana knocked on Tatiana's door. *"Soy yo mi hijita."*

Tatiana met Emiliana at the door and held her tightly. The top of Emiliana's head barely grazed Tatiana's chin. She tried to talk, but all that came were wracking sobs. Emiliana held her, whispering prayers and consolations she had learned from her Yaqui grandmother almost ninety years ago in Mexico. After a few minutes, Tatiana straightened and pushed herself away.

"Sorry, Emiliana, I feel so bad."

"It is good to cry it out. You cannot leave all that pain inside you. Your spirit is heavy and sad now," Emiliana murmured as she studied Tatiana's face: the swollen eyes, the pallid complexion, the tangled hair—and the fresh black bruise on her cheekbone.

"It was my fault! If I hadn't been driving—"

"It is not your fault! Liam said an elk was on the road. That is not your fault, *m'hija*. Your father says you do not remember anything?"

Tatiana nodded as she took a sweater from an antique wardrobe and slipped it on.

"I can only remember the morning of the accident. I found out I was pregnant." She looked away.

Emiliana hid her shock.

"I was upset because I was taking birth control pills," continued Tatiana. "After that, I remember being dragged out of the car."

"Where else were you hurt?"

Tatiana sat on the bed and lifted her sweatpants. Her shins were covered in angry, jagged red lines and stitches. "We flipped three times and landed on the roof. I remember waking up because my legs stung from the glass. I think this happened when Liam pulled me out of the car through the window."

Emiliana ran her small brown hands over Tatiana's left leg and looked closely at the stitches. She peered into Tatiana's eyes, urging her to go on.

"Well, my back and neck are very sore, and of course, I am bleeding and cramping because of the miscarriage. It was my fault, Emiliana! I could've gotten both of us killed! If I hadn't left—" Tatiana looked away, her face pensive.

Emiliana held Tatiana's shoulders. "You will heal, *mi niña*. You will also heal your spirit. It is never fast. It takes tears and time, but you will heal. Tonight, *te sobo*."

Tatiana walked over to the elaborate vanity on the wall opposite the bed. Sitting in front of the mirror, she applied concealer to the bruises on her face. "The truth is I didn't want a baby. I am not ready yet. But I feel terrible for Liam."

"Some things are not meant to be, and the accident is not your fault. You need to accept it. Time will help." She was too young to have a child, even though Emiliana herself had had her first at seventeen. It was good that women had careers and waited to become mothers. Not all of them wanted children.

Tatiana nodded, putting on pink lipstick. Emiliana still sensed she was troubled.

"Dinner is ready!" shouted Liam up the stairs.

"Let's go, Emiliana. Liam is a great cook."

They sat at the kitchen counter, side by side, with Tatiana in the middle. Emiliana's feet dangled above the floor. They ate looking at the dark yard through glass sliding doors as Mount Si loomed above; its peaks above the pines reflecting purple and pink from the setting sun.

"I hope we see the deer today. They are so tame! They're used to people and will come right up to you," said Tatiana.

"Yeah," said Liam. "The deer are a plague—just cute, overgrown rats that destroy my garden!"

"What a grouch!" said Tatiana rolling her eyes. "I love them! The other day one came up less than five feet away. A little doe!"

"A little doe just like you, pretty one," said Liam, giving her a kiss on the cheek.

"Do you like living here?" asked Emiliana.

Tatiana nodded, smiling. Liam poured wine for all three of them, exclaiming, "Of course she does! She loves nature and gets a break from Seattle."

"I don't think I should drink while on the medications," said Tatiana, pushing her glass away. Liam took the glass and set it back in front of her plate.

"Nonsense, pretty one, you need a little distraction!"

Tatiana frowned, took a sip, then started pushing the food around on her plate.

"I wish they hadn't made you come, Emiliana. I'm fine and I don't need babysitting."

"But you are my baby too. I raised your grandmother and uncles. Even some of your *primos*. I'll stay until you get better."

"We just need you to stay this week. I have to go survey a helicopter accident in Canada, and I don't want Tatiana here alone. She'll need company when the stitches are removed on Saturday," explained Liam. He stabbed at the pasta with his fork and washed it down with half a glass of wine.

"Why doesn't Tatiana stay with her mother?"

Tatiana glanced nervously at Liam. "Because this is my home! Liam works from home, so I am not alone. Also, my mom has her own issues. Her migraines and depression keep her in bed. You know that."

Liam chuckled at this and drew air circles at his temple with his index finger. Tatiana shook her head at him.

"What is your work, Liam?" asked Emiliana.

"I'm an aircraft insurance adjuster."

"He works for a British insurance company. He goes to plane and helicopter accidents and analyzes the scene and writes a report. Right?" asked Tatiana, looking at Liam.

"Almost right," said Liam, winking at her. He took Emiliana's wineglass and drank from it.

"You go to where people just died?" asked Emiliana, her interest stirred.

"Yes. I do the investigations for any small plane or helicopter accidents on the West Coast, from California to Alaska, including Canada." He dove into his food.

"Oh, I see now. I can do a *limpia*, an energy cleaning for you, so the dead don't follow you," said Emiliana.

"Excuse me?" Liam looked up, a forkful of pasta in midair.

"Dead souls surround you. I think they follow you from the accidents. I can help them go home and give you protection."

"You silly little thing!" replied Liam, laughing. "I don't believe in primitive superstitions."

Tatiana bit her thumb. "Can you please remind me, are you Yaqui or Zapotec? I was telling Liam I think you are both."

"I *am* both. My father was Yaqui, or Yoemem, as we prefer." Emiliana's history was complicated. Porfirio Diaz sold her grandfather and other Yaqui to a plantation in Oaxaca, there they'd mixed with the nearby Zapotec community. Emiliana was proud her father had fought with Zapata's army during the revolution, even though he was later betrayed and murdered by Carranza. Her gaze hardened, as she remembered fleeing with her mother and paternal grandmother to Pachuca. "I was raised by my Asu, grandmother, with both Yaqui and Zapotec traditions."

"I love how Mexicans deny their indigenous roots; they all say they are Spanish. In England, Spaniards are our maids," Liam snorted.

Tatiana punched Lian playfuly on the shoulder. "That's racist!"

"If I was racist, I wouldn't be with you," replied Liam. "You are a rare find—a *mestizo* with a Russian name, who looks like a model for a Latina magazine."

"*Ni de aquí, ni de allá.* Sometimes it's hard to know where I fit in."

"You carry all your ancestors in you," added Emiliana, smiling.

Liam took a forkful of pasta from Tatiana's untouched plate. "As long as those ancestors don't expect you to believe in any of that hocus-pocus bollix about spirits—"

"You will like it here, Emiliana!" Tatiana brought the salad bowl to the counter, giggling nervously. "We'll go for walks with Luna, feed the chickens, collect the eggs. You're going to love the fresh eggs!"

"Then I will stay until you go back to work."

"Well, then that'll be forever. I'm not going back to work," said Tatiana, frowning, as she served some salad.

"Are you going back to school?"

"No, Emiliana, I deferred my admission. I'm going to wait a couple of years."

"You said when you got married, you would still go to school to be a lawyer. You promised your father." No wonder Luis was upset, Tatiana was giving up her dream.

"But I *am* going! And Liam has promised to pay for all of it! Just not now. I don't want the stress of law school, and I can't drive, so I can't go back to work."

"Tatiana, you can drive. You need to face your fears and—"

"I won't ever drive again!" shouted Tatiana. "What if I kill someone?"

"You're scared, *m'hija*,"

Liam poured dressing on his salad. "She'll get over it. Just give her time. In the meantime, I'll drive you,"

"If you do not drive, then you live in the city and use the bus," said Emiliana.

"I don't think this is the time to talk about this," Liam stood up. "Tatiana and I have been through a lot. We don't need to talk about this anymore."

"Emiliana, I'll be fine. By not working, I can go with Liam to all the accident sites. While he works, I'll go sightseeing."

Tatiana picked up the plates and put them in the sink.

"Tatiana will be the first one in your family to travel and live a life of luxury," said Liam proudly. "And one day soon, we'll have a family."

Tatiana came over to Liam and Emiliana and put one hand on each of their shoulders. She kissed them both on the cheek. "Good night. I'll take care of those in the morning. I'm going to bed."

When she left the room, Liam poured himself the rest of the wine. His cold, blue eyes bore into Emiliana.

"I know your family doesn't like me. But no one will ever love her like I do!" He looked around the room and continued, "You people work hard; I'll give you that much. But none of you will ever be able to give her what I can. It's just the nature of things. I can take care of her."

"She can take care of herself. Her father is worried she's too young to be married. You got married without knowing each other. She had—"

Liam put down the glass and grabbed the old woman's bony shoulders. "I will prove to you and your family that I have her best interests in mind." Letting her go, he added, "And you too. Enjoy your time here."

"Yes," said Emiliana softly, rubbing her shoulder. "I am just here to *apapachar*, you know? Care?"

"Good night," he said as he left the room.

Emiliana shuddered. The English accent still haunted her. Was there something wrong with Liam and the tortured spirits from the accidents that followed him? Was the darkness his, or the demon *Tzitzimitl*? She would go to *Tenku Ania*, the dream world, to explore.

The house settled into the darkness, creaking and moaning as the wind's susurrations sounded a warning. *Tzitzimitl* was near—that deathly demon, born from the stars, who'd been present at every tragedy in her life as a *curandera*. From her medicine pouch, Emiliana pulled a smooth, red-amber pebble and held it, drawing on its protection as she tried to sleep. She tossed and turned in bed, remembering the last Englishman she knew.

## Pachuca, Hidalgo, Mexico, 1930

Cross-legged, Emiliana sat at the large oak table in the expansive, wood-paneled dining room, polishing the heavy silver until it glowed. The dining room was part of a large, Tudor-style manor house where her mother worked as a servant for the head of the Cornish silver mining company operating in Pachuca. After her father's murder, her mother and grandmother had fled with her to Pachuca in central Mexico. Every morning before dawn, Emiliana and her mother arrived at the mansion, and at the end of every day, they left in the dark after completing their litany of chores.

Emiliana set down a heavy silver pitcher, picked up a sugar bowl, and polished it with a worn wool rag. She tilted her head in concentration, humming a Zapotec song under her breath to drown out the noise coming from the master bedroom. She flinched when the crack of a slap and James's baritone voice thundered through the door in his Cornish-accented Spanish, "She's old enough. Eleven, right? And not bleeding yet."

Her mother burst through the door yelling, "Leave now!" Then in Zapotec, "Go to Asu. Run!"

James appeared behind her mother and shoved Belegui to one side. She caught the edge of the table to keep from falling. The large Englishman strode quickly toward Emiliana.

"Come here. It's time you and I got to know each other better," he growled in English. "Be a good girl, now."

Before she could react, Emiliana's diminutive mother rushed James, striking the side of the big man's head with one of the silver candleholders Emiliana had just polished. James stumbled forward, his hand at his temple. Belegui bolted past him and grabbed her daughter's hand without breaking stride.

Out the door they fled, through the walled garden and down the path to the gate. Locked! Desperate, they both shook it, but the lock held. Belegui surveyed the stone walls topped with broken glass and barbed wire. Emiliana turned toward the house. James was halfway to them, charging, wiping blood from his eyes, stumbling and cursing.

"Come back here, or I will kill you!"

"Ama!" yelled Emiliana. Even though James stumbled once more, he advanced fast. Belegui quickly kissed Emiliana on the forehead before swinging her up on her shoulders. She stood on tiptoe and propelled the child over the gates.

Emiliana flew over the sharpened rods of the wrought iron gate and thudded to earth on the other side, the breath punched out of her lungs. She stared back through the bars, coughing and gasping for air. Her tears flowed as James seized her mother by her braids and yanked her to him.

"*Déjala*!" Emiliana yelled, through the gate bars.

"*Chonxonj! Go* to Asu! Run!" Belegui yelled.

James flung her mother to the ground like an oversized rag doll, straddled her and wrapped his huge hands around her neck. Emiliana shrieked before turning and bolting through the scrub brush and cactus as fast as she could.

When Emiliana reached her grandmother, she told her what had happened in between great tremulous sobs. Her grandmother hid Emiliana at a neighbor's and told her to stay out of sight until she or her mother returned. Asu returned an hour later. She was shaking, pale; a haunted look darkened her eyes.

"We must leave now!"

"Where is Ama?"

Asu looked Emiliana in the eye, and in a low, gentle voice, said, "Remember when I told you our people, the Yoeme, believe in many worlds?"

Emiliana nodded, tears stinging her eyes.

"Well, your mama is now in *Teeka Ania*, the world from the sky up through the universe. The Englishman was a demon and he sent her there. We need to leave because he is coming for us."

Emiliana's eyes overflowed, her small hands over her heart. Her mother was dead.

"You will see your mama in the dream world, Emiliana, in *Ania*."

Emiliana stood her ground, stomping her foot. "If we leave now, she will not be able to find me!"

"Oh, *niña*, your mother is always with you. She is in every little piece of you, in your breath, in your heartbeat. She is here." Asu pointed at Emiliana's chest. "Even now, when you cannot see her in this world anymore. Now, *chiquita*, we need to leave."

Through every concealed back path Asu knew, they hurriedly made their way to the bus station in Pachuca. Asu bought two tickets for Oaxaca and found the most out-of-the-way corner to await their escape.

Once they were on the road, Emiliana asked, "Where are the Yoeme, Asu?" Glancing out the dirty window. "Are we going to see them?"

"No, I don't want to go back; nobody from our town is left. We're going to Cinacatlán in Oaxaca, where you were born. Your mother's family is there, and maybe the *curandera* can train you."

"Aren't you a *curandera*?" Emiliana's large brown eyes studied her asu's profile.

Asu nodded. "Yes, I know the sacred ways of the Yoeme. The *curandera* that delivered you told your mother you have a gift. If she takes you in, you will learn the Zapotec ways, and I will teach you the Yoeme ways. You can help more people."

Emiliana leaned against the window, picturing her mother. She cried herself to sleep, lulled by the steady thrum of the road and her asu's soft, healing songs.

Emiliana dreamt of her mother, Belegui, dressed in a colorful *huipil* and colorful embroidered skirt, her braids interlaced with bright ribbons, her smile serene and kind.

In the dream, Belegui stands on one side of a river. Emiliana on the other.

"Ama, come here!" Emiliana pleads.

"I'm here," answers a voice that seems to come from everywhere and nowhere all at once. Emiliana turns, anxiously seeking her mother and the voice, but she is alone on the banks. The water roars, tumbling in its rock-strewn channel. The wet cold seeps through her clothing into her bones. The darkening skies are shrouded and menacing.

"Where are you, Ama?"

"I am here. Don't be afraid. I am here in the rocks and in the water."

"It is cold here!"

"I know, *mi preciosa*. Listen to your asu. She will help you open your heart so you can become a healer. You have a gift and you can help our people heal."

"But Mama, I want you to come back!"

"I cannot come to your world in the old body, but I am still there, in you. Do you know what my name means?"

"No."

"I am *Belegui*, the guiding star. When you do not know what to do, look for me in the sky, and I will guide you even through the darkest night."

A tiny, soft, speck of white light emerged from Emiliana's forehead. The light expanded, shifting in shape, becoming a woman who looked like Belegui. From the center of the woman's chest, a shining star cast its light, encircling and suffusing Emiliana in a soft cocoon of warmth.

"Listen to Asu. Keep your heart open and nurture your gift. Learn to travel between the worlds. I will see you here."

Emiliana awoke feeling her mother's lips on her forehead. She looked out at the night, and sighed, her life would never be easy.

## Tuesday

Emiliana was drinking coffee and folding clothes when Tatiana came in.

"No, Emiliana, please, no need to do this!" cried Tatiana, snatching a lace thong from her hands and throwing it back into the basket. She whisked the basket to the laundry room and returned to sit at the kitchen counter. "We have people to do this."

"I will make you breakfast," said Emiliana as she headed for the fridge.

"Just coffee, Emiliana, please," said Tatiana wearily. "I can't eat and I need to lose weight."

"You are too skinny and you need food for the medicines. I will make something for you. I'm soaking black beans for tomorrow."

"I'll just have an apple," replied Tatiana, taking an apple from the fruit bowl. She sank her teeth into it, chewing delicately.

Emiliana prepared a small plate for Tatiana with rolls of turkey, cheese, and fruit. She poured coffee for both of them, set the mugs on the counter, and climbed up to the stool.

"Mmmm. Did you put *canela* in the coffee? *Gracias*, Emiliana. I feel like a little girl again."

"We should go for a walk when you are dressed. You need to go outside."

Tatiana nodded, sipping her coffee and ignoring the food.

"Tell me, why are you postponing school?"

Tatiana sighed, put down her cup, and curled her feet under her on the stool.

"Emiliana, I don't need the stress of law school right now, so I delayed my admission to next year. Honestly, I'm not sure I want to attend anymore."

"But you got good grades on that test for law school, and you wanted to help *nuestra gente*. You said you wanted to be an immigration lawyer."

"Immigration lawyers don't help our *gente*. They work for rich immigrants from Asia or Europe."

"Tatiana!" said Emiliana. "You are intelligent and hardworking. You wanted to change the laws for immigrants. What happened to you?"

Something stirred inside Emiliana, a warning. What was this girl hiding?

Tatiana's cheeks flushed. "What do you mean?"

"You went from being a lawyer in the city to getting married to someone you just met!"

"Arghhh!" Tatiana put her full plate in the sink. "Why does everyone care so much about what I do? I found a man who really cares for me. What does it matter how much time we've known each other? Or how much older he is? He loves me!" She patted her heart with her right hand.

"How about *you*? Do you love him? What do you know about him?"

Tatiana turned around to wash her plate, her movements nervous, tentative.

Emiliana remembered what she'd said about Liam. His work kept him moving every two years from country to country, Hong Kong, Berlin, Stockholm, Barcelona, and many cities she couldn't remember. He'd never been married. They met at the law firm where Tatiana had been a paralegal, and Liam was a client.

"Of course. I love him!" Tatiana dried her hands on a towel and looked out the window at the mountain. "When Nico died, I took over the house, the bills, my mother's care. Liam is the first person to ever take care of me."

"At what cost?" asked Emiliana gently.

Tatiana sighed, exasperated. "Liam has nothing to do with me postponing law school."

"Then why wait?"

"I grew up. I'm married now, and I better understand how things work." Tatiana paused, smoothing her apron. "Things have happened that you don't know and can't understand."

"So you will just stay here and cook and clean?"

"Oh Emiliana, of course not! We have help. Liam doesn't let me do anything."

"*Ya veo,*" replied Emiliana.

"What?" asked Tatiana.

"*Vámonos!* You're not eating. Get dressed and we will walk."

Tatiana and Emiliana put on their raincoats and boots and stepped out into the backyard.

Clouds clung stubbornly to the sheer face of Mount Si, trailing from the Douglas firs, larches, and Sitka spruces like wispy ribbons. The two women, young and old, crossed the rain-soaked grass toward the river. Barking furiously, Luna took off after a doe and her fawn, who easily outdistanced the golden retriever.

"Luna! Come! Luna!" yelled Tatiana. Luna gave up the chase and returned, shaking off the rain, a mischievous smile stretched across her friendly face.

"Don't chase the deer; they're our friends!" Tatiana hooked the leash to Luna's collar. "That doe and her fawn come here to eat from the apple trees." She pointed to the trees full of green and red fruit dwarfed by the towering pines.

The deer in the undergrowth gathered under a cluster of dark green cedars on the edge of the property. Something stirred in her mind. Was this mother and her offspring a gift of the spirits, watching over them? The deer's large, liquid brown eyes followed them as they passed.

"*Seyewailo*," said Emiliana, looking at the deer.

"What?" asked Tatiana.

"I am greeting them. For the Yoeme, the deer represent everything that is good."

Tatina smirked.

The two women walked down a narrow, stone-lined path through the garden to the banks of the river. The sky had been overcast most of the morning, a thick, solid ceiling of gray. The occasional sun breaks, however, teased color from the trees, shrubs, rocks, and the rushing river.

Emiliana breathed in the pine-scented air, heavy with humidity. The water was high and loud as it raced between the escarpment's face, the immense backyard, and the house.

"I love this mountain," said Tatiana. "I love how it shoots straight up—almost out of nowhere."

They walked along the bank. Emiliana kept a brisk pace. She was short, but her steps were compact, quick, and sure. She covered a lot of ground, quietly and lightly.

"This place has many spirits. The mountain and the river make it a powerful place."

Tatiana smiled and rolled her eyes.

Emiliana's heart sank. Her beloved Tatiana was seemingly oblivious to the mystical forces of nature all around them.

Fed by heavy rainstorms, the river's roar nearly drowned out their raised voices.

"Do you miss being a *curandera* and living in Mexico?"

"I do. I miss the people and the other *curanderas*." Emiliana bent down, cautiously testing the rocks before balancing on a log fixed against the riverbank. "In Oaxaca, people would get sick because of bad food or bad spirits or bad energy. I helped get the sickness out of them."

A pale light broke through the canopy of clouds above the river's torrent. In her raincoat, Emiliana could pass as a child, but her face was wrinkled and ancient, gentle and fierce, all at once. "In this country, the people have a different kind of sickness. They are missing something. There is—*cómo se dice?*—a space, *un vacío*?"

"Emptiness?"

"Yes!" said Emiliana. "Emptiness in people. I think it makes them suffer even more."

"But how do—"

"Miss! Hey!" A large man in a sheriff's uniform appeared on the ridge above them, huffing from the climb. "You live around here?"

"Yes, of course," said Tatiana. "My husband and I just moved into that house." She pointed back toward where they had just come.

"Well, I'm just warning people to be careful," said the officer. He spoke in a low tone into a device on his shoulder, listened, and mopped his brow.

"The river is very high and rising, and we expect it to flood by the end of the week. Don't let the sun breaks fool you. Lots more rain's coming," said the potbellied man, gesturing toward the dark western skies.

As if on cue, a drizzle began.

"Does the road flood?" asked Tatiana, biting her lip.

"It can, ma'am. If it does, we'll open up the old logger's road and close this one," the man said, bending to adjust his belt. "You want to stay out of the overflow channels from now on. They look like safe paths, but when the river jumps its banks, the water will pour into 'em in seconds."

He straightened up. "People in these parts know, but still anyone can get swept away before they realize it. Keep to the high ground. OK?"

"Is it safe now?"

"I wouldn't risk it, ma'am. Wait 'til summer. Safer then. Last year, 'bout this time when we had less rain than we've gotten this year, I saw a bull elk caught in the current." The man put his hands on his hips, gazing down the river. "Got swept away like a stick toy. Found his swollen carcass down close to the falls, under the Railroad Avenue bridge. Bloody mess to fish out before he really started to get sour. No sense in risking it." He paused, studying the two women. "You be safe." He shuffled away.

Emiliana closed her eyes, feeling the water's power. Tatiana walked to the overflow channel and shuddered.

"Luna and I have been on those paths almost every day for the last month."

Emiliana nodded, grateful that Tatiana had a familiar, unobtrusive guardian.

They walked back in the thickening rain, the ground spongy and sodden underfoot, the tree branches baptizing them with water. How could a place so beautiful be so brutal and dangerous at the same time? Nature was neutral, indiscriminate— like the *Tzitzimitl*—not cruel or compassionate. A *tsunami* would sweep away the just and the kind, as well as the wicked. The landslide buried the newborn and grandfather alike.

Emiliana healed people who were suffering from nature and the passage of time. Sadness from loss. Disappointment, disconnection. Liam's darkness was different; it was evil. She thought about the first time she had encountered such evil.

## Oaxaca, 1934

Squinting from the bright sun, Emiliana walked into the adobe house, anticipating Asu's wide, proud smile. Casting nervousness aside, she closed the heavy wooden door behind her and waited for her eyes to adjust to the dark interior.

This was her first time. Grasping her medicine bundle tightly, she shivered, her body shedding the heat in the coolness of the place. She tugged on her *huipil*, trying to stretch it over her skirt, which was now too small for her at fifteen.

A table occupied one side of the adobe and a mattress on the hard-packed dirt floor was pushed against the corner. A woman lay motionless on the bed save for her labored breathing. Emiliana approached tentatively and knelt down.

"Good morning, Aurelia. I am Emiliana. I have come to help."

Aurelia moaned but didn't turn her face as she spoke. "What for? Even the doctors in the city can't cure me. You are just a *niña*. Let me die in peace."

"I am already fifteen, Aurelia. I will be married soon."

"Go away!" gasped Aurelia as she struggled to pull a threadbare blanket over her head.

Rebuffed, Emiliana sighed. She stood and walked out into the bright sun, squinting through the glare at the figures of the family standing next to Asu who towered above them, slender and gaunt, like the mast of a ship.

"I'm sorry, Asu," she said.

"You must help her, please," implored a young woman to Asu.

Asu approached Emiliana and whispered in her ear.

"Go back in," said Asu. Her eyes were kind, but her voice was insistent. "*Hija*, do not come out until you have given her some comfort."

Emiliana nodded and reentered the dark hut. She closed her eyes and prayed to Belegui, to *Maaso*, spirit of the deer, to the Earth Mother, and to *Ania*, the enchanted flower world.

"Aurelia, let me massage you. If you do not want to heal, let me at least take some pain out of your bones."

"Just go," said a muffled voice under the blanket.

"I will go if you let me massage your back and your arms and legs."

Aurelia sighed and threw off the blanket. Emiliana lit some candles and studied Aurelia's gaunt, wrinkled face. She was in her late forties but had the weathered, defeated look of someone much older—someone who could sense the closeness of death.

Emiliana took out a *jicara* from her wool *moral*, filled it with water from a jug on the table, and set it on the floor by the mattress. She pulled out little bundles of dried herbs and flowers, breaking off buds and twigs and dropped them in the water.

"I don't have any energy to do anything," Aurelia said as she struggled to turn onto her belly.

Emiliana hummed a prayer softly, rhythmically keeping time with her hands as she rubbed them together, warming them. She passed her hands over Aurelia's prone body, shaking them at the door after each pass, flinging the tendrils of dark energy she pulled from the suffering woman into the *jícara*; the water swirled clockwise.

"I will start," Emiliana said as she placed her warm hands on Aurelia's back.

Aurelia flinched at Emiliana's touch before relaxing. When Emiliana reached her neck, Aurelia cried out, "Ay! It hurts."

"Yes, you have something stuck here. I will be gentle."

Aurelia's whimpers turned into sobs as Emiliana kneaded the emaciated muscles. Emiliana closed her eyes, slowed her breathing and heart rate. A dark emptiness, deep in Aurelia's soul drew Emiliana like a magnet, down, down, down, and deeper still. The dark void had a name. It was the woman's son.

"You miss your son. The sickness in you is his absence," said Emiliana gently, tears filling her eyes.

Aurelia turned over and struggled to sit up. Emiliana wrapped her arms around Aurelia's shoulders and helped her sit on the bed. She cradled Aurelia's head with one hand as she rocked her slowly back and forth. Aurelia emptied her tears on Emiliana's shoulder.

"He took his life because he could not live in this world," Aurelia sobbed.

Emiliana took long, full breaths, pulling black smoke out of Aurelia's body and into her own. The black smoke came in long, tangled tendrils through Aurelia's mouth, nose, and every pore and settled in Emiliana's torso.

A thread of smoke spun and swirled before Emiliana, coalescing into a demon. It had a skull instead of a head. Its eye sockets were dark blue holes, and tiny stars, like pinpricks, sparkled in its joints.

"Leave her to me. She is closer every day to taking her life," the demon whispered in her ear.

"No!" shouted Emiliana, the dark smoke flowing out of her mouth, floating back to Aurelia. She inhaled with all her strength. The demon transformed back into smoke and flew into her nose and mouth.

Emiliana became so heavy, she sat transfixed, unable to do anything but continue to breathe in emptiness. Nothing mattered. Despair weighed her down. There was so much to do, but nothing would make a difference. She was as doomed as Aurelia. Emiliana hurled into Aurelia's dark void, and there was nothing she could do to stop her plunge.

"Emiliana, *vente, no te quedes*!" It was her mother's voice. "Emiliana, *vente, no te quedes*."

She heard it again, this time from Asu. "Emiliana, *vente, no te quedes*!"

Invoking her ancestors, Emiliana grafted her spirit onto their voices as they sucked the darkness out of her. She opened her eyes and looked down at Aurelia, who was sleeping peacefully for the first time since her son had killed himself. Emiliana finished the ritual and quietly walked outside to look for Asu. She was shocked to be greeted by the crimson sunset and the cooling breeze of the coming evening. Her time with Aurelia had felt like only minutes but she had been in there for over half the day.

Asu and Aurelia's daughter sat beside the fire, waiting. A log popped and sent sparks into the air. It was done.

She nodded wearily at them and the daughter rushed into the hut. Asu and Emiliana drank some water from a *cántaro*. Holding hands in the fading light, they began their long walk home.

"I'm proud of you," said Asu.

"I'm not! I got lost in her sickness." Emiliana bowed her head. "A demon came into me! I am not made for this work."

"You are wrong," said Asu, stopping in the middle of the dirt path. "You have a gift, *mi niña*. You feel what they feel, their suffering. What did the demon look like?"

"It was taller than me, dressed in a dark robe. Its head was just a skull."

"Did it have stars on its joints?"

Emiliana nodded.

"Only the most experienced and gifted healers encounter *Tzitzitlime*. When you confronted the *Tzitzimitl*, you were fighting for that woman's soul."

"What are *Tzitzitlime*?"

"They are sky demons who come from the stars. Powerful spirits who bring illness and death. We heal, while they make people ill and die. Most of them are female. The male ones are attracted to despair and attach to the soul. Once they attach themselves, they flood the host with dread, until they are unable to ask for or accept help. When the hosts kill themselves, as they inevitably do, the *Tzitzimitl* will latch on to one or even all those close to the deceased. They are very difficult to exorcise."

"You and Mama were there."

Asu smiled and nodded. "We will always be with you. But, in time, you will learn how to help people without their darkness sucking you in. You will learn how to protect yourself from those that seek to harm you because of your gift."

"Will there be a time when someone is so dark, you can't get out?"

Asu nodded, staring at the darkened path before them.

"Some people are so broken by life that they fuse with *a Tzitzimitl*. They are the most dangerous of all and the hardest to spot."

Emiliana shuddered and pulled her *rebozo* tightly around her shoulders.

## Wednesday

Liam walked from his home office into the kitchen as Emiliana stirred a large pot. Tatiana sat on a stool nearby, watching the old woman cook.

"What are you making, Emiliana?" he asked, sniffing over the pot.

"I am making you *sopa de albondigas*. Tatiana says it is your favorite. It's done. I'll make rice now," Emiliana said as she worked the pestle in the black volcanic mortar she carried with her everywhere. "Special chiles," she added, her face red and sweating.

"Now I am really glad you are here!" he said, opening a bottle of wine and pouring two glasses.

"I want to get to know you more. I will make you a good dinner."

Emiliana served large bowls of vegetable soup with small meatballs. It was spicy and comforting. She sprinkled sesame seeds and oregano into all the bowls, and with a deft, almost invisible turn of her wrist, added a finely ground reddish-brown powder into Liam's soup, before setting them on the counter in front of them. Smiling, she encouraged them to eat.

"This is delicious, Emiliana!" said Tatiana between mouthfuls.

"Watch your figure, pretty one. I don't want to have to call you piggy one."

Nobody but Liam chuckled.

"This is outstanding, Emiliana!" He wiped the broth from his chin with a napkin.

"It's depressing to see people let themselves go," he added. "Some of Tatiana's friends look forty."

"Maybe they are busy with other things," said Emiliana.

"What could be more important than your health?" asked Liam, shaking his head, "Anyway, I like young, healthy bodies. Like yours." Liam patted Tatiana on the thigh. She gave him a half-smile and continued eating. "I will be leaving on Thursday for Vancouver, but I will be back Friday afternoon."

Turning to Emiliana, he asked, "Can you drive the pickup into town? Just so she can get the stitches out?"

Tatiana looked up, and her face clouded. "I'll just call an Uber."

"If you can get one out here," said Liam, a grin crossing his face. "If not, the keys are on the hook by the door of the garage. I want to know you have some transportation in case you run out of toilet paper. It's not in good enough shape for I-90, but it'll do the trick on our little country roads."

"I can drive," said Emiliana.

Tatiana sighed. "I wish you didn't have to go." She gazed at her husband.

"I will be back on Friday."

Abruptly, Liam unbuttoned his shirt collar. "I am feeling a little warm." His face flushed and a thin sheen of sweat formed on his forehead and upper lip. He rubbed the back of his neck.

Emiliana jumped from her seat. "Let me make you some tea."

Liam smiled and drained his glass of wine. "The lights seem brighter. I hope we aren't having electrical issues."

"They seem fine to me." Tatiana put her hand on his forehead. "You do feel a little warm."

"Why don't you go lie down and I'll bring up the tea?" asked Emiliana.

Liam got up from the stool and Tatiana took his arm.

"I will go to bed too, Emiliana," said Tatiana, leading Liam out of the kitchen to their bedroom. "Leave the dishes, the cleaning service comes tomorrow."

Emiliana prepared two different teas. She added rose petals to Tatiana's, praying over the three mugs. She took one each to Liam and Tatiana.

"This one will replace iron from blood loss, *m'hija*," she said, setting Tatiana's mug on her nightstand. She walked to the other side of the wide bed, where Liam was already under the covers.

"I'm feeling really heavy, I can barely lift my arms."

"Don't worry. Drink this." Emiliana lifted his head so he could sip the concoction.

"It is sweet," he said. "Thank you."

"You two sleep. I will sit by the door if you need me."

"No, Emiliana, please," urged Tatiana. "Go to bed."

"It's the only way to sleep, *m'hija*. I will stay here and have a *velada*."

Emiliana closed their bedroom door. She dragged a chair from down the hall and positioned it to one side of their closed door, where she sat sipping her warm brew, waiting for the guides to appear. Luna lolled at her feet; her eyes trained on the old woman.

Emiliana had sipped through half of her tea when a chill crept from the base of her neck down the length of her spine. She wrapped her wool shawl closer around her shoulders, closed her eyes, and prayed silently to the spirits.

"Spirits of my ancestors! Guide me, please. Show me—now!"

With a decades-long practice, Emiliana slipped into a trance. She relaxed but remained inwardly alert. After an undefined period of time that stretched and slowed, she was jolted by a nauseating sensation of falling. The sacred medicine in her tea freed her mind from the material world and its physical laws, plunging her into the infinite present where there is no separation between beings and every moment in time is accessible. Her eyes rolled back in her head and her breath became imperceptible.

She opened her eyes and looked through a very young Liam's eyes. He is standing in the crib, crying. The room is dark but he sees his mother on her knees pleading, "Please stop, please, not in front of—"

A blow connects to the side of her head. She falls against the changing table with a loud thud as his father growls, "I said shut up!"

The room is silent; the hatred suffocating. Father drags his mother through the door and shuts it.

Darkness.

She blinks and sees through Liam's ten-year-old gaze. Father is yelling in his face, "You're bad! A horrible little shit!" Father lets go of his arm and whips out his belt. It whistles through the air, stinging his thighs, his back, the soft part of his belly. "Your mother left us because you're evil!" Hitting him again and again. Father throws him against the wall. His head leaves a moon-shaped indentation in the sheetrock. Into darkness he plummets ... falling ... falling.

Emiliana spirals backwards, into a black vacuum. She spins and stops. She opens her eyes and Liam is with a girl who is passed out; her breath smells of brandy and vomit. He—

Emiliana yanks herself away, refusing to watch.

Emiliana blinks again. Liam is in a bar fight, not caring who gets hurt. He rages, a wild animal, punching, kicking, hurting as much as he can until he runs out the back to avoid the police.

Liam's petulance engulfs Emiliana. He is being discharged from the Royal Air Force for assaulting a junior officer. He leaves avoiding people's eyes. He drives away and waits in his parked car for his now ex-commander to drive up the lonesome, rain-soaked highway. When Liam recognizes the commander's car, he tears after it, overtaking it, forcing it off a high steep curve.

His first wife, on the floor, her nose broken, swollen, and dripping blood. She begs him to stop.

Emiliana has had enough but cannot disengage.

Cruel images swirl, shift, and change. Liam is twelve and is putting live frogs in the blender. He is twenty, swimming in a quiet lake in the mountains and then holding a dark-haired woman under; she scratches his hands but he holds her head down, looking into her eyes. The images of cruelty come faster and faster as Emiliana claws back to consciousness.

Liam approaches a man walking to his car.

"Ramon?"

When the man looks up, Liam punches him in the face.

"What the fuck?" says the man, blood pouring from his nose, he spits a tooth into his palm.

"You lying sack of shit! You lied to Tatiana, fucked her, didn't tell her you were married."

"Listen, it was all consensual. If you're her father, I want—"

But Liam punches him, over and over, until a security guard pulls him back.

Emiliana convulses as waves of darkness break over her. A hard cold, like frozen metal, weighs on her chest, crushing the light out of her. Her head and limbs are heavy. Liam's darkness is profound, blacker than any she has encountered. Fear rips through her.

Emiliana calls on her mother and her asu. She calls to their light. A small hope stirs inside her chest as she claws out of the void. Her eyes open into the here and now. The terror slips away but just as quickly returns at the thought that Liam lies on the other side of the door, snoring and sleeping next to Tatiana, her great-granddaughter.

Through the closed door, Liam muttered in his sleep, distressed. Emiliana called the souls that orbit Liam, sucked in by his dark energy and illuminated the path to guide them away from his soul's vortex. "I need to find a way to protect Tatiana!"

## Thursday

Emiliana was sitting at the counter with a mug of coffee when Tatiana walked in.

"What is wrong, Emiliana? Is it Mama? Papa?"

"No, Tatiana. They're fine. Sit down."

Tatiana poured herself some coffee and sat next to Emiliana. Her bruise was healing.

"Tatiana, you are in danger. Liam is not a good man."

Tatiana's eyes bulged. "You're kidding, right?"

"No, *m'hija*, I saw his visions. I know him."

"Emiliana, I love you and I am grateful for everything you have done for me, but Liam is a good man and you—"

Emiliana slapped the counter. "No! He is not good. First, I thought he was just lost in darkness a little. It happens to a lot of us. But he is all nightmare, *una pesadilla*."

Tatiana blushed and stood up, her hands shaking.

"Emiliana, this is superstition! Liam is just a man and you hardly know him. He's not perfect, but he has only been nice to me." She avoided Emiliana's gaze and braided her hair. "Where are you getting these crazy ideas?"

"I saw him!"

"What do you mean, Emiliana?" said Tatiana, sitting down again, a look of disbelief in her eyes.

"Did his mother die or disappear when he was a little boy?"

"Yes, his mother left when he was two or three. He never heard from her."

"Did he have a little sister that died?"

"His stepsister died of sudden infant death syndrome; he probably told you."

"When did he tell me? Huh? When?"

"I don't know but you are worrying me. This is crazy, Emiliana!"

"Does he hit you?"

"Of course not!" yelled Tatiana, a reflexive reach to her face betraying the truth. She got up to fill the tea kettle, avoiding Emiliana's gaze. "Why are you making things up?"

"Did his father hit him when he was a boy?"

Tatiana sat down next to Emiliana again. She took her hand and said, "There's nothing wrong with Liam. I think his father spanked him, but he doesn't talk about it. But Emiliana, my father beat me, remember?"

"Your father had a sickness. I healed him and he never hit you again, right?"

"Yeah, he stopped hitting me when I was fourteen," replied Tatiana, looking away. "After a teacher saw the belt marks on my legs and reported it to social services."

"I am so sorry, *mi hijita*. But I cured him. He no longer has the anger inside."

"Liam is not my father!"

Emiliana paused, gathering her strength. She needed to make her understand the danger.

"I looked into Liam. I tried to cure him like your father, but I cannot. Something very bad happened to him when he was a child. It made him open to evil."

"That's ridiculous! My dad hit me when I was only two months old. Am I bad?"

"No, you are good. You are light. But Liam ... he is bad. When his mother left, or died, he lost something. He needs you to feed his darkness."

Tatiana stood up, her face and neck red. "Stop! I can't deal with this anymore! Why do you want to help me now when you didn't care that my father was hitting me since I was a baby?"

"But I didn't know—"

Tatiana put her hands on her hips. "Really? Everyone knew! No one helped us; the family pretended nothing was happening. Where were you *then*?"

Emiliana blushed.

"My mother not only did nothing, she encouraged him. Yes! She would complain about us and tell your grandson to hit us. No one cared about Nicolas or me. Even after you moved in, you cared only for my father but ignored us. Liam is the only person who ever stood up for me, and if he hits me, I'm big enough to stop him."

"I'm sorry, Tatiana. I never knew you felt this way. But right now, you are in danger."

"Enough! I can take care of myself. I am going to check on Liam."

Emiliana watched her walk away, her hands shaking. Tatiana was in danger, the *Tzitzimitl* had possessed Liam. She would back off and keep her beliefs to herself, bide her time, until she could deal with Liam herself. But something stirred in her chest. Had she failed Tatiana and Nicolas?"

## Seattle, Ten Years Before

Emiliana arrived at her grandson Luis's house the night social services placed Nicolas and Tatiana in temporary shelter care. Luis lived in a working-class neighborhood in Renton with his wife, Estela, sixteen-year-old Nicolas, and Tatiana, who had just turned fourteen.

Emiliana had never been to Luis's house because they said the house was too small. She rang the doorbell, but there was no sound. The porch light was out, the bulb broken, glass shards still in the socket. She tried again and then knocked on the door. Heavy footsteps approached and Luis let her in, avoiding her eyes. Emiliana gave him a hug and stepped into a cloud of cigarette smoke. The house reeked of cheap tobacco, stale beer, and spoiled food.

"Thank you for coming. I don't know what is wrong with me, Emiliana," cried Luis in a pitiful voice. "I can't control my anger."

"*A ver, a ver!*" Emiliana said. "This is not about you. Where are the children?"

"The state took them. They won't tell us where and we have to see a judge first."

"Where is Estela?" asked Emiliana, glancing at the overflowing ashtrays. The dining room table was stacked with piles of paper, folders, and files, towers more than three feet tall.

Luis caught her gaze and said, "Her business papers. She took a sleeping pill and went to bed."

Luis guided Emiliana to the kitchen where they sat around an oval table that had a folded magazine underneath one leg to stabilize its wobble. She kept her hands off the plastic covering crusted with grime and striated with brighter patches where someone had used a spoon to scrape down a clean spot. They sat in mismatched chairs; she on an old, stained pillow because the chair's seat had been gutted of its filling.

Piles of clothes topped the dryer in the corner and leaning towers of yellowing newspapers cluttered the floor beside it. Atop the refrigerator, open cereal boxes collected dust and flies buzzed. A cat drank water out of the sink's leaky faucet; a rubber band and a towel held down the key.

Luis poured her water from a kettle that was covered in kitchen grease and had little left of its original colors. He handed Emiliana a jar of instant coffee and a cracked sugar bowl. Pouring himself a cup, he sat beside her at the table. The cloudy windows veiled everything but the street light.

"What happened?" she asked, taking his hand. How could they live like this?

Luis lowered his head. "Someone saw belt marks on Tatiana's legs during gym and they called social services."

"Why does she have belt marks, Luis?"

Luis looked up at her and said, blushing, "Because I cannot help myself! I—"

"Luis, I did not ask about you! Tell me what you did to Tatiana and Nicolas."

"I hit them. Nicolas more. I always have. Tatiana was only two months old the first time I spanked her." Luis bent his head to his chest. "Because she was crying during the night—"

Emiliana nodded, closing her eyes as she reminded herself to listen with compassion, fighting the desire to shake him.

"When they were little, I just spanked them with my hand on their bottom, but when Nicolas was five, I started hitting them with my belt. I would hit them if they fought, if they broke something, if they talked back to their mother. Once I used a fly swatter on Nico because he woke me up from my nap. He was sick—Oh!"

Luis choked as loud shattered sobs erupted from some hot mantle of emotion that until then had found only one outlet. Emiliana let him cry. After a few minutes, she got up and brought him some bathroom tissues and poured him more coffee.

"Why does Tatiana have belt marks?"

"She was arguing with her mother and I lost it. I took off my belt and started hitting her on the legs until my arm was tired." Luis looked down at his mug, his fingers tightly gripping it. "I was so angry. I just wanted them to shut up. To leave me alone!"

He raised his head and sighed, looking at Emiliana. "I know it was wrong, but half an hour later, I asked her to forgive me. I was crying and she did."

"So after you hit her, you make her feel guilty for making you upset?"

Luis hung his head.

"Luis, you need to make this right. You have to talk to a lawyer and do what they tell you to get the kids back. I will move here to help with the house and the kids, so Estela can focus on work."

Luis nodded looking relieved, his eyes bloodshot.

"Most important, I will help you with that dark presence inside you. I can help Estela, too, if she wants."

"Thank you, I accept, but you know Estela. She has never been comfortable with anything from Mexico."

"I know! She even refuses to speak Spanish." Emiliana stood up, sighing. "I will help, but you must never hurt Nico and Tatiana again."

## Thursday Evening

Thursday evening, they sat at the counter eating chicken mole and rice and looking out into the evening. Emiliana had spent the day making it because it was Tatiana's favorite. A peace offering. Her eyes were red from grinding the different chiles that sat in bowls on the unused dining table.

Tatiana cleared her throat and said, "I have been thinking a lot and I *am* going to go to law school. I'll start next fall."

Liam's eyes narrowed as he set his spoon down and looked at Tatiana in surprise. "Really now? Thinking a lot about it? Has anything changed in the last twenty-four hours?"

Tatiana took out her phone and showed it to Liam, beaming, "I got an email from the law school. I have the highest LSAT scores of my class, so they offered me a full scholarship."

"Congratulations! I'm so proud of you!" said Emiliana, studying Liam's face.

"How do you plan on getting to the university?" asked Liam.

"I will drive. Emiliana is right; I need to conquer my fear."

"After what happened, I'm not sure you are safe behind the wheel. But we can talk about it when I get back."

"I need to call admissions tomorrow so I was thinking—"

"Fuck! I can't fucking believe this!" said Liam, standing up so fast his heavy stool crashed on the stone tile.

Tatiana leaped from her stool and cowered behind Emiliana, whose heart pounded in her chest. But Liam was not looking at them, he was bolting up the stairs to his office. Then dashing back down, carrying a gun, and shouting, "Those damn deer!" as he charged out through the large glass kitchen door. His angry rush triggered the motion sensors, and the light on the back porch came on, revealing a doe on her hind legs reaching to her full height and pulling an apple from the tree. Her fawn stood next to her. Liam approached within a few feet of the doe, who gazed up at him, unafraid.

Liam stood still, lifted his right arm, and aimed the gun.

"No!" Tatiana yelled, running toward the sliding glass doors as Liam fired. The doe staggered for a second before falling, a mournful cry escaping from her slackening mouth. The fawn scampered away as Liam raised the gun and fired again but missed. Liam stormed back inside, slamming the door behind him.

Emiliana and Tatiana glared at him.

"Why? Why did you have to shoot her? She had a baby!" Tatiana yelled, her eyes wide.

Emilina pressed her hand against her chest, breathing slowly, her gaze on Liam.

"That's what happens when you mess with me. I'm just teaching them a lesson."

"What's wrong with you?"

"With me?" he scoffed, "What's wrong with *you*? Do you think any decent law firm will hire you after they know you slept with a married partner and a client at the same time?"

Tatiana stepped back, as if punched. "That's cruel!" She blushed a deep red, avoiding Emiliana's gaze.

"I may be cruel, but you know I'm right. Your not-so-little indiscretions will follow you forever."

"That's not how it happened," she cried, now looking at Emiliana.

"I believe you," Emiliana hurried to say, Tatiana needed to know she was on her side.

"That's how it appears. You may get into law school, but no firm will ever hire you." He picked up the bottle of wine and, with the gun in his other hand, started walking up the stairs. "Come to bed. *Now*."

Tatiana looked at Emiliana and then at Liam.

"Don't go, *hija*!" whispered Emiliana, taking her hand.

"Don't worry, I know how to calm him down. I'll be fine." Tatiana pulled her hand away and went upstairs to find Liam.

Emiliana watched her leave, seething, her powerlessness scorching her stomach. Wisdom and the spirits could not compete with a gun. She took off her shoes and ventured into the storming night. She prayed over the fallen doe and promised to look after her fawn, who called pitifully from the grove of trees. A gust of wind rushed at her, roaring like a train barreling through the forest. Pine boughs flew through the air like autumn leaves. The towering cedars groaned as their ancient trunks bent to the wind's will.

Emiliana looked toward the river obscured by the night. She raised her face to the pelting rain and prayed, "I call on you, Spirit of the River, Spirit of the Wind. Help me stop the *Tzitzimitl* that threatens my great-granddaughter."

Something hit her back. A pinecone? A small branch? Emiliana took shelter under a cedar. A rattling sound, barely audible in the roar of the wind, startled her. Fear clenched her heart, pounding in her chest. Terrified, she knew she would have to confront her old enemy, *Tzitzimitl*. The demon materialized in front of her. Clothed in a black veil to hide the blood stains, a necklace of human hearts hung below her fleshless face.

Blue eye sockets stared at Emiliana with an evil glee. She rattled her skirt made of shells.

"I am here, Emiliana," she said. Her voice had a strange quality; it seemed to drift and land on the ears all at once.

Emiliana faced her, ready to fight for Tatiana and exorcise this demon from her life at last.

"I am not a threat to Tatiana," said the demon, reading Emiliana's mind.

Emiliana froze; her heart beat faster. "Then why do you follow Liam? He is abusing Tatiana!"

"Foolish old woman! It is not Liam I follow, but *you*."

"But why?" Her shoulders sagged with weariness, yet her senses were on fire. Open.

"You must find the answer yourself. Think about the first time we met."

Emiliana closed her eyes, forcing herself to ignore the storm around her and in the house.

She was delivering a baby that was breached. The hospital was too far and now too late. She prayed to her ancestors. After a couple of tries, she turned the baby, delivering a healthy boy. She laid the squalling newborn on his mother's chest.

"I robbed you of a mother and child that day," said Emiliana.

"Do you remember how you felt?" asked *Tzitzimitl*.

"I was happy and relieved."

"That's it? Do you remember feeling powerful? That you could defeat death?"

"I don't remember anymore. Why are you asking me this?"

"Because you need to understand when this started and how it evolved." The demon flexed and turned toward her. "You need to see your part in this."

"Mine? But I was only trying to help."

"Have you ever failed?"

Emiliana remembered the night Nico called her, two years before. She was living with a great-granddaughter, helping her with childcare and housekeeping, so that she could work as a nurse. Her husband had brought the phone to her room. "It's Nico," he'd said.

"What's wrong, *m'hijo*?"

"Why do you always say that when I call?"

"Because you never call me." Nicolas was silent, so she said, "Nicolas? Is everything alright?" Another pause. "Where are you?"

"I'm driving."

"Where?"

"Austin."

"Nicolas, what's going on?"

"I need to ask you something. When you came to live with us and got dad to change, how did you do it? Was it something inside of him? I thought it was the drinking but …"

"Nicolas? Are you OK?"

Nicolas sniffed and cleared his throat, "No actually, I'm really not well. I hit my little girl today. I lost it. Like Dad. I'm just like him."

"Oh Nicolas, how is she? Please calm down, you can get help."

"She'll be better off without me."

"Nicolas, you're her father. She needs you."

"She needs to be far away from me."

"Nicolas, listen to me! Your father changed, you can too."

"Please tell Tatiana that some people are born evil but not her. Tell her I love her."

"Let me help you."

"You can't. It's too late. It's inside me."

"*Nico*? Nicolas?"

He had disconnected. She tried calling him back, but the line went straight to voicemail.

Emiliana looked at the demon with hatred. "It was you! He went off the road into a ravine and died. You did it."

"I was there, but it wasn't me," intoned the demon, swaying back and forth. "Nicolas took his life because he was damaged from the abuse. No one helped him. You didn't help him."

The wind roared, slamming a branch against the house.

Emiliana stared into the blue holes of the spirit's eye sockets. She fell into the dark and saw herself. She saw her pride when she'd stolen the woman and baby from *Tzitzimitl* and the arrogance that started to bloom. She'd believed she was indispensable. If she'd only been humble enough to realize Nicolas and Tatiana needed help, counseling—or something she could've provided—things might have been different.

"I thought I was a healer," cried Emiliana, sinking to her knees.

"You are only the vessel. It is the spirits that heal through you."

"So you punish Tatiana to get back at me," said Emiliana bitterly, although nothing could be worse than knowing she'd hurt her loved ones.

"You foolish woman! Your pride also made you forget that *curanderas* and *Tzitzimitl* work together. We are not evil, we are the spirits of women who die in childbirth. We keep the balance, or the spirits of nature will retaliate. We take lives, but we also cure the sick through you."

Emiliana shook her head. "I don't understand."

"I was never your enemy," uttered the demon. "I have haunted you because you tied me to your pride. *You summoned me every time you blamed me for your mistakes.*"

"But Liam—"

"Liam has a demon passed on from his father. It has fed on the power of this place and on Tatiana's shame."

"Then help me fight him."

"You are still blind, Emiliana. This is not our battle. Haven't you learned? If you fight this for Tatiana, she will only find another broken man, maybe worse than Liam."

The apparition dissolved in the night. Emiliana shuffled into the house and changed her soaking clothes. She sat up all night, listening for sounds from Liam or Tatiana so she could intervene, thinking about what the *Tzitzimitl* said.

## Friday

Emiliana waited until she heard the garage door close and saw Liam heading down the driveway on the way to Vancouver. She slipped out of her room and went to the kitchen, where Tatiana sat at the counter, drinking coffee.

"*Estás bien?*"

Tatiana nodded and poured them coffee.

"I want to tell you everything."

"You don't have to," said Emiliana, climbing up on the stool beside her.

"I fucked up." Tatiana flushed and looked down at her hands, "I'm sorry to swear, but I did. Big time." Looking straight ahead, as if playing it in her mind, she recounted.

"I met Ramon, a partner at the firm, when they assigned me to one of his cases. He asked me out, told me to be discreet because he was a partner. I was thrilled that a seasoned lawyer like him was interested in me. We were together for two weeks when I found out he was married and that everyone knew about us. I wasn't the first paralegal that fell for him. That day, I was leaving the building, crying, when Liam saw me. He was the firm's client."

She sighed. "Liam beat up Ramon in the parking lot when he left work. I didn't know until he showed up at my apartment with bloody knuckles. Ramon agreed not to press charges if I quit. I was so stupid!"

Emiliana poured them more coffee, waiting for Tatiana to continue.

"It happened so fast. Liam is so charming and rich, and before I knew it, we were married and had this house. He's right, I could never be a lawyer."

"You made a mistake by trusting some bad men, but it doesn't mean your life is over or that you need to stay married to Liam."

"I need you to help me," said Tatiana.

"With what, *hija*?"

"I need to know what happened on the day of the accident. I need whatever you take to get into people's minds. I want to do that. I want to know before I leave him."

"Let's go now before Liam comes back."

"I need to be sure first, before I hurt him. He won't be back until Sunday. Can you help me?"

"The medicine I use is not for this; it's for healing." Emiliana took the girl's face in her hands. "I have been so proud. I misused the medicine by trying to control people, as if only I knew what they needed. I thought I could save your family by myself. I was too blind to see you and Nicolas needed help."

She sat back and sipped her coffee. "I also realized it doesn't matter who Liam is. You are the one who has to decide if you want him or not."

"What has this got to do with me knowing Liam's mind?"

"We don't need to know others' minds, *querida*, just our own. That is the only way to heal."

"Then help me know my own mind. Help me remember."

Emiliana nodded and left to get her medicine bag. She returned and took out her mortar and pestle. Into the mortar, she placed some shriveled brown fungi from a small pouch and ground them as she sang in Zapotec.

Biting her nails, Tatiana watched, a fine sheen of sweat moistening her brow and upper lip. Her large, brown eyes were as trusting as the murdered doe's.

"Do you have peanut butter?" Emiliana asked as she continued to grind. Tatiana rummaged through the cupboards until she found it. She opened the jar and set it in front of Emiliana, who took a spoonful and mixed it in the mortar with the little twig-like mushrooms.

Emiliana offered the spoon to Tatiana. "Eat."

The younger woman swallowed the mixture and drank the entire glass of water Emiliana offered.

"Lay down, *m'hija*."

Tatiana lay on the sofa next to the floor-to-ceiling window and stared into the green landscape. The pine, the rhododendrons, the hawthorn—everything so green and dripping with rain, with life. Her great-grandmother poured tea into two mugs. She left one on the coffee table next to Tatiana.

"Don't drink yet," Emiliana said. "Wait to see if you need it." She hovered by Tatiana's side sipping her tea, and Luna curled into a ball at the foot of the couch.

Tatiana kicked off the throw to cool off. Both closed their eyes.

Emiliana could now see through Tatiana's eyes.

She is in the dark, in space, she *is* space. There is a flash of light and planets are spinning, dancing.

"*Tatiana vente, no te quedes!*" She is drawn to the voice, to the call. It's cold and raining. The night is black beyond darkness. Tatiana bolts to her car; she presses the on button when Liam jumps into the passenger seat. "Don't go, please, I'm sorry."

Tatiana advances down the driveway. "Get out! I'm going to my parents."

"No! I'm going with you."

Tatiana turns unto the one-lane road. Emiliana is Tatiana, she sees through her eyes.

The wipers work furiously, yet barely whisk the water off the windshield as Tatiana speeds parallel to the North Fork of the Snoqualmie River. On the right, the car passes the shadowy outline of a horse farm and the brightly lit windows of homes. On the left rages the river obscured by a curtain of torrential rain. The headlights behind her flash, blinding her, forcing her to accelerate past the 55-mph speed limit of this country road.

"Turn the car around now!" snarls Liam from the passenger seat, his face flushed in anger. A wave of fear sweeps over her. She grips the steering wheel and fixes her large brown eyes on the road.

"I'm sorry I hit you, but I was only protecting you from doing something stupid." Liam pauses, watching her intently. When she remains stonily silent, he continues in a conciliatory tone, "You have to understand, pretty one, after being abandoned by my mother and—" he swallows.

A surge of pity washes over Tatiana.

"I've always wanted a child," Liam continues huskily, "to raise him in a different way, to finally have the family I've never known."

Tatiana touches the throbbing bruise growing on her cheekbone. "I'm going to stay with my parents for a while until we work this out." Her hands tremble and she clutches the wheel even harder this time.

"So you're leaving me to stay with the father that beat you until you were a teenager?"

"That's different! My father changed. He got help and he is sorry."

"Well, I'm sorry too. How come you can forgive your father but not me? I just reacted when you said you wanted to leave me and kill our baby."

"Oh my God! Please! I am not leaving you!" she yells, banging the steering wheel. Tatiana's thoughts are loud in Emiliana's mind, I just don't want a baby now, and it's my fucking body! Fear and desire to appease Liam fill her. "I just need some time away to think."

"You're such a selfish bitch!" Liam pounds on the dashboard. "I knew you were damaged, but I never thought you were so broken and fucked up! You're staying with me and you're having my baby! Turn the car around!"

Liam grabs the steering wheel and jerks it hard to the right. The car leaves the road, airborne in the darkness.

Tatiana's screams mix into the smell of wet earth, blood, the grinding sound of metal on rocks, the smashing of glass, the crushing pressure of the vehicle on her body.

"There was no bull elk," sighed Tatiana, opening her eyes.

"You already knew that, Tatiana. What else do you need to know?"

Tatiana tried to get up, but Emiliana held her down gently as tears flowed down Tatiana's face. "It's me! I'm my own curse!"

She blew her nose and wiped the tears on her sleeve. "All my life I felt that if only I could be good, better, perfect, then my mother would love me. When my father beat me, and then when Liam did it, I thought I deserved it. That it was my fault. And Nicolas tried to tell me before he died."

Emiliana sat next to her, stroking her hair.

"I bought into the idea that I was responsible for calming Liam, but I can see it now. He doesn't love me; he wants to own me. I remember now why I was driving the night of the accident. He hit me that night because I argued with him."

Tatiana sat up slowly and turned to plant her feet on the floor.

"I made a mistake, and instead of owning it, I gave up and hid by getting married. I don't want this life of luxury! I want my life to mean something."

Emiliana rose from the couch. "Go pack. I am going to get my things. We are leaving."

Emiliana walked out of her bedroom trailing her suitcase and froze. Fear flooded her chest. Liam was standing in the kitchen entrance, his back to her. He was between Tatiana and the front door where a suitcase propped open the door. Emiliana saw Luna waiting for them in the old pickup.

"Where are you going, pretty one?" he asked. His friendly tone sent a shiver down Emiliana's back.

"You scared me!" said Tatiana blushing.

"Must be your guilty conscience."

Tatiana coughed nervously.

"Where are you going?" he demanded, his tone no longer sweet but huskier, threatening.

"What are you doing here? I thought you would be in Vancouver by now."

"Liars answer questions with questions."

"I'm taking Emiliana back home," said Tatiana, moving to put the table between them. "I just can't stand all her superstitions. Why are you here?"

"Don't lie to me. You know I hate liars." He stepped toward her.

Tatiana stood her ground. She stood straighter and lifted her chin. "You're right. I shouldn't lie. This is my life and I've decided to go to my parents."

The slap thundered on the side of Tatiana's head, flattening her ear. She spun and held on to the table. She felt him come up from behind her, muttering, "You don't think! I think for you. You're not leaving."

Tatiana grabbed the bowl full of ground chiles, guajillo, pasilla, mulato, negro, ancho, de árbol, cuaresmeño, piquín and threw them in Liam's eyes, turning away as the powder landed on his face.

Liam howled and rushed to the kitchen sink. Tatiana bolted out the door, Emiliana behind her. They jumped into the old pickup where they'd tied Luna. Tatiana turned the key in the ignition, her hands shaking.

Emiliana placed her hand on her arm and said, "You are strong and brave. Go! Go!"

Tatiana sped down the driveway, cycling through the gears. Liam ran out of the house with a water bottle and dish towel and got into his sports car. Tatiana turned onto the road, losing sight of him. She pressed her foot on the accelerator.

The roads were choked with standing water from the rains, and she kept hydroplaning. "The tires are old!" she yelled over the sound of the wipers and motor. She slowed as she drove parallel to the North Fork of the Snoqualmie River. The same road on which they'd had the accident. Emiliana gripped the door handle.

Tatiana shoved in the clutch, braked, and pulled abruptly to the left, parking on the bank where, in summer, fishermen and teenagers accessed the river. She turned to Emiliana and said, "Get out now! Take Luna and hide behind the trees. Wait for me to come back."

"Call the police!"

Tatiana shook her head, "They won't make it in time. I need to stop him." She hugged Emiliana tightly. "Don't make a sound. Let him think we broke down and we are running on the trail."

Emiliana got out in the pouring rain. Big furious raindrops stung her face. Her pants below her raincoat were quickly saturated and dripped into her boots. Standing on her toes, she took Tatiana's face in her hands, murmuring a Yaqui prayer. "Walk in flowers. Walk with Asu and Bele-gui." She let her go and sought a hiding place in the trees far from the trailhead where she tied the faithful Luna.

Emiliana sat beneath a tree and took off her boots and wool socks, planting her feet into the cold, wet earth. Closing her eyes, she summoned her mother and grandmother. Two ghostly shapes shimmered on either side of her before speeding to encircle Tatiana.

The oldest and tallest had a long, gray braid that flowed over her left shoulder, down her white cotton dress. She was tall and slender like Tatiana. "I am Asu. I am in you, Tatiana. You have the power of the Yoeme and the spirit of the deer."

The other woman was short and very dark. Her two braids were interlaced with red and yellow ribbons. Her large, almond eyes were a deep brown, a mirror of Tatiana's. In the center of her chest pulsed a bright, white light. A star. She said, "I am Belegui. You have my light. I once saved Emiliana from a man who lost his soul. You can do it too. We are in you, as are all your ancestors. Use our strength."

"*Vente*, Tatiana!" Emiliana called. Her inner vision sharpened and she saw through Tatiana's eyes. They were one.

Tatiana flings off her raincoat and her sweater and leaves them in the truck. Liam's sports car barrels down the road, a flying V of water streaming behind it. Tatiana makes sure she is seen before darting onto the path. She runs in the pelting rain, over sodden ground, her clothes quickly waterlogged. Unable to see more than a few feet in front of her, she stumbles and crashes headlong into a puddle of water. Her hands sink through the soft moss into the viscous mud below. It is soft and cool and—alive. Something awakens within her.

She rises, yanks off her shoes, and bolts without looking down, trusting her feet as she leaps over rocks and dips in the path. Every rock, plant, and root vibrate, expanding into an energy field that guides her.

The rain-swollen river roars a warning. Liam's steps crash through the vegetation behind her. He pants like a beast, enraged, tracking, hunting. Tatiana becomes part of the forest, communicating with the plants through the mycelium beneath her feet, urging her forward.

"He is close," they say. "Run faster!"

He is so close, his sweat, his musk, his excitement from the hunt engulf her. The river roars behind them even louder.

The forest whispers to her as the rain comes down faster and harder. The trees lean in behind Tatiana, as if blocking Liam's path. Roots surge through the ground to trip him. Stones dislodged from their muddy cradles roll loose, making him stumble and slip. Thorny blackberry brambles scratch and tear his skin and clothes.

Tatiana jumps into one of the river's runoffs. Liam follows, closing the gap between them. The ground trembles underfoot, echoing a loud rumble, as if a herd of elk were stampeding down the mountain. Liam closes in; he grazes Tatiana's hair but he trips over a rock, falling a few feet behind.

Grunting and gasping for breath, Liam yells in a deep growl. "I'm going to look into your lying eyes when I kill you."

Tatiana peers over her shoulder and trips over her own feet, crashing on her side. Her ribs throb. She glances behind as Liam advances, grinning. Scrambling to her feet, she limps, holding her side.

Liam is within arm's reach when he falls; his boot ensnared in a tangle of the cedar's roots. Thunder fills the valley as a roaring wall of water advances on them, dragging trees and boulders. Tatiana leaps and catches a low-hanging cedar branch. The branch yanks her out of the runoff and flings her to safety.

As Liam desperately tries to yank his foot free, the river devours him, smothering his last growl, flinging him tumbling down the river and over Snoqualmie Falls.

Emiliana opened her eyes as Tatiana walked on the road back to the pickup, limping and sodden but alive. They held each other until Emiliana sank into the earth singing to the spirit of the river.

Tatiana took out her phone and dialed 911. "Please help! My husband was swept away in the runoff trying to save our dog. The dog got out, but he didn't. Please help!"

# A Safer Place

**YESSICA CUDDLED HER SISTER** Araceli's baby against her chest, one eye on her uncle's weathered hands steering the SUV. She couldn't wait to leave this flat, dusty, brown place. I'll never complain about the rain in Snoqualmie again, her nose and eyes gritty from the dry heat. She sighed heavily.

"As soon as we get the car seat, we can leave for Snoqualmie; if we take turns, we'll be there by tomorrow night," her uncle Enrique said, his eyes almond-shaped and brown, identical to Yessica's. He was burly and solid, the gray in his mustache and hair softening his rugged features.

Yessica shrugged. Driving twenty-eight hours to El Paso was better than picking blueberries in the summer heat before her sophomore year. Her mother said she was good at high school only because she hated working. But Mami was clueless, she liked school because if she got to college, she'd have a better life; I'll never pick crops again.

"It isn't your fault Araceli had to stay in Mexico," tio said, "and it isn't your fault that the *migra* caught her."

Yessica blushed and stared out the window, long blond strands with dark roots hiding her face. She scratched her knee, visible through her torn jeans, and swallowed. Her mother, pregnant with Yessica, had left Araceli in Mexico when she crossed the border fifteen years before. Yessica complained her mother only cared about Araceli, resenting the hand-me-downs and money sent each month for her care. But now, she was confused. When her grandmother, who cared for Araceli, died, the eighteen-year-old set out for Snoqualmie, but the border patrol detained her and her three-month-old baby. Separated from her baby and facing deportation, Araceli had begged her mother to take Isaac. Yessica squeezed her eyes; Araceli in her loose orange jumpsuit, gaunt, with dark circles under her eyes, haunted her. Araceli's eyes had darted around as she whispered about guards groping and beating her. Could it be that Yessica was the fortunate one? The gifts and money for Araceli consolations for being left behind.

"What's going to happen to Araceli?"

Tio Enrique lowered the volume of the accordion music blasting from the radio. "They'll send her back, and she will try again so she can be with her son. It isn't fair but that is life. Life isn't fair."

Yessica whipped her head around. "Why didn't Mami bring Araceli? How could she leave a three-year-old behind in Oaxaca?"

"*Basta!*" said tío Enrique as he gripped the wheel and stared ahead, his jaw clenching and unclenching.

Yessica gazed at him, startled. He'd never shown much emotion, especially not anger. She wrapped her arms around baby Isaac and stared ahead, pressing her lips.

"Your mother did the best she could," he said, his voice softer. "They killed your father in front of her; shot him as he left the house. She had to leave immediately."

"But why would they come after her? Wasn't my father the leader?"

"They both organized the community to strike against the power company. Your mother couldn't cross the border with a three-year-old. She didn't even know she was pregnant with you at the time."

"My father died for a stupid waterfall!"

"It was more than that! Your parents were fighting to keep our *pueblo* alive. Losing the waterfall meant the community would disappear, and it did."

"Why didn't he just come to the US like you?"

"*Ay niña!*" he groaned as he slapped his forehead with his left hand. "We never wanted to leave Santa Catarina. That *pueblo is* us. Without our *pueblo*, we'll never grow permanent roots," he sighed. "You were born here and don't understand."

"But you've done so well! You've got papers, your own landscaping business. You're the one we go to for everything."

"I only came because someone needed to make money for the family." He stared wistfully at the road ahead, his eyes on the cars. "I always planned to go back, but there is no one left there, and my daughters are here."

Yessica stuck her finger in the torn vinyl seat and felt the metal frame. "You paid for the coyote to bring my mother over, right?" she asked.

He nodded.

"Why didn't you pay for Araceli to come?"

"It wasn't the money," he said, pursing his lips, which he did when he was uncomfortable.

"Then why didn't anyone bring her? Why keep her away from her mother and sister?"

"Something happened to your mother when she crossed the border. She won't speak about it, but it was bad—" He paused, shaking his head. "—so bad she tried to talk Araceli out of coming."

Yessica shuddered as images of her mother and sister raped and beaten in the desert flooded her mind.

"That's all I know," the finality in her tio's voice closed the subject, and she knew not to push him.

Tio Enrique searched on the radio until he found a banda station.

Yessica hated that music. "Can we listen to something else?"

Tio Enrique turned off the radio. "You should listen to Mexican music; it's part of your culture. You kids can't even speak Spanish anymore."

Yessica frowned. How could he miss Mexico? That dusty, poverty-stricken place everyone was trying to leave for the US. "El Chico Muñoz says everyone is killing each other, and no one has money."

He grimaced. "That good for nothing? Please don't tell me you're seeing him."

Yessica's cheeks burned; her uncle was strict about boys, and he hated Chico because he'd been in jail and deported. So had her youngest uncle, but the family had sent him money for the coyote. Her mother forbade Yessica from seeing him, but it didn't stop her. When she was with Chico, she felt grown-up and alive, his desire for her a new power. A pleasurable tingling coursed through her when she evoked his brown hands roaming her body. He was like a drug; when she was with him, nothing mattered.

"You don't get it."

"I get that he's in gangs and drugs and is too old for you."

"He's only five years older than me! The same age difference between my parents."

"He's nineteen, and you're a child. That man has been in prison; he brags about the people he's killed.'

"Ughh!" Yessica didn't know what she hated most, being called a child or negative comments about Chico. They didn't know him as she did. He'd hurt others, he claimed, killed men but only to survive, and he swore he'd never tortured anyone. His stories about the border terrified her.

The baby stirred, and she adjusted her seat belt below his face. I wonder if he'll be traumatized by the detention center? She dried the sweat from her chest and the baby's head with a cloth diaper. Humming, she traced his little nose with her index; he'd barely moved since they picked him up. She swallowed, remembering the tantrum she'd thrown when her mother told her Araceli was on her way and would be moving into her room.

"Where am I going to sleep?"

"You'll sleep with me. Araceli and Isaac need their own space."

"You snore, and I need privacy! It's not fair!"

Her mother's slap had shocked her into silence. "You selfish girl!"

Yessica sulked the rest of that evening, furious. After her mother left for her night shift, she'd biked in the dark to the basement Chico rented in a house in town.

They made out on Chico's bed. When he unbuttoned her jeans, she grasped his hand. "Do you have protection?"

Sighing, Chico rolled off the bed and searched his backpack and the bathroom. "I'm out." He sat next to her and tugged at her jeans' zipper. "Come on; I promise I'll pull out."

Yessica shoved his hand away and sat up, crossing her arms. "You know the rules." Yessica rarely said no to Chico, often doing things she didn't want to, but she held firm when it came to condoms. There was no way she was ruining her life with a baby.

"Fuck!" he said, getting up and putting on his sneakers, "I'll run to the store. Before I forget ..." Chico lit a *veladora* in front of a twelve-inch statue of La Santa Muerte, the patron saint of death, sitting on a chest of drawers. The female skeleton wore a black cape and held a scale and a scythe with her foot resting on a globe. "My mother is having surgery tomorrow; watch over her *flaquita*," he said, kissing his fingers then touching the statue's head, an eyeless skull.

"Do you believe in her?" Yessica asked.

"I owe her my life! When I was in Juarez, a rival cartel kidnapped me and were going to kill me. I watched them torture and kill my friend; I was next, so I prayed to her." Chico waved his left hand missing the pinky. "They spared me but left their mark."

"The priest said she's blasphemy against religion and a cult to the devil."

"Who do you believe? A pedophile priest?"

Yessica shook her head.

"You can't trust your fucking mother for sure!"

Yessica cringed. Her mother was annoying but hearing Chico swear at her made her stomach shrink.

"La Santa Muerte accepts everyone, drug dealers, murderers, poor, rich. She doesn't care who you are or what you request. Ask her anything, you'll see." Chico pulled on a hoodie. "You stay right there while I go get more condoms."

"We're here," Tio Enrique interrupted her memories as he drove into a Walmart parking lot, packed on Saturday morning. He steered slowly, yielding to a man with a cart loaded with cases of beer, then slid into a place in front of the giant store. With the AC blasting, he turned to look at her, his right fingers on the keys. "You are smart and I'm proud of the effort you've put into school; you need to help Araceli and Isaac now."

"I will. At least Isaac is in a safer place," Yessica said, patting the baby's back. "I'm going to save the money I make this summer to help pay for Araceli's coyote."

Enrique turned off the engine, and they descended into the hot, dusty desert air. Yessica held the baby on her left hip, the sweat rolling down the back of her neck. She grabbed her purse and a small blanket to protect the baby from the blast of AC that would hit when they entered the store.

"Don't you think he's too quiet?" asked Yessica. "Not even a whimper."

"*Pobrecito*, probably gave up when no one answered his cries in the detention center."

They entered the giant store, crammed with brown people speaking Spanish, pushing carts piled with groceries, dragging children and grandma behind.

"Let's get the diapers first and then look for a car seat," tío said.

Yessica shifted Isaac in her arms. Even though the nurse at the detention facility had told them the baby was underweight, her back ached from carrying him. Her arm trembled.

"*Tío,* can we get one of the things to carry babies, like the—"

Bang! Bang! Bang! Fireworks from the parking lot? Uncle Enrique froze. The bangs started up again, this time louder. Someone yelled, "Code brown!"

A thunderbolt knocked Yessica over and back. She held on to Isaac as she grasped empty air with one hand, landing on something soft, her uncle. Turning over, she curled herself over Isaac and felt her chest and stomach; there was nothing, only a dull pain on her tailbone from the fall.

"*Tío!*" whispered Yessica, reaching to shake his arm, but he barely budged. Lifting her head a few inches, she made out his face, eyes open, unblinking.

"Shooter!" someone yelled and ran toward the store entrance. Gunshots thundered. Screams echoed.

Yessica prayed silently, "Please, God, please save us! Please don't let Isaac be dead. Let him live. Let me live." Again, and again, she prayed, not daring to look at the quiet, unmoving bundle beneath her or at the warm, uneven circle of red spreading around and beyond them.

Police shouted and rushed into the store as Yessica lifted Isaac, his body limp in her arms. She stopped praying, a sob catching in her throat, remembering that night in Chico's room. After he left to buy condoms, Yessica knelt in front of Santa Muerte and asked, "Please keep my sister and her baby Isaac from coming to Snoqualmie."

La Flaquita had delivered with cruel indifference. Yessica clung to Isaac as the EMTs struggled to pull him from her arms, muttering, "I take it back. I take it back. Take me instead!"

# Honor Your Mother

**"MAMI!" ASHLY SCREAMED, BOLTING** upright in bed, eyes wild and awake. The shaking disoriented her until her eyes settled on her brother's face.

"Stop shaking me! What the—?"

"We've got to get Mami!" her brother said, biting his lower lip.

"What do you mean?" she asked, stretching her short legs, substantial thighs, and hips. Built low and anchored to the earth; better for keeping her dream-filled head from floating away.

"They evacuated Mount Si Estates!"

Ashly combed the wild curls into a bun on top of her head, "So? They won't evacuate the town."

"I'm not worried about us, stupid!"

Ashly looked at him, insults locked and loaded, but kept quiet. Worry oozed from him. Not the time for verbal warfare. Instead, she fixed him with her brown eyes, replicas of his own.

"Mami cleans a house there."

"They'll turn her back. Now get out so I can get dressed." She said, shoving him toward her bedroom door.

"Wait!" He anchored himself to the doorframe. "Listen, dammit!"

Ashly stepped back. He rarely stood up to her. He's scared! His fear caught and ignited in her stomach.

"Mami went to clean the Taylors' house and doesn't know they're evacuating. She walks up the back trail, through the woods. If we don't get to her, she'll burn to death while she's vacuuming!"

"Have you called her?"

Christian rolled his eyes. "No signal on her crappy burner."

Ashly's eyes narrowed, her mind racing. If people evacuated, there would be firefighters and alarms, maybe cops. But her mother would avoid authorities because of her legal status. If she wore her headphones while cleaning, she wouldn't even hear the calls to evacuate. The Taylors, more worried about their possessions, had likely forgotten the maid that walked to their home three times a week; she was their human appliance, an invisible presence that cleaned, not a mother with two kids.

"Let's go!" Ashly said, running to the bathroom. She pulled on jeans, a T-shirt, and tennis shoes and met Christian at the door. They avoided looking at the table their mother had laid out for them before leaving for work. Foil-covered plates hiding *huevos con chorizo*, empty Dona Maria jars waited to be filled with juice and individual bowls piled with diced fruits.

Ashly opened the door into a hellish dystopia. Thick smoke obscured the trailer across the driveway, and ashes like gray snowflakes fell on cars and trees. She squinted in the pale, bilious light, the acrid air stinging her nose.

"Get a jacket!" ordered Ashly. "It's cold."

"It's July!" protested Christian, but he pulled a jacket from a hook by the door.

"The smoke's blocking out the sun," she explained as they climbed into the old Honda Civic that had ferried her back and forth from Wazzu. Twenty years old, her same age, rusting and peeling in places, the car nonetheless meant freedom. She cranked the tired AC to keep out the acrid smoke that stung her nostrils and chafed her lungs. Pulling away from the double-wide trailer, their home since Ashly had started high school, she maneuvered past the trailers that circled a playground, only the top part of the slide stood out from the smoke.

Ashly blushed as she remembered the screaming arguments she and her mother had when she decided to enroll at faraway Wazzu instead of nearby UW. She'd come up with many reasons for the move, but mother and daughter both knew Ashly was going to Pullman simply to be away from home. The truth of it had gone unsaid, too painful to acknowledge. Their bond was fraying; the daughter seeking her way, Mami holding on.

A few miles later, Ashly turned on the country road and sped east toward the Cascades that towered over the Snoqualmie Valley. She glanced at Christian, who continued to bite his lower lip and strained forward in his seat, willing the car to go faster.

"She'll be fine. I'm sure she's walking home right now." Awkwardly, she patted her brother's shoulder, the gesture too alien for their undemonstrative family, so different from the punches they gave each other when playing. Christian shrugged her hand away, scouring the roadside for their mother's familiar figure, her short, stocky body so much like Ashly's but with a long, heavy braid down her back. Ashly focused on the smoke-shrouded roadway. Mami will be alright. She's tough, resourceful.

"She cried herself to sleep last night," said Christian, mournfully, his voice cracking.

Ashly nodded, "We ruined her birthday."

"We?" spat Christian, eyes flashing. "Your birthday present to her was coming out!"

"I didn't plan it that way, but she just—" Ashly sighed. Her mother had mocked a gay coworker. As with almost everything her mother said lately, Ashly felt personally attacked, so she had blurted out that she was a lesbian. She'd known for a year, had planned how she would tell her mother after she graduated, but anger had derailed the plan. Confused, Ashly gripped the steering wheel harder. College was changing her; it was supposed to make her mother proud, not force them apart. Mami had told her to make a better life, but it seemed she wanted Ashly to stay the same obedient little girl.

"Why'd you have to tell her on her birthday? Fuck!" Christian pounded the passenger door.

"Fuck you!" screamed Ashly, going from love to hate at light speed, as only siblings can. "What about you dropping out of school? Getting a girl pregnant? You think that made her happy?"

"She doesn't know about the baby yet," he said, "and she wasn't that mad when I dropped out of school. She was relieved that I wouldn't turn out like you."

"Oh, you mean educated, with a good job and a degree?"

"No! A know-it-all superior bitch who tries to tell us how everything we do or say is wrong."

Christian's fury pounded Ashly into silence. Her mother often called her Miss Perfect and a know-it-all, but it stung to hear him say it with such conviction. Her visits home, her phone calls with her mother, usually ended with Mami begging for her to stop scolding her. Had she changed so much she no longer belonged? She swallowed hard.

"What are you going to do about the baby?" she asked, trying to shove the argument away from her.

"Jenny wants to keep it."

"But you're only sixteen!"

"Jenny's seventeen, and I have a job."

"With *Tio* Juan?"

"Yeah, I'm part of the crew." He sat up higher, prouder. "I get paid for every tree we cut."

"Is that enough?"

"We'll manage. *Tio* Juan does."

"Barely."

"He's alright. Didn't he pay for the coyote to bring us over?"

"That was twelve years ago before the pandemic broke everybody!"

"I'll figure it out. How much money are you going to make with your women's studies degree?"

"Fu—"

"Stop!" he said, pointing to a paved drive that snaked up a steep hill. "That's the road!"

Ashly gunned the car uphill, the fancy, old-timey streetlamps giving off a sickly yellow light, too weak to pierce through the smoke but casting a nauseating glow on hanging baskets of wilted flowers. She stopped in front of an immense wrought iron gate, blocked by two police cruisers and a fire truck. They left the car and approached three officers standing by their parked vehicles.

"This neighborhood has been evacuated. Can't go in," announced the youngest of the officers, acne scars covering his lower jaw and neck.

"Our mother is in there. We came to get her," explained Ashly.

"You live here?" the young officer asked, icy blue eyes daring them to lie.

Ashly snorted her annoyance, a sarcastic remark cut off when Christian answered, "Our mother is cleaning one of the homes."

"Everyone's been evacuated. No one's here. You need to go."

The officer started to turn his back when Christian shouted, "No!" His face was red and sweat rolled down it. "Our mother's there, and she doesn't know about the evacuation."

The officer glared at him when a truck hauling a horse trailer interrupted their standoff. It roared up the hill and stopped behind Ashly's car. A tall blond woman opened the truck door and leaned out, shouting, "I'm here to pick up my horses."

"You need to move," said the older officer to Ashly.

"You're letting her in to save horses, and you won't let us rescue our mom?" asked Christian, anger and disbelief marching across his face, making him look older this time. From the corner of her eye, she glimpsed the younger officer flex his meaty right hand around his holster.

Ashly stepped in front of Christian. "Please, officer, won't you just let us check to see if our mother's there?"

"Only escorted residents can go in, but he can send someone to check," said the older cop, nodding toward the younger one.

The young officer sighed and spoke into his radio. "What's the house?"

Ashly looked at Christian, who answered quickly, "The Taylor home, up on the hill, by the ridge."

As the young cop spoke into his lapel radio, the older officer said, "While he's checking, please move your car, so this lady can get in."

Ashly moved the car. The paved drive on the other side of the fence snaked downhill between estate-like homes with perfectly manicured lawns. The only sound was the chatter from the officers' radios. The young officer came over and said, "Someone checked the house, rang the bell, shouted, and knocked on the door. It's empty."

"Are you sure—"

"There's nobody there. You need to leave."

Ashly and Christian climbed into their car.

"Maybe she realized there was a fire and left," Ashly said.

"What if she didn't?"

In silence, they drove back to their trailer. Fear clenched Ashly's heart. She promised to be kinder to her mother. To listen, not scold or judge. She recalled an incident when she was five. She had slapped her mother in an angry outburst, the first of many. Her mother held her offending hand and said, "Honor your mother, or your nightmares come true." Her mother had hundreds of strange sayings like this, things Ashly was sure Mami made up. Like, "If you look too long in the mirror, the devil will appear" or "Provoke an impure thought with your body, you pay for that sin." These three had stuck with her; their dark messages menacing her memories. She shuddered. I wish I believed in God now so I could pray to someone, something, anything to keep Mami safe. She slowed the Honda to a crawl along the wood-lined road, hoping to spot their mother, but it was empty and unnervingly quiet, as if the creeping specters of smoke had sucked away all life.

"Why didn't she ever learn to drive?" asked Christian.

Ashly parked in front of their trailer. "The bullshit machismo she was raised in."

"It's not fair! I fucking hate Papi; I wish he—"

Christian's phone buzzed.

"It's Mami!" he said, swiping to answer.

Their mother's voice crackled over the phone.

"Christian?"

"Mami, where are you?"

"I had to leave the house. The fire, *hijo*!" she huffed.

"You need to get out of there, Mami!"

"I'm trying! I went back the same way, but the flames!"

Wrestling the phone from Christian, Ashly shouted, "Go to the main entrance, walk to the main gates!"

"What? Ashly?"

"Mami, go to the main entrance. There's police. They'll help."

"Okay, I'll try. *Voy.*"

Ashly and Christian stared at the phone. The speaker echoed with their mother's steps and ragged breath. Huff, huff, cough, cough, a stumble, and a muffled grunt.

"I can't get to the main road; it's all on fire," their mother croaked hoarsely.

Ashly shuddered, a memory about mothers and nightmares slithering through her brain, but she yelled away, "Where are you, Mami? What's the street?"

"There's fire everywhere. I can't see," Mother coughed.

"Look for a street sign! We'll tell the police to find you!"

"I can't, *m'hija*; *everything* is burning. *Hijole*!"

"What happened?" yelled Christian, his nose almost against the phone's screen, trying to climb into it.

"A house just exploded! I'm going to the river. Meet me there."

"But Mami—"

"Meet me there!" More coughing, but this time it took longer to stop. "I'm hanging up."

"Stay on the line!" yelled Ashly as Christian howled. "No!"

"Can't"—cough—"talk"—cough, cough—"river."

"Mami, wait!" yelled Christian, but she'd hung up.

Ashly gave him the phone and fired up the tired old Civic.

"Where?" she asked as she gripped the steering wheel to keep her hands from shaking.

"The north fork, behind the development. It's steep, but if she gets to the water, she'll be safe, right?"

"How do I get there?" she asked, avoiding Christian's eyes.

"Drive back the way we came. I'll show you."

Ashly drove until Christian signaled her to turn on a dirt road that jangled their teeth as the car drove over it. The car's dust wake mixed with the acrid smoke. Ashly turned on the wipers to swish away ash. Tiny embers, like angry red fireflies, flickered everywhere. A deer ran in the opposite direction, its terror-filled eyes glancing at them in warning. *It thinks we're too stupid to flee from fire,* Ashly thought. Branches and bushes leaned in, caressing the car as it rattled toward the north fork. When they came to a stone barrier meant to keep teenagers and drunks from crashing their cars into the water, Ashly parked.

"What now?" she asked Christian.

"It's down there," he said, pointing to a slope behind a clump of pines. They stepped toward the roaring river, the smoke thicker, the embers burrowing tiny holes in their clothes. Ashes fell like old snowflakes that had dried up in some attic while they dreamt of becoming snowmen.

"Wait!" yelled Ashly as she went back to the car and pulled out two face masks leftover from the pandemic.

Christian and Ashly slid down the steep embankment. The flowing waters rushed in front of them, gray and ash encrusted. The far bank hid behind a thick curtain of smoke, appearing and disappearing for seconds at a time, like a stripper teasing an audience. During one of those times when the smoke cleared, their eyes traced the steep embankment up to the sky, flames blasting high above the tree line. The fire's furnace spewed its heat, pounding Ashly and Christian into a crouch near the water's edge. Ashly's chest heaved as she surveyed the scorched far bank. Reason fought hope as she clung to the notion that her mother was invincible, would always be there, that life was fair and wouldn't heap another tragedy on this woman who'd already suffered so much, that bad things like this only happened to people on the news and in movies. She knelt and dipped the masks into the freezing water. She pushed a mask into Christian's hands, who held it to his face as he stared across the river, the strong current dragging blackened trees and branches, leaving wakes along the ashy surface. They waited, every sense straining, the river's roar now accompanied by crackling flames.

"Mami!" yelled Christian, his voice breaking, the last syllable cracking with hysteria.

Ashly cupped her hands around her mouth and shouted, "Mami! We're here!" Drowning in her panic, she tried to imagine a way out of this, some way in which Mami would survive. Mami was tough. She'd survived crossing the border, supported two kids when her husband left. So nothing could happen to her, right?

A black figure crashed through the burning brush. Not human, thought Ashly, panic leaping from her stomach to clench her heart. But even across the water, past the charred flesh of the figure, the stocky frame was unmistakable.

"Mami!" the words came out of Ashly's mouth as she tried to convince herself she was mistaken. This burnt, hunched figure could not be her mother, but Ashly's body knew what her mind denied, and her mouth shrieked, "Mami!"

"*Mis hijos*!" cried her mother in a harsh screech, her head jerking up, her ear burned away but still homed into her children's voices. She reached her fingerless hands in front of her, her burnt corneas useless in the dark caves left on her scorched face. Red flames exploded behind her, igniting the trees that towered above. She stumbled forward and plunged headlong into the water. The river dragged her away, steam rising from her smoldering back.

"Mama!" yelled Christian, plunging forward. Ashly grabbed his jacket and yanked him back. She held him while he sobbed, and the river swept away their mother. Was he remembering all the things their mother had done for them? How when Papi stopped sending money to Mexico because he had a new family, Mami had saved to pay for a coyote to bring her and her kids to the US. "I can make a living in *el norte* too," she had told them. How she worked nights canning fruit and yet, in the morning, had waited with Ashly and Christian until the school bus picked them up, their lunch boxes packed with *tortas* she'd made while they got ready for school. The summers when they worked with her in the fields, picking strawberries, then blueberries, and finally blackberries that tattooed bloody scratches on their arms above the glove line. There were fall weekends filling crates with apples and pears that Mami or another worker canned at night. She had always insisted Ashly and Christian keep their wages to spend on themselves. How despite heartache, poverty, and struggle, she'd forged a happy childhood for them, full of comfort and cheer.

Christian fell to his knees. Ashly lifted him by one arm.

"We need to get out of here! The fire is gonna jump the bank any minute."

Ashly dragged him to the car, and they drove back to the main road.

"This can't be happening!" cried Christian, his tears leaving tracks on the soot on his face.

"She's gone," Ashly said lifelessly. "We didn't honor our mother, and our nightmares came true."

# Soul Sacrifice

## June 21, Mount Si State Park, Washington State

**LUZ LEAPED OUT OF** the car as Patrick rolled to a stop next to her mother's old Camry, surrounded by yellow police tape. She bolted through the parking lot as Patrick huffed behind her, trying to catch up. Underneath the canopy, the muggy, dark trail twisted and tunneled upward. Sweat rolled down their faces and backs, sticking their clothes to their skin, and Luz's hair curled and frizzed into a brown halo. Gasping, she stopped and leaned against the trunk of a cedar so tall, its crown disappeared above her.

"Are you alright?" Patrick wheezed, catching up to her.

"Just nauseous."

"You shouldn't be up here. We didn't even bring water."

"Pat, I'm pregnant, not sick!"

"You should sit down."

Luz shrugged. "I just hope they found Mami."

"What could she be doing here?"

"No clue," she said, biting her bottom lip, trying to make sense of the last twenty-four hours since her mother disappeared.

"Well, it looks like we'll have some answers soon."

They continued up the empty trail, which was usually crawling with the hikers and runners who drove forty-five minutes from Seattle to climb Mount Si and catch a glimpse of the Snoqualmie Valley stretching to the west. Saving their breath, Luz and Patrick hiked in silence, their footfalls, an occasional bird call, and wind rustling the trees the only sounds.

"Are we going all the way to the top?" asked Patrick.

"No, we need to take the trail to Roaring Creek; it is just a few more feet. My father would bring us here to camp when we were little. I can't understand why my mom's here. She hated it! She only came along once or twice."

"I always knew your mom was depressed, but I never thought she'd do something so strange."

"I know! I'm worried it could be early dementia. Or a mental breakdown."

"Dementia?" Patrick asked between pants. "Isn't she too young?"

"Yeah, she's only fifty-two. But it could be early-onset Alzheimer's." Luz bit at her fingers and tore off a sliver of skin from her thumb, a habit triggered when she was stressed.

Patrick took her hand, and they walked until Luz stopped to take a scrunchie out of her purse. She gathered her unruly curls and made a bun on the top of her head.

"It would be sad for her to have a grandchild and then not be able to enjoy her."

"Her?"

"Or him. As long as they don't get my crazy hair!" she said, trying to tuck in some curls that were resisting the bun.

"I hope he has your eyes." Patrick put his arm around her but she pushed him away, impatient for answers, and picked up the pace. Finally, they found the trail spur to the creek. The narrow path was easier to climb than the steep, rock-strewn switchbacks up Mount Si. It led them through lush ferns, giant pines, and the occasional clump of maples along the clear-cut, mycelium-colonized ground. The dark earth was soft and cushioned underfoot, a welcome change from the main trail's hardpack.

As they approached a group of people clustered around a firepit, a tall man with salt-and-pepper hair speaking to a police officer—her father, raised his hand. Luz bit her lip. When did he get old? She dashed to him, searchin for her mother.

"Papi! Did you find her?"

Marcelino turned to embrace her. "No, *hija*, just her clothes."

Luz hugged him. They were both tall, Luz at five feet, nine inches and him six feet, both broad-shouldered, their large, round brown eyes dominating their faces. If Luz could have grown a mustache, she would have looked like her father's younger, curvier brother.

"What do you mean just her clothes? What's going on, Papi? I saw her car in the parking lot."

"Someone found her car. They sent police to investigate, and they found her clothes at this campsite."

"What clothes, Papi?" she asked, panic creeping into her voice.

A middle-aged officer approached them. "Evening! Is everyone here?"

"We're only missing my other son."

"What's going on? Can you please tell us what you found?" asked Luz.

"We'll give you a summary as soon as we get you folks together. We also would like to ask you some questions. So just give us a few minutes."

As he walked away, Marcelino said, "I feel like I'm in a nightmare and can't wake up."

"I know, Papi." Luz huffed as she sat down by the firepit. She wiped a layer of sweat from her brow, breathing slowly as nausea rolled in her stomach. "Nothing makes sense! Why would Mami come here and leave her clothes and her car? Do you think she was kidnapped?"

"I don't know. I know your mother, and she would never have left us. Especially now." He frowned and looked away.

Patrick walked over and offered a water bottle as he sank next to Luz on the rocks that ringed the firepit. "Have some; I got it from the cops."

Luz sipped noisily while Patrick gently massaged her back. They were an odd couple. He was Vietnamese, slender and agile, slightly shorter than her, while Luz had brown skin, long legs, a tiny waist, and curves that kept her from being fashionable. Introverted and mild-mannered, he was fascinated by Luz's passion and intensity, anchoring Luz with his stability. They leaned into each other.

"Can I get you some water or something?" Patrick asked his father-in-law.

Marcelino shook his head, glancing nervously at his watch. "She wouldn't have come here on her own! She used to say, "*yo soy flor de asfalto*, remember?"

Luz nodded.

"Christian must have been three the last time she came camping with us." He sighed heavily. "Patrick, can I use your phone to call Christian? I'm going to tell him to meet us at the house instead of here."

"Sure, let's go down the trail a little where there's a better signal."

Luz watched them walk away as her younger brother Joe sat down next to her and offered her a cigarette. She shook her head and looked at her hands.

"You quit?" he said, taking a puff. He looked more like their mother, short and stout, except for the curls he cut down to a stubble. His jeans were dirty, and he wore a plaid shirt with the sleeves rolled up to his elbows. "Holy shit! Are you pregnant?"

"Yes! We haven't told anyone yet. I just found out yesterday."

"This is great news! How long have you two been trying?"

"Two long years."

"Congrats, *hermanita*." He wrapped his arm around her shoulder and kissed her loudly on the cheek. "I am going to be an uncle."

"I can't believe Mami isn't here for this!"

"I know. Bizarre!" He took another long drag, adding, "I got the job yesterday afternoon, just as Papi was calling the police."

"I'm so happy for you!" Luz gave him a one-arm hug.

"I still can't believe it. I knew it was a risk to quit the job at the restaurant; only Mami encouraged me to try to find a job in film. Now I can't tell her I got it!"

"When do you leave, Mr. Hollywood?"

Joe put out his cigarette in the pit and stood up. "I have to be there in two weeks. Hopefully, Mami will be back before then." He stretched his arms above his head. "Remember all those scary stories we used to tell around this campfire?"

Luz nodded and leaned down to pick up the cigarette butt from the pit. It felt wrong to leave it there. Next to the butt, she felt something hard and pulled out a stone the size of a nickel. She inspected it closely.

Sparkles winked as she turned it over; her fingers traced the sharp edges of the crystals, iron pyrite. Without thinking, she put it in her pocket.

"Christian would get so scared, he'd piss in his sleeping bag," Joe said dreamily, a grin on his lips.

"Does Papi think Christian is going to come?"

"A junkie's parents never stop hoping."

"That's part of the problem."

"No one can predict what Christian will do. Papi called him, and Christian started crying. He told Papi he was going to rehab, but he would come up first to help look for Mami."

"Well, I hope he does go this time, for his and Papi's sake."

"Yeah, heroin's a bitch! I'll be right back, baby mama. Gonna irrigate those trees."

"Don't ever call me that again." Luz pretended to kick him when he passed by her.

As he walked away, Luz took out a small bottle of painkillers. She emptied the pills into her bag, and with the empty bottle, scooped up some of the fine ash from the pit and hid it in her purse. Why did I do that? Maybe it's the hormones. As she was wiping her hands on her jeans, an officer called the group to gather around a small, portable table he had set up and which looked out of place in the middle of the forest. Stiff but alert, Luz and her family stood in front of the officers. Please give us good news; Luz prayed.

"Mr. Marcelino and family, thank you for coming. First, we would like to ask you a few questions, and then we will share what we know."

Luz startled everyone with a slap. "Sorry, mosquito," she said as she rubbed her neck.

"Yeah, let's try to get you out before it gets dark. Do you see anything familiar at this campsite? Anything odd or out of place?"

"Honestly, we haven't been up here since we were teenagers. So I wouldn't notice anything," offered Joe.

Luz nodded. "Same here."

"Is there any reason to believe your mother would leave on her own?"

"My mom would never leave without telling someone. She was afraid of driving in the dark and hated camping and hiking." Then, realizing they expected answers from them instead of the other way around, Luz said, "You gotta help us here!"

"I understand your frustration, and we're doing the best we can. Here is what we know so far. Yesterday, June 21, at around two in the morning, Mrs. Alma Rodriguez was seen by a neighbor, Mr. Davis, putting a large bottle into the trunk of her car. She was alone. This morning a park ranger found her car with the door open and the keys in the ignition. An hour later, he found her clothes, which you've identified, neatly folded in a pile on that boulder. He also found an empty bottle of lighter fluid and a flashlight that you identified as missing from home. We've not been able to find any clues or footprints except for those of her shoes, and they stop here. We are as lost as you. Can any of you think of any reasons she would act like this?"

The group looked around at one another; their silence accentuated by the sound of the creek and birds.

"Any documents she wanted to destroy?"

The family looked at him with blank faces.

Joe stepped forward. "Could someone have incinerated her in the firepit?"

"How could you say something so gruesome?" growled Marcelino.

"I'm sorry, but someone had to ask the obvious question. We are on the mountain from Twin Peaks."

Luz stepped between her father and brother. "Just shut up!"

"Let me assure you we have found no signs of violence. Also, a fire-pit cannot create the heat necessary to incinerate a body. We usually find garbage and half-burned logs in these pits, but this one is pretty clean. It's warm to the touch, but there is only ash. No other sign of burning."

They stood silently, cops and family waiting on one another for answers.

"Anything else?" The officer paused. "Well, please contact me immediately if you can think of anything or remember something," he directed, passing out his card. "Sometimes people may be going through something, and then they come back."

"You don't know the first thing about my wife," Marcelino said through clenched teeth. "You should be trying to find who took her."

"Mr. Marcelino …"

"Mr. Rodriguez. Marcelino is my first name."

"I apologize, Mr. Rodriguez. We have no reason to believe someone abducted your wife. There was no forced entry into your home, and we have a witness who saw her leave. There is no sign of violence or struggle."

The younger officer chimed in, "It's as if she vanished into thin air."

"Which is impossible!" corrected the older officer. "You have my word; I will keep investigating." He offered his hand, and Marcelino shook it, glaring at him.

They trekked down the trail in silence, the dropping temperature and downward slope making the return trip physically easier. Shadows lengthened as their dread deepened, each of them in turmoil, trying to come up with an explanation for Alma's disappearance.

## Twenty Years Later

Luz rested her head on the steering wheel, waiting to cry, hoping to bawl her eyes out, but nothing came. I'm dead inside. The university's parking lot was empty now that finals were over, and the summer students had a few weeks before they were back in class. She'd left a memorial for one of her students, the third this year. It's too much! How many more young lives cut short by suicide? This one had been even harder than the others. She'd known him, having counseled him a few times at the beginning of the school year, but she was only allowed to provide short-term therapy as a college counselor. Now, almost eight months later, he'd jumped off an apartment building.

"Fuck, fuck, fuck!" she yelled, hitting the steering wheel. Could she have made a difference? His psychiatrist and therapist hadn't, so probably not. The doubts about her work snowballed. Nothing seemed to cure the depressed and anxious students; the medications just tempered the symptoms.

Sighing, she started the car and drove home. What home? Her two-year relationship with Mark was waning; the passion that precipitated her divorce from Patrick dead. Mark was a lecturer of philosophy at the university. Introverted, solemn, and quiet; her opposite. They shared a bed in his house but, for all practical purposes, lived apart. Mark spent the time when he wasn't lecturing writing his obscure book on epistemology.

Luz picked up Thai food; she wasn't hungry but still felt compelled to fulfill her womanly duties and feed her man. So she parked in the driveway and went straight to Mark's study. He was bent over the keyboard, his salt-and-pepper hair falling over his forehead as one hand pecked away furiously while the other stroked his beard.

"Do you want to have dinner?" she asked because she always did, even though he always said no.

Without looking up from the screen, Mark shook his head. "I'll just grab something later. Need to finish this chapter on intuition, or as I call it, fake knowledge."

"I got pad thai."

"Mmmm."

She watched him type; his eyes fixed on the screen. "I'll leave you a plate in the microwave."

Luz went back into the kitchen, prepared two plates, and sat at the counter, staring out at the tiny backyard. It darkened suddenly from the passing of a cloud, as if someone had used a dimmer. She forced herself to eat a forkful of papaya salad, sour and spicy; like the jicama with lime and tajin her mother would make her. I can't believe it's been twenty years! She glanced at the ceiling; I miss you, Mami.

The landline message light blinked, so she pressed the button.

"Hola, Luz! It's your aunt Lula, call me! It's urgent. I think you are two hours ahead, no? Please call me. It is Tuesday, about four in the afternoon here, *Dios mio*! I hope it's not too late there."

That's strange! For the last twenty years, since her mother disappeared, she phoned Aunt Lula, her mother's sister in Mexico, the first Sunday of the month. The only time Lula had called her was when her husband died. Something must have happened. She dialed her aunt.

"Luz? Yoali is gone!" Her aunt's voice trembled.

"What do you mean gone? Did you call the police?" Luz held her breath; the possibility that Mexico's rampant femicide had claimed a member of her family sent a shiver down her spine. Yoali was her twenty-two-year-old niece and her aunt's granddaughter. Her aunt Lula had raised Yoali after her mother died in a car accident. She visited Luz in

Seattle for a week every summer but had pulled away in her teen years too busy to travel.

"She went to Sinaloa to find out about her father. I'm afraid she'll try to kill herself again!"

Something seized Luz's stomach, twisting. "What do you mean again? What is going on?"

"It's been so bad," she sighed, "but I didn't want to worry you. You had so much on your plate getting divorced, and you work all the time."

Luz closed her eyes. There it was, Lula's usual jab coated in disapproval.

"Yoali went downhill since she started looking for her father's family. She tried to kill herself with a gas overdose, but a neighbor found her before it was too late."

"What?" That's all Luz could say. She swallowed. Why didn't I stay in touch? I could've helped them. "*Tia*, this is serious. You should have told me. Tell me from the beginning."

"When she stopped visiting you in Seattle, she became like those Goths, always in black, pierced all over, sleeping all day, saying she didn't have a reason to get up. I took her to the psychiatrist, and they gave her pills but they don't work, and she gets mad when I ask if she took them."

"I'm so sorry, *tia*. Where could she go? Who are her friends?" Luz asked, taking a glass from the dish rack and filling it with water.

"I never met her friends; she's always moody and on her phone or laptop."

"I'd love to help, *tia*, but I wouldn't know where to look for her."

"I'm not asking you for that. I'm asking you to come and help as a psychologist."

"I'm a counselor, remember? And I'm not that good."

"Luz, we need you."

"Let me see what I can do. I call you back."

She hung up as Mark walked into the kitchen carrying a shot glass and a bottle of tequila.

"For me?" asked Luz, sitting down and pouring a shot. "What's the occasion?"

Mark warmed his food in the microwave. "I'm done."

"With?"

"My book. I finished it."

Luz almost choked on the fiery drink. "You did?"

"Yes."

"Congratulations!" Luz finished the shot, and halfway up to hug him, she sat down. "How does it feel?"

"Like I just woke up from an eternal dream. Twenty years."

"Wow! Huh," said Luz. It was hard to imagine a future in which he wasn't working on it at least ten hours a day.

"I was thinking about Cabo for a week to get some sun, then maybe Spain, no wait, too hot in the summer. How about Machu Picchu?"

"Now? This summer?"

Mark nodded, his mouth full of food.

Luz's cheeks burned. "I can't. I'm going to Mexico."

Mark dropped his fork. "Since when?"

"My aunt Lula left a message. Yoali has disappeared and I need to go."

"Is this the niece who used to come every summer?"

Luz nodded.

"I could come, or we can go when you return. I was thinking we should get married; we could go on a honeymoon."

"What?"

Mark got on one knee. "I'm serious. This is what you want, right?"

Luz stared at him, mouth open. It was so unexpected that she almost burst out laughing but held back.

"You look horrified," said Mark as he struggled to get back in his chair, "Am I that bad of a catch?"

"It's not that. It's just you and I barely speak to each other. We have separate lives."

"It's not that bad." Mark got a beer from the fridge and twisted off the cap.

"What did I do last weekend?"

"Come on, that's not fair; I was busy finishing the book."

"Alright, tell me what we did for my birthday. No, I'll make it even easier. When is my birthday?"

"You're ridiculous. You know I don't care about those things."

"That's fair, but I do. Ok then, what kind of future do you imagine?" Luz sat on her hands to keep them from shaking as her heart pounded in her chest.

"We can retire to my cabin on Orcas Island. Enjoy life."

"I'm not ready to retire; I'm only fifty-two!"

"You can still do your counseling thing there," said Mark, taking her hand.

He's dismissing me! Heat rose from her stomach to her head, and she yanked her hand from Mark's grasp. "You're right. I should just throw away my ten-year career at the university, my PhD, and all my experience so I can help rich women face their wrinkles."

"That's not what I meant."

Luz got up so quickly, her chair toppled over, crashing on the floor. "What did you mean then? That I should be a good little woman and give up everything to follow someone who has ignored me for the last year?"

Mark got up from the table, red-faced and breathing hard. "You're too emotional. We can talk when you're calm."

But Luz had smashed the valve restraining her emotions and the trickle of resentment was now a firehose that she couldn't turn off. Hands on her hips, she blocked his exit and glared at him with blazing eyes. "Let's talk now! You no longer have your book as an excuse to flee."

Mark tried to go around her, but Luz stood in his way, arms crossed.

"I said we'd talk later."

"No!" Luz said, poking him in the chest with her index finger, nostrils flaring. "I'm calm. Tell me what you meant."

"You're not calm!"

Luz took a deep breath, crossing her arms to hold in the current that rushed through her body. "I'm calm now."

"Listen! I thought that is what you girls want, to get married, the ring."

"Can you hear yourself? Do you think we *girls* of fifty-two want a ring? Security? I can buy any fucking ring I want. We have the same retirement plan!" Luz paced. "I can understand why you want to get married; married men live longer, but women don't! You just want someone who will leave their work to entertain you."

"You're irrational!"

"Maybe I am, for putting up with your shit for so long."

"I had to put up with a lot too!"

"You? What?"

"You leaving all the time to see your sons, giving them money and buying them everything they ask for, even though they never thank you."

Luz chuckled, but it came out like a strangled laugh. "I guess I should let you manage my money, so I don't waste it on my kids."

"That's not what I meant."

She exhaled. I need to stop, it isn't worth the energy, no use stirring the embers in a fire you want to put out. Breathing deeply, she drank a glass of water and leaned on the kitchen sink.

Mark left his beer bottle in the sink and poured himself half a glass of scotch.

Luz sat at the table again and put her head in her hands. "I don't want to marry you; I'll move out."

He poured her another tequila. "You don't have to. We can stay as we are now."

"It's time. You don't even like me."

"That's not true," said Mark, finishing his scotch. "It's just some parts of you that are problematic."

"I need to get my own place where my sons are welcome."

"I'm sorry I said that before; you know I like them, right?"

Luz got up. She didn't want to hurt Mark, but she wasn't going to lie either. "We tried for two years; it's time to let go. I'm going to bed; I have an early day tomorrow."

The next day, Luz rummaged through her office for items she might need during the summer break and placed them in a canvas tote. She threw in a water bottle, her headphones, and an open bag of almonds.

Her dean knocked and opened the door. "Can I come in?"

"Please," said Luz, taking the tote off a chair.

"I have bad news," said the dean, crossing her legs.

"No! I didn't get the director's position." Luz slumped back in her chair. Her life seemed to be taking some wrong turns.

"I'm sorry, Luz, remember it's just an interim position; when it opens six months from now, you can still apply."

"What for? It's obvious the committee doesn't think I'm director material."

"Then become director material. You have the next six months."

"What do you mean?"

The director ruffled her short blond hair. "Work on your skills. You can be very opinionated and passionate, and it turns people off."

"I see, you mean the committee doesn't like women with opinions."

"It's not that, but you can be intimidating."

Luz was grateful she'd run an extra two miles that morning, taking advantage of the good weather because it helped her contain the anger building inside. She took a deep breath and grit her teeth. "Thank you for your honesty."

"One piece of advice. Stop questioning all the experts; we may not get the results we want all the time, but their methods work. Maybe you're just a little burnt-out."

"I'm not sure the parents of the dead students think our methods work."

The dean scowled and stood up. "Aggression is a sign of burnout. Sorry for the bad news, but I hope you have a relaxing summer."

Luz bumped her way through the crowd, scanning the faces in front of Mexico City's airport arrivals. Fearful she wouldn't recognize her *tía* Lula, she spotted the older copy of her mother right away. A hollow feeling set up in her chest. That's what her mother would have looked like now.

Lula pecked her cheek. "*Ya llegaste.*"

Luz hugged her back, bending over her pear-shaped aunt; her short, thin legs and meaty arms so typical of older Mexican women. Lula kept her short hair dyed brown, a gray fringe at the hairline presaging a visit to the stylist. Dark circles framed her eyes and her clothes hung loose.

"You must be tired," Lula said, turning toward the parking lot without waiting for Luz to answer.

Luz followed as they skillfully maneuvered around men pushing dollies packed with bags and large families trying to stay together. They walked by shops, money exchange booths, and restaurants from which wafted tantalizing smells of bacon, freshly brewed coffee, and salsa. The loudspeakers warned passengers not to leave packages unattended and increased the sense of urgency in the air. Lula walked confidently ahead, never stopping, expecting people to get out of her way, and they did. She guided her through the maze of the airport and parking lot until they arrived at a steel gray VW Beetle. It was a model from the seventies, bare metal, and glass, no-frills but immaculate. Not a scratch or a stain on the cloth upholstery. Luz swung the suitcase into the front-end trunk and sat by her aunt.

"Thank you for picking me up. I could've taken the bus to Pachuca."

"Nonsense!" said Lula. "I'm so grateful you came; this is the least I can do. And it's only seventy kilometers."

"Have you heard from Yoali?"

Lula shook her head and gripped the steering wheel with eyes stuck on the traffic ahead. The Popo, cone-shaped and majestic, smoke rising from its crater, appeared to float above them as they drove northeast on the modern highway toward Pachuca. Cottonwoods and cactus trees lined the road. Occasional tents sheltered and fed hungry drivers with *barbacoa* and flavored *nieves*. They passed the turnoff to Teotihuacan, where the Sun and Moon Pyramids were once the centers of the world.

Luz checked her messages and read Mark's latest. "Get your shit together and come back. I'm here, but I won't wait forever." Luz swallowed hard but didn't reply. Instead, she texted her sons that she had landed and was safe.

As they approached Pachuca, the Sierra appeared out of nowhere. The Otomies and Chichimecas founded the capital of Hidalgo in the narrow valley that was essentially a wind tunnel and gave the city its nickname: *La bella airosa*. Conquered by the Mexicas and then the Spanish, it was rough land accustomed to hardship. The arid, rugged hills hid rich silver and gold veins. A sixth of the world's silver was mined here on the backs of Indians, Black slaves, and Mestizos. International companies ran the mines dry and left toxic mounds of refuse, on top of which people built their brightly painted homes.

They left the rural landscape and reached the outskirts of the city, where cheap motels and improvised shacks lined the highway. Lula drove the VW Beetle at ten miles below speed limits as they left behind malls and large grocery stores that soon gave way to recently built McDonalds, Domino's Pizza joints, and Walmart.

She maneuvered through the main avenue where long-established businesses fought a losing battle against global corporations: *Mercado Revolución*, a coffee mill that gave off whiffs of freshly roasted beans, a pharmacy, little shops, and homes. Then, they turned down a narrow cobblestone street and parked in front of an immaculate house. Clay pots, flowering with red and white geraniums and multicolored begonias, lined the walls. Inside, the scent of roasted chiles hung in the air.

"I made the bed in Pedro's study for you. I'm going to check on *la comida*."

They sat at the heavy, formal dining room table. Lace curtains let in rays of the afternoon sun that ignited the swirling dust into shimmering motes. The bell from the nearby *Basilica* rang, announcing 2:00 p.m. Luz closed her eyes and for a moment was back in her grandmother's kitchen, visiting with her mother. She thought she heard Alma's raucous laugh.

"I made you a typical meal," said Lula. "I hope you eat Mexican food."

"Of course I do! It is my favorite. You shouldn't have bothered. Thank you, *tía*."

"What else do I have to do but worry about Yoali."

In front of her, Lula placed a bowl with a red-stained bundle trussed in string and sat at the head of the table with her bowl. As Luz opened the bundle, steam saturated with the aroma of chili ancho, garlic, cloves, and oregano rose, tickling her nose.

"I know you gringos don't eat spices nor chiles … Luz, what is the matter?"

Luz smiled, sweat trickling down her face and neck. A blush spread across her cheeks. "It's just a hot flash, *tia*; it'll pass."

"When your mother was here the last time, we were both having *bochornos*. One of us would get one, and the other would follow. They seemed contagious."

Luz wiped the sweat from her forehead. "They're driving me mad!" She bit her taco. "Mmmm. *Tia*, this is delicious, thank you."

"I'm glad you like it. I was worried you'd only want hamburgers and hotdogs. How is your father, Luz? And his new wife?" asked Lula.

"Oh, he's doing fine. His wife isn't that new; they've been married fifteen years now. She takes good care of him."

"I can't believe it! How long has it been since your mother?" Lula asked, raising her right eyebrow.

"Twenty years, my mother was my age when she disappeared."

Lula sighed. "What if Yoali never comes back?"

"She will, *tía*. Can you tell me more? Was she seeing a doctor?"

Lula nodded. "I made an appointment for you to speak with him tomorrow."

"Does she have a boyfriend? She hardly spoke to me since starting college."

Lula arched her eyebrows and pursed her lips. "You should talk to her anthropology professor; I bet he knows where Yoali went."

"Her professor?"

"She's fascinated with him! She couldn't stop talking about him. I think they were having an affair."

"Are you serious?"

Lula nodded. "Can you believe that?"

"Yuck! Maybe I'll go check that asshole out." She hated the professors with frail egos who surrounded themselves with young admirers, often taking advantage of them. One of the things that attracted her to Mark was how immune he was to his female students' charms.

The next day Lula drove Luz to meet with Yoali's psychiatrist. The doctor was in his forties, balding and wearing his doctor's coat. Luz was surprised at how eagerly he talked about his patient, reading from a paper file, with no concern for her privacy.

"I started seeing Yoali when she was in high school; the school psychologist referred her to me for cutting. I diagnosed her with generalized anxiety disorder and clinical depression and started her on a couple of medications."

He lowered his glasses and turned to Luz; she nodded to show she was following.

"She responded well to the medications, but six months later, the effects wore off, and she was back in the same place. So we doubled her medications, and again she responded. A year later, she attempted suicide. We swapped her medication, then six months ago doubled it."

"Have you considered that when she felt better after starting a medication, it was a placebo effect? That's why it wore off after a few months."

"Yoali is a very sick person; when she is depressed, she reports not having a reason to live!"

Luz walked to the office door. "Let me know when you find a pill that gives someone a reason to live." She shut the door behind her. Fuck! Poor Yoali, searching for meaning and instead getting pills. She knew people who benefited from medications, but in this case, they'd made things worse.

That evening, Luz squeezed into a tiny square table in the corner of the kitchen, while Lula flipped *tlacoyos* over a hot *comal.*

"*Tia*, what was my mother like growing up?"

"Alma?" laughed Lula. "Alma was the opposite of me! Your mother was the rebel of the family!"

"She was the oldest, right?"

"Yes. I am the youngest and the only one left; After Alma came Magda and Claudia. Both of them died of cancer, and your mom, well, you know better than me." She looked wistfully ahead, as if replaying memories. "Your mother was a contrarian! She hated school, never got good grades like the rest of us. She was the first one to drive and she smoked and cursed a lot!"

"I had no idea my mother was like that," Luz said, leaning in.

"Alma was the only one who left Pachuca and married a *gringo*."

"My father isn't a gringo, he's Mexican."

"No, Luz, your father was born in the US, and so were you. You're not Mexicans."

"In the US, I'm Chicana."

Lula poured *café con leche*, in Luz's cup. "You're a *pocha*, Luz."

"I guess *ni de aquí, ni de allá*. It must have been hard for Mami to move to a new country and live with a man she barely knew."

"I kept expecting her to leave him and come back, but she loved Marcelino and marriage meant something back then."

There's the jab once again. Luz sipped her coffee. "Did my mother ever tell you why she was so unhappy?"

"She missed Mexico and the family. Hated the weather, said she could never get warm. She expected to live in a big US city but ended up living on a ranch."

"Back then Snoqualmie was a *rancho*. It's still rural but it's grown into a suburb of Seattle. My father was a manager on a farm, so he bought this little rambler in a place where it took an hour and a half to walk to the little town. I can see how my mother must have been bored."

Lula placed a plate of *tlacoyos* in front of Luz. "Bored? She wished she could be bored! She went with someone with papers, expecting to have the great American life and ended up working for fifteen years cleaning the farmer's house."

"I remember going with her to clean the big house."

"Yoali and her mother were here when your mother came to visit the week before she disappeared."

Luz sipped her coffee. "Do you remember how she was? Did she say anything?"

"Ay, *m'hija*." She sighed. "Those were very dark times for all of us."

"My dad said the police talked to you on the phone, *tía*."

"They did. They wanted to know if your mother had moved back or told us of any plans. But she never said anything about leaving. She was very worried about all of you. Your father had the cancer, you couldn't get pregnant, and your brothers had drug problems."

Luz picked up her plate and washed it. "Just Christian. He's been clean since Mami disappeared. But what cancer? My father has never had cancer."

"I may be wrong but I'm sure she said he had cancer in the liver or pancreas. She was very distraught. And I wasn't much help as I was dealing with my own problems."

"How long was she here?"

"Alma was only here for a week. After she disappeared, I wondered if she came to say goodbye. Maybe it was too much for her?"

"Do you think she left us?"

Lula, gaunt and pale, emptied her almost full plate in the trash and handed it to Luz. "I don't know what happened, but the Alma I knew would never consider leaving her family. When she was here, she was worried, scared even. I think something evil happened to her. The day she disappeared was also the day my Eleonora died." Lula made the sign of the cross.

The harsh light of the kitchen accentuated the lines on Lula's face. "Eleonora was only twenty-four years old when she died, still a kid. She was fleeing Culiacan with that man." Lula pressed her lips, blinking rapidly. "That man was one of those *Narco Satánicos* who murdered the gringo; they were going to arrest him."

Luz frowned; she'd never heard this before. "Was that man Yoali's father?"

Lula nodded stiffly with a downturned mouth. "He was driving too fast and blew a tire. The car flipped over and over on the side of the road and landed on its hood. Eleonora's head was crushed, and the coroner said she died instantly."

"I'm so sorry, *tia*. I hadn't heard the whole story. It must've been so hard," Luz said softly, patting her aunt's hand.

"They found Yoali crying next to the wreck, calling for her mami. She was bruised and scratched but she didn't even need a Band-Aid."

"And the driver?"

"He was crushed, part in and part out of the car, screaming in agony. It took them almost four hours to free him. He died in the ambulance." She smiled, then frowned, looking away. "Eleonora wasn't a bad girl; she just fell in with a bad crowd." Her shoulders slumped, and she lowered her voice to almost a whisper. "But Yoali's father and his gang weren't *rebeldes*, they were evil."

Luz squeezed Lula's hand. "I know she wasn't bad, *tía*. We all have our battles. For some, it is harder. Yoali is lucky to have had you and Tio Pedro."

"We were lucky too. After losing Eleonora, Yoali brought us comfort and joy. My Pedro became young again; he doted on her." She looked away wistfully, probably remembering the good times before a stroke extinguished Pedro's light like a candle in a rainstorm. "My Eleonora died the day your mother disappeared. That was why I wasn't able to come stay with you. I wish I could have been there to comfort you and your brothers."

"I understand, *tia*," said Luz, wiping a tear from her eye. "Thank you. I wish I could have been here for you when Eleonora died."

Lula sighed. "If I had only told Yoali about her father, she wouldn't be in Sinaloa speaking to those awful people. He was pure evil!"

"Why do you think Eleonora fell for him?"

She crossed herself. "Satan isn't ugly and mean, he's charming! That's how he tempted Eve—"

Lula excused herself and returned a few minutes later with a stack of about ten letters tied with a faded violet ribbon. She placed them in Luz's hands.

"Your mother and I wrote each other every month. They're yours now. I hope you can find some answers."

Luz stayed up in bed reading her mother's letters from the year before she disappeared. They contained daily descriptions of her life, chores, and her fears and worries for her family. The last letter outlined her last trip to Pachuca and finished with the news that Marcelino had been diagnosed with pancreatic cancer. Fear stitched the last few lines as she described an upcoming appointment to meet with a specialist.

Luz couldn't sleep; hot flashes made her sweat and kick the blankets off the bed. She flipped over so that her head was on the cool bedspread and her feet on the hot pillow and lifted her nightgown below her neck, letting the air cool her stomach and chest. She checked her phone. It was 1:00 a.m. She rolled down her nightgown and went into Yoali's bedroom. Where are you? String lights hung over Yoali's bed; her desk was neat and clean, probably organized by her grandmother. Flopping on the bed, she hugged a stuffed elephant, one of a menagerie of animals that slept on the bed. What am I doing? I'm stuck in my job; my sons don't need me; I don't know where to go from here. She picked up Yoali's pillow to take to her bed and saw a leather journal, with only the first five pages filled with Yoali's neat script. Poems or lyrics thanked someone with hazel eyes for saving her life and promised enduring love. Luz left it where it was; Yoali must be in love. Finally, around three in the morning she fell into a fitful sleep.

In the afternoon, Luz borrowed Lula's car and drove to the university to talk to Yoali's professor. She meandered through the campus, its modern facilities crowded with students, until she arrived at the Sociology Department, where a receptionist informed her Professor Ivan was at his community project.

Rush hour traffic congested the streets, as Luz sat in her aunt's beetle, massaging her left leg unused to the clutch. She chewed on the corner of the page with the address for a community garden downtown. I hate that idiot professor! Glancing out the window, she strained to see above the cars in front of her, afraid she wouldn't make it.

She arrived at Cubitos, an informal settlement on a hill where the working poor built colorful houses, one on top of the other. Some lacked running water, and most with improvised cables "borrowed" electricity from the power lines. Following a sign pointing to the Ecological Reserve,

Cubitos Park and Community Garden, she arrived where a group of college students and residents were busy planting and hoeing.

Luz stood on her toes, searching for someone who looked like a professor. Spying a man in a suit at the far end of the garden, she rushed to him but tripped over someone crouched in the brush. Luz flew through the air, then broke her fall, scraping her palms and elbows. Her purse spilled its wallet, cell phone, comb, and makeup bag on the ground.

The crouching man rushed to help her up. Luz was already on her knees beet red because the man was handsome. He wore jeans and sandals, and a light blue chambray shirt with only the top button open. Thank God he wasn't one of those gold chains on a hairy chest type. His almond-shaped eyes blinked at her as he offered a weathered hand; a salt-and-pepper braid fell down his back.

"Are you alright?" he asked, holding her arm until she was steady.

Luz laughed and dusted herself off. "I didn't see you."

The man let go of her arm, got on all fours, and passed her the objects from her purse. When he gave her the canister with the ashes from the firepit where her mother disappeared, Luz panicked and searched through the bag for the pyrite pebble, but it wasn't there.

"My pebble!" she cried, getting down on the ground and looking for it in the dry earth.

"What pebble?" asked the kind man, little wrinkles formed in the corner of his eyes. His large, slightly hooked nose gave his face power.

Luz got up and sighed. "It's useless; I'll never find it."

The man handed her a water bottle. "I'm sorry, how can I make it up to you?"

Luz looked for the man she thought was a professor, but he was nowhere.

"Fuck! I missed the creepy professor!"

"What professor?"

"Ivan something, they told me he was here."

"You mean that creep Ivan de la Sierra?"

Luz nodded.

The man shook her hand. "I'm Ivan de la Sierra; nice to meet you."

"Shit!"

Ivan arched his eyebrows.

Luz blushed, but then remembered why she was there. "My name is Luz Rodriguez, and I need to talk to you about one of your students."

Two young women approached with shovels and pails. Ivan turned to them and gave directions, then turned back to Luz. "I'm almost done here. But, first, let me make sure everyone returns the equipment, and then I'm all yours."

Luz walked through the community garden. In one corner, an indigenous couple taught two young men how to properly water the new corn. Instead of a fence, eight-foot tall *nopales* interlocked their arms to enclose the garden. She waited by the entrance as Ivan chatted with the students returning shovels and hoes, relaxed but never inappropriate.

Ivan locked the shed and walked over to Luz as the overcast sky gave off a low grumble. "There's a coffee shop just down the street. Would you like to talk there?"

Luz followed him down the cobblestone street to a cozy little cafe where her mouth watered at the aroma of roasted coffee. They sat in a corner; the table so small, their knees touched under the table. She sipped the dark roasted coffee and gazed at him over her mug. She could understand why his students would be attracted to him; even though he was in his fifties, he was fit and strong with a quick smile that softened his rugged features. He's fucking hot, she sighed, and interested in twenty-year-olds.

"How can I help you?"

"My niece, Yoali, left home. I'm hoping you might know something about where she went."

"Why are you looking for her? Is she in trouble?"

"I don't know. She's going through a lot and her grandmother is worried."

He offered her half of his sugar cookie. "Do you think I'm having a relationship with her? Is that why you called me creepy?"

"Are you?"

"No! I assure you. I've never blurred the line between professor and student."

Luz bit the cookie, wanting to believe him but not ready to trust him. She enjoyed listening to his soft, low voice, his quick smile, and the kind way he treated the servers. But Lula was right, charisma wasn't a virtue.

"You seem to enjoy being around young people."

"I do. I dislike people that complain about them. These young people are witnessing the destruction of our planet, all the while they are the most isolated but at the same time the most connected generation. So, who are you, Luz *Tía* de Yoali?"

"I'm a counselor at the University of Washington in Seattle."

"Ah! So you also like working with young people."

"Is there anything at all you can tell me about Yoali? Her grandmother is worried and we have reason to believe she may be in danger."

"I'm sorry. I honestly don't know where she could be. She was in my class and we have talked a couple of times, but that's about it. Is that why you came to Mexico?"

Luz put her elbows on the table. "Yes. If you think of anyone that could help find her, will you let me know?"

Ivan nodded. Luz thought she should leave but didn't say anything when the server refreshed their mugs. "What about you? Why anthropology?"

"Easy! Anthropology has allowed me to connect to my culture and my roots. And through teaching, I'm helping my students connect to their roots."

Luz nodded, sipping the coffee. She licked her lips and saw him staring at them.

"I'm Yaqui on my father's side and was fascinated by his stories of our people. I have been researching our family and tribal history and culture in Oaxaca."

"But aren't the Yaqui from the north?" Luz asked.

Ivan beamed at her. "Yes, my people were from Sonora and Arizona, but Porfirio Diaz enslaved them and sent many of them to Oaxaca to work the plantations. My father moved here in the 1950s to work in the mines. I was born in *El Real*."

They chatted for a while about Pachuca and the surrounding towns. Luz glanced at her phone. "I should leave; I'll take some *pastes* for my aunt for *la merienda*."

"The *mole* ones are the best. Yoali wrote a paper on a local legend; if you want, I can email you her paper."

"I'd appreciate that." Luz wrote her email on a paper napkin, then rushed away with a warm bag of meat pastries. She had an uneasy feeling in her stomach, then realized it was desire.

That night Luz sat in bed reading Yoali's paper. It started with how pre-Hispanic tribes had mined for obsidian to make tools and weapons. When the Spanish invaded, they worked the Indians to death, then replaced them with slaves stolen from Africa. They dug deeper and deeper until they exhausted the mines. Years later, Cornish and American companies returned with new technologies to access the minerals and precious metals, precipitating the first labor strike in Mexico in a mine in Pachuca in 1776.

The paper was well-written and detailed. In 1920, a fire spread through the deep shafts of a mine worked by an American mining company in *El Real*. The managers sealed the tunnels to starve the fire of oxygen. The blaze was extinguished but at the expense of dozens of incinerated miners, whose charred remains were found strewn where they fell when the bosses opened the mine after six days. There were six survivors. The legend of the Bordo fire and *el minero* was born.

The survivors said that when the mine caught fire, eighty-seven men ran to the elevators to escape. Tenoch, repelled by the heat and smoke, bolted in the opposite direction, deeper into the mine's heart. Tenoch knew the stories about how his ancestors sealed the underworld to protect the Earth Mother from rapacious humans and that the gods left fire serpents to guard her. Tenoch sprinted deeper and deeper into the earth's womb, away from the fire.

When Tenoch stumbled into a dead end, he fell to his knees, wailing to the earth to save him. A slash opened in the wall, and the Great Goddess appeared. On her head rested an enormous headdress from which spiders dangled from silken webs; an owl perched on her shoulder.

She wore a red *huipil* embroidered in gold thread. Taking pity on him, she offered Tenoch water and told him she would grant him a wish. Tenoch asked for his life. The Earth Mother agreed but warned that she had to keep the natural balance of life, that for every gift there was also a price. In return for his life, Tenoch would have to guard the mine entrance for eternity and offer wishes only to those he deemed worthy. Tenoch agreed. The Earth Mother handed him a leather pouch from which he could pull iron pyrite crystals to give to those requesting help. Since that time, Tenoch lived by the mine where only those with pure intentions can find him to ask a favor.

Luz's heart accelerated; she had found a pyrite crystal where her mother disappeared! The one she had lost today. She read on until she fell asleep and dreamt her mother was walking into a mine, disappearing into the darkness, the howls of the burning miners reverberating against the rock walls.

The following day Luz and Lula squeezed back into the tiny square table in the corner of the kitchen. They drank strong, black coffee and stabbed cubes of aromatic red papaya with a fork. Lula, in a faded nightgown and slippers; Luz crossed-legged in black yoga pants and an oversized T-shirt.

"Why do you think Yoali was having an affair with her teacher?"

"Because she's never had a boy over and talked about that Ivan all the time."

"Did she say anything to make you think they were seeing each other?"

"I told you she's very private; she didn't speak about anyone else so I assumed."

Luz felt lighter. "Do you know anything about the *minero* and wishes?"

Lula choked on her coffee. "Why are you asking me this?"

"I read Yoali's paper on the legend of the miner who gives out wishes. Did my mother ever go to the *minero*?"

"Your mother went to see him the last time she was here." She crossed herself. "I think he did a *trabajo* on her, cursed her because a week later Eleonora was dead and your mother disappeared."

Luz left the dishes in the sink, then sat and took her aunt's hand. "Tell me what you remember."

"*Ay hija!* It was so long ago! I remember she was intent on going, even though I begged her not to."

"But why *tia*?"

"That place is evil! The miners dug so deep, they let out millions of spirits who now live in the abandoned mine."

"You don't believe that, do you?"

Lula yanked her hand away and glared at her. "I'm not a superstitious old woman! Some say the ghosts of dead miners live in its bowels; if you'd been there, you'd know."

Luz emailed Ivan asking if he knew where she could find the miner from Yoali's paper. A half hour later, he offered to take her. Butterflies fluttered in her stomach but not from fear.

Ivan picked Luz up and drove to El Real or Mineral del Monte, a small mining town at almost 9,000 feet in the Sierra de Pachuca. Red, tin-roofed homes dotted the mountainside along narrow twisted roads that crisscrossed the small town like a drunken snake. They stopped at the market and bought a warm blanket, a rain poncho, and some *pastes*, a Mexican version of Cornish pasties filled with potatoes and chiles. Ivan meandered through the stalls and bought a bottle of pulque.

Ivan maneuvered his pickup out of town and up the mountain, slipping past meadows where families and friends gathered to enjoy the weekend. Luz replayed the fun times with her cousins when they would come on vacation, the soccer and volleyball games, the horseback rides, and the hikes, *the carnes asadas*. The adults would warn them to stay close and watch out for the *tiros*, mine shafts big enough for a person to disappear into the dark forever. She shuddered just as Ivan turned onto a hidden dirt road.

"I almost missed it!" he said as the car fishtailed in the dirt. He slowed to a crawl, and they rattled and shook down the narrow, rutted path until he stopped at a rusted wheel that straddled the width of the primitive road. "Now we walk."

They hiked through the *oyamel* trees, pines that looked like the shorter cousins of the majestic conifers in Snoqualmie. Ivan offered his hand to help her over a fallen tree; his touch sending a buzz through her body. It was the rainy season, and everything was green and blooming. The narrow path, thick with mud, was barely visible through the overgrown grass, wildflowers, and many mushrooms erupting from the moist earth. Pine and *ocote* rode the gentle breeze that sculpted the clouds above, infusing a cleansing aroma into a show of light and shadow on the trees. They circled an immense boulder and stared at the boarded-up mine. Luz's face drained of color; it was the cave from her dream.

"Wait here," said Ivan, walking away.

Luz stared at the mine entrance, the hair on the back of her neck standing on end. She flinched, startled, when I van shouted. "Tenoch! Don Tenoch! *Es* Ivan!" She burst out laughing, all of this was getting to her. She was wiping sweat from her brow when Ivan appeared, holding the arm of the oldest person Luz had ever seen. His bent, skeletal frame topped four feet at most; his face was a dark mask of wrinkles and bushy white eyebrows that shot out like cat's whiskers from beneath his straw hat. He walked slowly but sure-footed and straight in child-sized Skechers shoes. Ivan placed the wooden chair he was carrying and helped him sit down. He motioned for Luz to bring their offerings. Luz approached with the clothes and food.

"*Buenas tardes,*" Luz said.

"*Buenas tardes, m'hija,*" he said in a clear, strong voice. His teeth were almost all gone; blackened stumps filled the gaps. His left ear was disfigured by flaky gray and white growths.

Ivan motioned Luz forward. "This is Luz. She brought you some gifts."

Luz placed the poncho and jacket on the older man's lap as he stared ahead with eyes clouded by yellow cataracts. He felt the clothes, then took her hand. A blush crept up Luz's neck as a hot flash burst from her solar plexus, sweat running down her face and neck.

"You are changing. Good." He smiled, nodding, his blank eyes staring into nothing. "Menopause is when a woman's power is at its peak."

"Really? Where I come from, it's the exact opposite. It's when you're done." Luz tried to pull her hand away, but he tightened his grip and pulled her closer. Luz held her breath, avoiding the stench coming from the pit of his mouth.

"The heat, the fire, is just energy. It is there for you to use. It is the time to create something new." He released her hand and threw back his head, croaking out a phlegmatic laugh. "Luz, you have two choices: you can become a wise woman or a bitter, old crone."

Ivan gave him the bottle of pulque, and he took a long drink. "Food?" he demanded. Luz took out some of the *pastes* and watched him tear off a piece and jam it in his mouth, crumbs spraying on his jacket.

"You want a favor?"

"No, Don Tenoch. I came to ask you about my niece, Yoali. She came to see you a few weeks ago."

"Yes," he nodded, smiling again, "she always brings me chocolate. But you're not here for her, are you?"

Luz swallowed. "Have you heard from Yoali? Do you know where she went?"

"You want to know about Alma. She wanted a big favor."

"How could you remember her?" Luz's cheeks burned.

"I don't forget anything. It's part of the sacrifice I still make!" A dark look surged over his face and Luz took a step away from him. His blank eyes and crooked grin quickly replaced it. "I have worked at this mine since 1918."

"Can you tell me why Yoali came here?"

"She came like everyone else to ask for a favor from the Great Goddess *Nantli*. So did your mother."

"What did she ask for?"

"That is between her and *Nantli*."

"Can I ask Nanti?"

"*Nantli*," he corrected. "Our Mother. See? You did come for a favor."

"I guess I did."

"You are searching for your mother; Yoali, for her father. But in reality, you're searching for yourselves. Yoali thinks she can reach him in Mictlán with *teonanacatl*."

Ivan leaned in, his face pale in the afternoon light. "Did you give them to her?"

Don Tenoch looked up with eyes white from cataracts. "I gave her a wish and sent her away. The mine's fruits are only for the protector of the mine."

Luz stared at Ivan, a thousand questions swirling in her mind but before she could articulate them, Don Tenoch yanked out an old leather pouch from his jacket pocket. His deformed, arthritic fingers struggled to loosen the ties, until something the size of a quarter spilled onto his palm. He offered Luz a pyrite pebble, fool's gold. It shone in the afternoon light, just like the one she'd found in the firepit when her mother disappeared.

"It is the firestone. It contains the fire of the earth and the power of *Nantli*. Use the firestone to ask *Nantli* for your favor. You will know when it is time." He waited until they nodded, then added, "Remember that the Great Goddess must keep a balance, so there will be a price to pay for whatever you ask."

Luz stowed the stone in her pocket. A feeling of disappointment overcame her; she knew nothing more than when they had started. I shouldn't buy into the fantasies of an older man who should be in a nursing home. I'm an American and an educated person.

"Take me back to my home," he said, staring ahead.

Ivan gathered the gifts and the food in one arm and gave Don Tenoch his free arm to help him back to his *jacal*. When he returned, they walked back to the car.

"What did you mean when you asked him about the teona—"

"Teonanacatl, flesh of the gods, magic mushrooms."

"You think Yoali is using mushrooms?"

Ivan shook his head. "I don't know anymore. What did he mean when he said you were looking for your mother?"

"The week before my mother disappeared, she came to see him."

"Are you searching for your mother?"

Luz shook her head. "She died, well, disappeared, twenty years ago. You don't believe he was the miner from 1918, do you? That would make him over one hundred and fifteen years old."

"Does it matter? Culture is about people agreeing to believe in certain things, whether they're real or not. People come to see him because they believe, and the Earth Mother grants them favors and they heal."

"Isn't believing in legends and stories a crutch?"

"How about your stories? About Freud and psychology? Are they real? Do they heal?"

Luz bit her bottom lip. What do I believe? The science she'd built her practice on was infective and inaccessible. The rain fell fast and hard, and lightning and thunder boomed above them as they drove back to Pachuca.

An hour later, Luz and Ivan sat across from each other in a restaurant when her phone buzzed. Aunt Lula rushed into a litany of warnings about the miner until Luz stopped her by saying, "I already saw him. I'm fine."

"It's because I've been saying a rosary since you left! Anyway, Yoali called. She's in Sinaloa, went to find her father's family and is coming back."

Luz slumped in her seat as a weight fell off her shoulders. "Thank God!"

"She should be back by Monday. Why don't we go this weekend to Arcelia's house in Huasca for the weekend?"

"Go spend time with your daughter and grandchildren; I'll stay here and visit with friends."

Luz hung up and filled Ivan in on the details, casually mentioning she was alone and without plans for the weekend.

Ivan pressed his index finger against his mouth with his eyes semi-closed. "Good! That's good news."

The waiter brought a breadbasket to the table and took their order. Luz felt hungry for the first time. They ordered and shared stories about university life and students. Ivan was a good listener, and before Luz could stop herself, she'd shared most of her life's story. In contrast, all she knew about Ivan was that he was divorced and faculty.

The waiter arrived with their food. Luz took a bite out of the small cheese-filled chiles.

Ivan put down his fork and looked Luz in the eye; she blushed as a hot flash spread through her body. "Excuse me."

Luz darted down a corridor and into what she thought was the restroom but went out the back exit instead. She leaned against the door until she cooled down, wiping the sweat from her brow. When she tried to get back in, the door would not open from the outside; she pulled and banged on it until her hand hurt, then ran through the rain to the front entrance.

Ivan looked up from the table as Luz sat down with curls dripping water and her black top plastered to her skin.

"What happened?"

"I'm sorry. I accidentally locked myself outside." A waiter gave Luz a couple of cloth napkins, and she used them to pat dry her face. "There goes all my work straightening my hair!"

"Please excuse me for commenting on your appearance, but I love your curly hair."

Luz smiled at him, and they locked eyes until she tore hers away, unnerved. She liked him a lot. I think he likes me. At least, I hope he does.

"I've always hated my hair, spending hours trying to tame it."

"Don't! It suits you."

Ivan insisted on paying their bill. While they waited for the check, he said. "Would you like to spend the weekend at my house in El Chico? It's a drive but beautiful."

Luz managed a controlled smile. "I'd love to. What's your address? What can I bring?"

"I can pick you up."

"I'd rather drive myself," she said, wanting to have a ready escape if things went wrong.

"Then just bring hiking shoes and leave your hair like it is."

On Saturday, Luz drove to El Chico, the first national park in Mexico located in the highlands of La Sierra de Pachuca, covered in white pines locally called *oyamel*. At almost 10,000 feet above sea level, visitors often perched on high points to look down at a carpet of clouds below.

She coasted through the tiny town of El Mineral Del Chico slowing to a crawl because of the tourists trying to navigate the narrow cobblestone streets. Rustic brick and stone homes and shops with red metal roofs surrounded the plaza and climbed up the hillside. After crossing the town, she came to a crumbling stone wall that gave way to a courtyard in front of a stone house. A creek babbled nearby.

Luz took a deep breath of pine and *ocote* scented air. Images of Snoqualmie, where she'd grown up, filled her mind. Ivan flung open a rustic wooden door.

Ivan rushed to grab her bag, then led her into the cabin-like house. Colorful, warm Zapotec tapestries hung on the white stone walls. Dark, lustrous hardwood floors peeked through wool area rugs, and massive wood beams arched into the vaulted ceiling. The floor-to-ceiling windows on the far wall shimmered in the afternoon light, which filtered through the trees and fell on an ebony-colored dining table. A chocolate-colored mutt with only three paws jumped over to them.

"Kahlua, meet Luz. Kahlua is the master of the house." Ivan swung her bag and left it on an antique wooden trunk by the entrance.

Luz scratched the dog's ears while trying to gauge Ivan's mood: was she there as a friend? Or as a lover? He seemed attracted to her, but he hadn't made any moves.

They spent the day hiking, and Ivan grilled fish for dinner and poured wine. The conversation flowed easily between them, covering different topics. Neither of them brought up romantic relationships. Luz studied his face. Could she be misinterpreting his signals?

After dinner, Ivan poured them glasses of wine and invited her to the yard.

"Oh my God!" cried Luz, looking at the night sky.

"What?"

"The stars! It's so dark here. I can't remember the last time I saw a sky like this." The skies in Seattle were either cloudy or polluted by the blaze of too many city lights, but here, the mountain was cloaked in darkness.

He took off his jacket and spread it on top of the grass in the courtyard, then turned off the outdoor light and sat down on the ground. Luz joined him and they laid side by side, staring at the sky.

"How old are you? It's just that most men I know can't get up and down from the floor like you."

He chuckled. "I'm fifty-six, and it's yoga. Look at that!"

The stars twinkled back at them. They watched in silence, aware of each other, their breath, the warmth where their arms touched until Ivan turned to her and said, "This is even more beautiful." They kissed. After a while, they went upstairs to his bedroom.

Luz sat up in the bed, screaming in pain. She opened her legs and pushed herself up, looking between them at Don Tenoch. He stood in front of her, ready to catch the birth.

"Push! You can do this, push!" he said. So she pushed and felt herself break in half as rocks, fire, and lava erupted out of her.

She woke up with an intense hot flash, the kind that would leave the sheets soaked. Wiggling from under Ivan's arm, she opened the door to the balcony and stuck her head out, breathing in the cool air. Ivan touched her shoulder.

"Are you alright?"

"Yes, just a little warm."

He opened the door and stepped out naked, offering her his hand. "Come on! No one can see us here."

Shivering with relief, Luz stepped out onto the cool night and lifted her heavy mass of curls to let the breeze dry the sweat from her body. She stood like a statue until the flames retreated inside her solar plexus. Then, as her body cooled, she leaned into Ivan, searching for his warmth.

"You're beautiful."

Luz blushed in the dark. "This was probably a bad idea, but of course, I say that after we made love."

"Why was it a bad idea?"

"I just ended a two-year relationship."

"So, it's over, right?"

Luz nodded, biting her lower lip. "It's just so recent."

"Was it you who ended it?"

Luz nodded, then started biting the skin around her thumb.

"In your heart, how long has it been over?"

"Honestly, it never was a full relationship." Luz stretched against the railing, her curls tumbling down her light brown back. Ivan looked down at her round bottom and looked up again to her face. "It even started wrong," she continued. "I started seeing Mark when I was still married; typical friends turned lovers, then divorced, realizing that Mark was just a symptom of the problems in the marriage." Ivan took hold of the thumb Luz was biting and kissed it. She crossed her arms and leaned against the rail.

"The first years with Patrick were great! But we got so involved in our jobs, the kids, that we stopped working on our marriage and became roommates, taking each other for granted. I'm glad we divorced, but I regret cheating on him. Patrick didn't deserve it." She paused and looked into the darkness. "I think I stayed with Mark not to be alone. Once the novelty wore off, there was nothing left. I won't bad-mouth him; we just had nothing in common, no shared culture, no values. I don't think we even liked each other anymore. Does all this make sense, or is it TMI?"

"You want to make sure you don't jump into a relationship with me because you're afraid of being alone."

"Exactly!" She turned to him, fearing she'd disclosed too much too soon.

"I understand. I haven't been in a committed relationship since my divorce four years ago."

Before Luz could ask him to elaborate, Ivan said, "Look."

They watched the trees as the outline of the Sierra appeared above. With the approaching dawn, the light went from purple to violet to pink. Suddenly a bluebird appeared singing as it called other bluebirds who joined her, swooping and flying as the light turned to gold. They watched in silence.

"Thank you for sharing this with me. I'd like to get to know you better."

Luz sighed. What could she answer? Her life was a mess and she wasn't about to start another failed relationship. But she liked Ivan, the attraction was overwhelming. She took Ivan's hand and pulled him to the bed; at least her love life didn't need any healing.

They spent the weekend hiking, making love, and sharing stories. Sunday night Luz was sleeping in Ivan's arms when his cell phone startled them.

Ivan listened, nodding. "I'll be right there." He hung up and pulled on his jeans and sweater. "Yoali is in the hospital."

In a fog, Luz put on his sweater and searched the room for her jeans, finding them in the bathroom. "Who called?"

"Andrea, her best friend. She drove her."

Uneasiness flooded her. Why had Yoali's friend called Ivan? Why did she have his cell number? "I'll drive," she said, digging her keys out of her bag.

They got into her aunt Lula's VW Beetle and Luz started the car, but instead of driving, she stared out the window. "Why did Yoali's friend call you?"

"Andrea and Yoali were in my class, and—"

Luz glared at Ivan, a curl fell across her face and she pushed it away. "I asked you why she has your number? Why would she call you?"

"Because this may be my fault, and—"

"Get out!"

"Wait, hear—"

"Get the fuck out of my car!"

Ivan got out but held on to the passenger door. "I told you I'm not with her; you have it all wrong."

With screeching tires, Luz took off down the mountain, the thrust slamming the door shut. She wiped the tears from her face with her hand. "What's wrong with me! I'm a fifty-two-year-old woman!" Her stomach churned and she pulled over and opened the door, vomiting last night's wine. She took deep breaths until she was ready to drive.

Luz bolted into the small private hospital. A man with deep circles under his eyes called a doctor, and a few minutes later, a young woman in a white coat arrived. They stood in the empty reception area, the harsh lights reflecting off the green walls, casting a deathly hue on their skin. Doctor Molina was pretty and young; her confidence and kindness won Luz over.

"How is Yoali?"

"Yoali is in a coma. We pumped her stomach and have her on fluids and are monitoring her closely."

"What happened?"

"Her friend," the doctor turned to look at a young woman sleeping on three plastic chairs lined up against the wall, "brought her in; she found her unconscious. Apparently, Yoali took a combination of pills, mushrooms and alcohol. We may administer an anti-sedative. As soon as I know more, I will be back."

Luz watched her walk away. Biting her lower lip, she wiped the sweat rolling down her face as a hot flash took hold of her body. They were more frequent when she was upset. She studied Yoali's friend, then shook her shoulder gently.

"Hi, I'm Yoali's aunt. Can we talk?"

The girl opened her eyes and sat up, pulling the hood over her dirty blond hair. Her hazel eyes blinked rapidly.

"Where's Ivan?" she asked, looking over Luz's shoulder.

"He couldn't come."

"Who are you? Is Yoali OK?"

Luz sat down on one of the chairs. "I'm Yoali's aunt. Ivan told me you called him. What's your name?"

Guarded, her eyes roaming over Luz, she said, "Andrea."

"Can you tell me what happened?"

"Are you the aunt that lives in Seattle?"

Luz nodded.

Andrea sighed, she slumped in the seat. "I knew Yoali was having a hard time but I never thought she'd do it."

"What? Please tell me; her grandmother is worried sick. I flew from Seattle to help."

"Yoali told me she had enough ambiens and Xanax saved up in case things got bad; I didn't think she'd do it, you know?" Andrea shook her head, a tear trickled down her cheek and trembled on her chin. "When she came back from Sinaloa, she was desperate."

"What happened in Sinaloa, did she tell you?"

"Yeah, nothing. She was bummed. She tracked down a woman who was her father's cousin but didn't know anything. All she heard was what a bad person her father was. That he was a narco, Satan-worshipper and enjoyed torturing his victims before killing them."

Andrea stood up. "I need to smoke."

"I'll go with you."

They walked out and stood on the street; only a few cars drove by. Andrea offered Luz a cigarette and then lit up after Luz shook her head. She blew out a cloud of smoke that dissipated in the cool air. "When she couldn't find anything about her father, she got it into her head that on a trip with psychedelics, she'd find him in Mictlán and confront him. I should've stopped her!"

Luz waited, listening, as her counselor skills kicked in, trying to read Andrea's body language, taking in every detail.

Andrea wiped a tear. "Yoali got some purple mushrooms and read online how to prepare for a trip; I was her sitter. At first, she was very still, eyes closed. I thought she was sleeping, then she cried and cried. She told me she'd been to Mictlán, that her father was evil and she was like him. I tried to talk her out of it. She told me she'd not only taken the mushrooms, but all the pills she'd been saving. I called an ambulance and then Ivan."

Luz touched Andrea's shoulder. "You're not responsible for this."

Andrea nodded, her eyes filling with tears.

Luz patted her shoulder. She's a child just like Yoali, who was the same age but short and stocky like her grandmother. I abandoned her in the last few years. Shame flooded her. "Did Yoali ask you to call Ivan? Do you know how long they've been together?" Luz couldn't help herself with the last one.

Andrea smiled through the tears. "No! Ivan sent an email to our class asking us to call if we heard from Yoali. Yoali isn't into men. We're together."

Luz sighed, leaning against the hospital's wall. Fuck! Ivan's face when she screamed at him floating in front of her eyes. The lights of the few cars that sped down the street fell on them like searchlights.

Andrea stepped on what was left of her cigarette and returned to the waiting room.

"How did Yoali get the mushrooms?"

"Yoali has been trying to do a peyote or ayahuasca trip but couldn't find any; so she got the purple mushrooms from the mine. I begged her not to do them; they're dark magic, you know?"

"What are you talking about?"

"The magic mushrooms that grow inside the Bordo Mine, they grew on the corpses of dead miners and the spirits that were released by the explosion. Yoali thought they'd help her reach her father."

"Why those?"

"Because those mushrooms take you to Mictlán, the underworld, and she wanted to see her father."

The doctor returned and updated them on Yoali who was in a coma in a private room where they could visit. She encouraged them to talk to her, play music, and make her aware of their presence.

Luz got them both coffees, and they sat on the fake leather couch staring at Yoali in

her bed.

"Do you know who sold her the mushrooms?"

"Yeah, he's a drug dealer that lives in a shack by the cemetery in El Real. It looks like a tire repair place, but it's just a front. He's very—"

Lula burst into the room with two of her daughters, crying and calling to Yoali. Luz updated her, then left to shower and change and visit the drug dealer.

Luz parked in front of the dilapidated front shop; its red-tin roof sagged, and the metal door's paint had surrendered to rust. The once, whitewashed wall now crumbled exposing the brick underneath. A skinny gray cat glared at her from the rooftop. Luz banged on the metal door and waited. Only the low grumbling of the afternoon rain clouds answered her. So she banged on it again, this time as hard as she could.

The door was yanked open and a man in his twenties glared at her. Black tattoos covered every inch of his skin; Luz shuddered imagining the needle on his bald scalp. Skulls, owls, scales, scythes, and hourglasses were some of the images that covered him like a wetsuit. Rail thin, the man barely filled his black jeans and Adidas sweatshirt. He studied Luz.

"You sold mushrooms to my niece. I don't want any trouble; I just want to know what you gave her. She's in the hospital in a coma."

The man took a step back and opened the door inviting her in.

Luz looked around at the empty street, the cemetery's stone wall looming like a warning. From where she stood, the shop was a dark cave. "Can we stay out here?"

The man made to close the door in her face but Luz held it open. He again stepped back and Luz walked into his bizarre world. There was a single mattress with dirty sheets on the floor and what looked like hundreds of candles flickered from an altar to La Santa Muerte. The female skeleton was dressed in black, holding a scythe in one hand and a scale in the other. On her shoulder perched an owl and at her feet was a globe and an hourglass. The black holes in her skull followed Luz. Offerings of cigarettes, joints, and alcohol bottles littered the surface beneath the candles while photos, pictures of saints, and handwritten notes begging for a favor from the saint of death decorated the wall. The hair on the back of her neck stood up and she shivered. The place felt wrong. It reeked of cigarettes and weed, almost masking a dark, putrid smell leaking from the walls.

"I just want to know what you sold her."

His voice was raspy, as if he had a frog stuck in his throat. "I don't sell the *flaquita's* magic; she gives it in exchange for a sacrifice."

"Whatever. What did you give her?"

The man grinned, displaying his metal teeth. "I gave her the purple mushrooms from the mine so she could meet her father."

"What are they?"

"I told you they are purple mushrooms, a combination of blue from psilocybin and the red from the blood and fire of the mine."

"Well, they fucked her up and she's in a coma now."

"I only gave her the mushrooms; she's responsible for what she asked them to show her. She must be trapped in Mictlán."

Luz walked to the door; her skin crawling, and a voice shouting in her mind to get out of there, now!

"You can bring her back, you know."

Luz turned to him. "How?"

"I can give you the same mushrooms so you can find her and bring her back."

Luz scoffed and opened the door. The afternoon rain was like a curtain between her and her aunt's car.

"You'll never see her alive again."

This is bullshit! Still she waited.

The man offered her a plastic bag. "Take these and you will find her; but a warning, Mictlán could trap you both."

"How much?" asked Luz, taking the bag that felt as light as if it was empty.

"I told you I don't sell the gods' flesh. All I ask from you is a kiss."

Luz shook her head.

"Then give them back," said the man extending his hand.

When Luz offered the bag, he grasped her wrist, yanked her forward, and pressed his mouth against hers. Ice cold lips shocked her, as freezing waves engulfed her, draining her of hope. He let her go, laughing. "I crave the fire of a changing woman; it's the only thing that warms me."

Luz rushed to the car and got in, wiping the man from her mouth. She didn't have any hot flashes that night, just a chill that settled deep in her bones.

Later that evening, Luz parked and dashed to the hospital but froze when she spotted Ivan standing in the entrance. He raised his hand, flashing her a strained half-smile that made her cheeks burn. She forced herself to walk up to him.

"I have your things in my car," he said, pointing to a pickup parked across the street.

"Thank you. I'm very sorry." Luz was relieved he'd brought what she'd left when she rushed out.

"Let me get your things," he brushed past her and crossed the street returning with her overnight bag.

"Can we talk? Please?" she asked.

"What for? You don't believe what I tell you and jump to—"

"I know, I'm sorry, it's just you have an unusual relationship with Yoali, and when you said it was your fault she tried to kill herself, I just assumed …"

"I told you I didn't have a romantic relationship with her. I was teaching Mexican Shamanism and I shared my experience with mushrooms; that's what I meant when I said it was my fault. I don't know the men you've been with before, but I'm nothing like them." He turned to walk away, then stopped and said, "I care for my students. I thought if anyone would understand it was you, but I was wrong."

Luz watched him walk away. "Fuck!" she said under her breath as a heaviness descended on her. Walking to Yoali's room, she groaned, Why can't I stop myself from jumping the gun? Years of therapy and she still rushed to react, the impulses too strong to control. Ivan was very different from any man she'd been with: considerate, great listener; he engaged her intellectually. And, sexually. And she'd ruined it.

That night, as she settled in to spend the night with Yoali, she logged into the university's library and researched the newest peer reviewed articles on psychedelics and mental health. The results were overwhelming. Psychiatrists, neurologists, and psychologists worldwide reported incredible success when using LSD, psilocybin, DMT, and ketamine in treating PTSD, addiction, and existential anxiety for those on the brink of death. Fascinated, she saved articles to read later as she looked for information on the purple mushrooms, but there was nothing.

From there, she went on to various interpretations of what happened to the mind when on psychedelics. For some it was only chemistry and dangerous, but others, like Carl Jung and a collection of psychiatrists and psychologists, believed entheogens were a portal to the collective unconsciousness. Some stated you could access all the information stored in our DNA, while others believed it allowed the mind to transcend time and space and experience reality without the filters of our body and cultural programing.

Luz grasped Yoali's hand. "Yoali! Yoali!" The monitor's beeps, steady and regular, were the only sound. "Come back, we love you." She put her laptop on the floor and rested her head on the bed. "I'm sorry I wasn't there for you; I should've stayed in touch."

"Wake up, Luz!"

Luz opened her eyes. Where am I? She lifted her head, the beeps reminding her she was in the hospital.

"Help me!" said Yoali.

"Yoali! You're awake. Let me call—"

"I don't have much time. I'm stuck in a bad place and I can't get back."

"Yoali, you've been in a coma, you must—"

"Listen to me!"

Luz's head jerked back, as if she had been slapped. Yoali no longer had oxygen nor an IV; she was standing by the bed, in black jeans and T-shirt with a colorful skull. On the bed, another Yoali lay quietly.

Luz shook her head and squeezed her eyes shut, but when she opened them, there were still two Yoali's in the room. I'm dreaming, she told herself.

"Help me, Luz. If I die, I'll be stuck here forever."

"Come back; it's all in your mind."

"There is no light here, it's nowhere. I don't know how to get out of here and he's coming for me."

"Who? Where are you?"

"My father. He wants me to stay with him in Mictlán!"

Luz shuddered. "Wake up, Yoali! Come back to us!"

"He's coming!" Yoali gasped, her eyes wide with fright. "Help me, Luz! He's coming!"

Luz opened her eyes, Yoali's shrieks still ringing in her ears. Her niece was in the same position as before, her gentle breathing barely perceptible. Luz rummaged through her purse and dug out the bag with the dried purple mushrooms. "I'm coming to get you!"

Luz rinsed her mouth with the sugary drink she'd bought at the gas station, her stomach roiling at the taste. Looking in the rearview mirror she grinned, running her tongue over her teeth. She was parked outside Ivan's house, watching him arrive an hour ago.

Luz pulled on the hemp cord to a copper bell; it's ringing drowned by the wind stirring the trees, making them whisper secrets that sent shivers down her spine. Dark clouds grumbled and ozone tickled her nose announcing the rain. Please don't make me drive back in this, she prayed, ringing the bell again.

Ivan swung open the door, barefoot, in jeans and a T-shirt, his brown hair loose. "You?" he asked, wide-eyed.

"I'm sorry. I know I'm a terrible person and I'm really sorry but I need your help."

"What?" asked Ivan, shaking his head.

"Can I come in?" Luz tried to look over his shoulder but he blocked the entrance with his wide chest.

"I'm with someone."

"No you're not! I've been watching your place all day."

Ivan stared at her, speechless, mouth open.

"Please, I'm not asking you to take me back; I know I fucked that up. I need your help. For Yoali."

Ivan stood to the side and opened the door. Luz walked into his living room and sat where a few days ago he'd done things to her that now made her blush. She crossed her legs.

"Can I get you something?"

Luz shook her head, a wave of nausea crashed over her. "Do you have any crackers?"

Ivan returned with a box of pita chips. He sat across from her on the floor and played with the fire, poking it probably to avoid looking at her.

"How is Yoali?"

"Not well. The doctor said that if there are no changes by tomorrow, they'll move her to a long-term facility and we should give up hope."

Ivan left the fire and sat next to her on the couch, his hand on her back. "I'm so sorry. How is your aunt? Andrea?"

"Not well, as you can imagine. Lula and Andrea are with her tonight. I came because I need your help. Yoali took purple mushrooms from the mine and is trapped in a bad trip. I got the same ones and I'm going after her."

"Are you crazy? The mushrooms will poison your mind; they won't help you communicate or whatever you think you can do with Yoali!"

"Can you really say that with absolute certainty? Not even neuroscientists can explain consciousness! The more I read about this and about physics and quantum theory, I—"

Luz looked around the room, wiping away a tear. "I wasn't here for Yoali when she needed me. I'll do anything it takes to save her life."

"I understand, but you don't know what you're getting into! The purple mushrooms are extremely dangerous."

"I already took them," Luz looked at her phone. "It's been half an hour."

Ivan's eyes bulged and he yanked Luz up by the arm. "I'm taking you to the hospital to have your stomach pumped."

"Stop!"

Ivan let go of her arm.

"It's too late! The nearest hospital is an hour away and I will have already digested the mushrooms. I need to do this for Yoali, help me!"

Ivan sighed; they both sat on the couch.

"How are you feeling?"

"Fine. I mean nothing yet. I'm scared."

Ivan sat next to her, his brow furrowed. "I'm not sure I can help you. Mushrooms are sacred medicine; they're so powerful that you're supposed to prepare, do it in ceremony, and have a Shaman guide you."

"We'll improvise! Please, tell me about your trip."

"I was fortunate to participate in a ceremony with a very compassionate *curandera* who died a few years ago. She helped me heal after my daughter's suicide."

"I'm so sorry. I cannot even begin to imagine what … thank you for telling me." Luz wanted to grasp his hand but she'd imposed a lot on him already. He'd agreed to help her, not take her back.

"I thought I would never recover. For a year, I couldn't speak about it; I couldn't even go to therapy. Lina killed herself while we were in the house sleeping. We had an argument and I grounded her. She also had trouble with a boyfriend and school but we didn't know." Ivan sighed, staring ahead. "Lina was seventeen and was pulling away from us, shutting us out. She took my wife's sleeping pills. When we found her the next morning, it was too late, and she was declared brain-dead."

"I became a bitter, angry man, pushing others away and drinking every night until I passed out. I was mean and impatient with my students, faculty, and the few friends who stuck around. My wife left me. I was in Oaxaca doing research on sacred medicine traditions when I interviewed a *curandera*. Thankfully, she took interest in me, or perhaps it was compassion. One look at me and she told me my spirit was sick with regret. She held a ceremony and changed my life."

"What was it like?" asked Luz, blinking, the lights seemed brighter, rays shooting into her eyes.

Ivan stared at the portrait of a young girl with curly hair. Luz wondered if it was Lina. "It was scary at first. I spoke with Lina. We forgave each other. I then could let go of so many things." His voice cracked. He went to the kitchen and poured them both glasses of water, placing them on the wood coffee table in front of them. The patterns on the wood swirled then stood still.

"There were moments of euphoria too, experiences I can't describe. Ineffable."

Kahlua jumped on the couch next to her and placed his head on her lap. She scratched behind the dog's ears as Ivan's face transformed into that of a man with a similar face, slightly shorter, then into a woman with long braids and dark eyes exact replicas of his, then an ancient face, wrinkled and brown, a deer headdress weighing on his crown. Luz blinked and saw Ivan again.

"I changed, tried to become more loving and patient and open; no longer angry at the world. I poured my energy into fighting against injustice, abuse, and poverty. I still have dark days and bouts of depression and anger, but it got me unstuck. That is why I care so much for my young students. Yoali shared with me her depression and coming out; I wanted to help her!"

"I'm so sorry," said Luz, wrapping her cardigan around her, shivering.

"Me too. I like you but you're very impulsive and that scares me."

"I know, every time I think I have a handle on myself, I fuck up again." Luz's teeth chattered.

Ivan took another blanket and wrapped it around her shoulders. "Mushrooms can make you cold. Can I make you some tea?"

Luz shook her head. "I'm freezing. Do you have any advice?"

Ivan grabbed his laptop and started typing. "Let me do some research; this really isn't my thing."

"There's an article on how to help someone on a bad trip; you should read it." The room stretched out suddenly, the ceiling so low Luz could touch it with her fingertips while sitting down.

The light from the screen fell on Ivan's face; his skin melted off revealing his skull. "It says to remember it is your mind. If something frightens you, ask what it has to teach you."

"Ivan."

"Remember you are in a safe—"

"Ivan, it's started."

Ivan left the computer and helped her lay down on the couch, placing a pillow under her head and covering her with blankets. He sat on the floor next to her and took her hand.

"I'm sorry I'm so impulsive; you're a good man, Ivan."

"Let's get you through this trip so you can make it up to me."

"Just don't ask me to cook; you have horns growing out of your head." Luz smiled when a wave of sensations overcame her leaving her paralyzed and plunging her into darkness. Closing her eyes, she tried speaking but her mouth refused to obey. Terror gripped her and her heart pounded in her ears. But Ivan's warm hand grasped hers, so she monitored her body. I'm breathing, she told herself, I'm not completely paralyzed.

She stood in front of the mine, but it was different, the vegetation was foreign, flat, as if an alien planet. The entrance yawned, threatening to devour her. "Yoali!" she yelled, "Yoali!"

A voice on her left said, "You must go in the mine." Luz looked around but was alone. The voice was female and familiar. Mist emanated from the mine, forming a cloud that climbed the mountain, leaving whisps stuck in cliffs and on ledges.

Luz stepped inside and almost plunged into a lava-filled pit. People screamed as they struggled while the melted rock scorched them. A hot flash crept over her body, starting at her feet, slowly climbing. Howls and cries came from the pit, the cave walls amplifying them. A dark horned figure, more of a void than a presence, as if it was a hole in the fabric of the universe, rose in front of her. Red slits for eyes stared into her soul. "Sinner! Accept your penance!" the deep growling voice yelled, "Here you will toil for eternity in penance." The voice was that of a priest from the parish her grandmother attended.

"My mind is creating this version of hell learned in my childhood." The pit disappeared and Luz walked across firm ground deeper into the mine. "Yoali! It's me, Luz!"

A light broke the darkness of the cave and Luz rushed to it, coming upon a window to a room where a gray-haired woman lay in bed. A burly orderly came in and changed her diaper, never muttering a word. As he left, the old woman asked, "Has anyone come to see me?" The man shook his head. "Poor old bat, always the same question and no one has come in the last five years."

"Who is that?" asked Luz, but before the voice on her left answered, she had recognized her face under the lines and ravages of old age. That was her personal version of hell, being alone at the end of her life. "It doesn't have to end this way," the voice on her left said. The images dissolved.

Luz yelled again, "Yoali! Yoali!"

A mumbling came from deep inside the cave, growing, voices advancing toward her, loud, angry, reproachful. "You didn't help me!" "My son killed himself because of you!" "I told you I was suicidal!" "You knew my pills were making me worse!" among the phrases she could make out. Dozens of angry students and parents charged her, surrounding, yelling at her, demanding. "I'm dead because of you," said a student with a face bloated and purple, a rope hanging from his neck.

"I'm sorry!" said Luz, falling to her knees. "I'm sorry!"

"Sorry won't bring my kid back," said a mother.

A girl, with deep bloody gashes down her forearms, pointed at her. "She couldn't even save her own niece."

Patrick, her ex-husband, shook his head. "Selfish cheater ruined her sons' lives." Her sons stood behind him, glaring at her.

Mark joined them. "You're a cold bitch; you deserve to die alone."

Luz caved in on herself. They were right; she was a failure as a wife, mother, and counselor. "I can't save anyone!" she said out loud, "I can't even save myself." Shrinking into the dark, she hung, suspended. "I'll stay here forever. It's peaceful." There was no space, no time. Nothing. She was there for eternity or maybe for an instant.

"Luz! Tia Luz?"

Yoali's voice broke through the dark cocoon, tickling her ears. But she could not move, nor speak, she was the weight of the world; she would never move again.

"Help! Luz! Help me!"

"I can't," thought Luz, surprised by her thoughts breaking the stillness.

"Luz!" sounds, bright white, surrounding her, breaking into the rainbow. She drank each one, the flavors distinct, impossible to describe but in one word: red was passion, orange joy, yellow health, green beauty, blue love, purple wisdom, and violet peace. Each flavor burst in her solar plexus bathing her in sounds, chimes, notes, that vibrated in her, shedding the leaden blanket pulling her down.

"Luz!" That same female voice, it wasn't Yoali.

Luz sat up, and she smelled and touched her name for the first time. I am light, Luz! she said, the texture of light, tingling from her fingertips to her toes. She called out, "Yoali!"

Yoali stumbled into her view, Luz's words falling on her like flower petals kissing Yoali's face. Luz opened her arms; Yoali rushed and embraced her. "You came for me!"

"Your call brought me back," said Luz. She let go of her. "Let's get out of here."

Yoali clutched her hand. "He won't let me! He says this is my world."

"Who?"

"My father! He promised me to the devil when I was born."

"Think! You are a college student. What about free will? You are your own person!"

"But I've tried to escape! And I can't find myself anymore."

"Nonsense, Yoali! You called me, remember? Call yourself back!"

Behind Yoali, a male figure appeared, in place of a head, a skull with a scorpion tattooed on the bleached bone of his forehead. Luz recognized it from the descriptions of Yoali's father. "It's useless, Yoali; your mother's family doesn't understand the power they are up against. I named Yoali, Night, this is where you belong."

"Night is a beautiful thing, Yoali; it's when we replenish, rest, love, and dream. Your grandmother kept your name because you are good and beautiful like the night," Luz said.

"You have me in you, Yoali; you can't erase me," said her father.

"You have your mother in you; she made terrible mistakes but she loved you."

"She never loved me or she would've kept me away from him!"

"Then do it for your grandparents, for me, for Andrea!"

Yoali looked from her father to Luz. "Do you really think I can have a different life than my mother?"

"You already have."

Yoali took Luz's hand. "Let's go."

"One of you has to stay; that's the price."

"I'll stay," said Luz.

"But Luz—"

"I've lived my life and it's been pretty good. The world needs someone like you, Yoali, more than me. You go!"

"No!" father yelled, the voice echoing through the cabin, like thunder in the mine. "Yoali can never leave! She belongs here."

"Let's go!" cried Yoali.

Yoali's father clapped and everything went dark, a black so deep, there was no up or down, nor sound.

Luz's thoughts spun in a void. There was nothing. Only emptiness.

"You will never leave!"

"You can't keep us here! You have no power anymore."

A dot of light appeared on the horizon, slowly expanding into a line that grew upward. Luz understood. "Yoali! Your father only has the power we give him; he can't keep us here. You get to choose, don't choose him!"

Luz grasped Yoali's hand and yanked her toward the light, her father's howls fading into a toddler's tantrum. As they ran, the light grew until they came to a subterranean cave, where a gentle river flowed between boulders, lapping at the moss-covered banks. Light streamed through a gap in the stone hundreds of feet up, where an oak grew, it's crown hidden from view. A *catrina,* dressed in a flowing purple hooded cloak, raised her hand.

Yoali froze. "It's *Nantli*."

"The Great Goddess!" said Luz.

Nantli held out her hand to Yoali who placed the firestone in the skeleton's hand. The Earth Mother pointed at a clay pot by her feet.

Luz and Yoali stared into the pot; the water's surface shimmered, then cleared. Yoali's father was speeding down the highway, his eyes wild and enraged. Eleonora kept glancing at Yoali in her car seat in the back. "Please, I'll go with you, but let's leave Yoali with my mother."

"She's coming with us. Those *cabrones* will never take me alive. If I leave you two, they'll use you against me."

"No one has to know! Please!"

"Shut up!" he screamed as he punched Eleonora in the chest weaving out of his lane. He overcorrected and the car flipped over twice landing on the median strip.

Yoali looked at Luz, tears trailing her face. "My mother loved me."

"You may have your father in you, but you also have her."

Yoali nodded.

"Go back, go now!" said Luz, giving her a shove. Yoali ran and disappeared into the light.

*Nantli* pointed a bony finger at Luz, then at the same pot. Luz gave her the pyrite pebble and peeked through the door into her parents' bedroom. Her mother, Alma, was in her fifties and scarred by the toll of a lifetime of hard work. While Luz, now at the same age, could pass for being in her early forties, her mother looked sixty. Her short, gray hair was disheveled from the bed, and deep creases lined the middle of her forehead and around her mouth.

Alma listened to Marcelino's snoring, then gently pushed off the covers, bending over to kiss him, but she stopped, kissing her hand instead and touching it gently to his head. Changing into pants, a sweatshirt, and sneakers, she grabbed a bottle of lighter fluid from the garage and put it in the trunk of her car. Headlights shone on her as a car passed.

Alma parked in the empty dirt lot at the Mount Si trailhead, then climbed, a flashlight in one hand, the lighter fluid in the other. She tripped. Sweeping the flashlight back and forth, she searched for the trail as her heart pounded, shaking so hard, her teeth chattered.

Alma arrived at the campsite. The night was quiet, the wind beyond still as a half moon, shrouded by high clouds, shed an eerie gray light on the little clearing. She removed her clothes, folded them neatly, and placed them with her shoes on a boulder. Stepping into the pit, she poured lighter fluid over her head, then opened her hand to look at the pyrite in her palm.

Alma held the stone up to the sky and shouted, "Hear me, *Nantli*. I ask you for many favors, and I am willing to pay the price. I ask that you cure my Marcelino of cancer and my son Christian of his drug addiction." She swallowed, swaying on her feet. "Save my sister Eleonora and her daughter Yoali from evil." Her hand shook, gasping. "Make my Luz a mother." Tears streamed down her face as she shouted, "Finally, I ask that my son Joe finds a career. I beg you!"

A hot flash started in her belly; the strongest Alma had ever felt. The powerful wave spread over her body, radiating from her solar plexus and intensifying to temperatures no human can endure. She burst into a white flame that rose above the cedars, making them gyrate and pulse in a shadowy dance. As fast as it ignited, it went out, casting the woods into darkness. The flash, however, remained emblazoned on Luz's retinas.

"Mami!" she yelled, recognizing her voice as the one guiding her through Mictlán. She dashed to the firepit and ran her hands through the warm ashes. Leaning in, she plunged into the dark pit.

Sometime later, Luz opened her eyes, her hand grasping Ivan's. He helped her sit up, propping cushions behind her.

"Can I get you something?" he asked.

"Tissue," said Luz, wiping tears that flowed effortlessly down her face.

Ivan brought her a box, sitting beside her on the couch. He touched her cheek. "You scared the shit out of me."

Luz tried to tell him what happened, but so much was impossible to describe and it was fading quickly. Ivan brought her a legal pad and a pen, and she wrote down as much as she remembered, filling only a page.

Luz's phone rang, startling them. "It's three in the morning!" said Ivan.

Luz smiled, picking it up. "It's Lula. Yoali's awake."

Luz tried to sleep, but even the relief of Yoali's recovery couldn't keep away the images that intruded on her every time she closed her eyes. It was six when she finally fell into a restless sleep with her head on Ivan's chest.

After breakfast, Ivan offered his hand to Luz. "Come with me."

They walked into the yard where long tendrils of green beans laden with orange and salmon-colored blooms bent over the top of the wall. Tomatoes stuck out through a wire fence. Bees buzzed. Flowers bloomed in blues, yellows, reds, pinks, and purples indicating a loving hand. Sitting on the rough grass to take in the sun before the afternoon clouds covered it, they listened to the creek at the end of the lawn behind a twisted cottonwood.

"This is paradise," said Luz, stretching her arms above her head. "Did you plant the flowers?"

"I did. Flowers are important to the Yaqui."

Luz lay on her back to watch the clouds above. Ivan laid down next to her. "When do you go back to Seattle?"

"In two weeks."

"May I see you while you're here?"

"I would love that, but I need to make time for my *tía* and Yoali."

"Would your *tia* be willing to come up here? I would love to cook for the three of you next week."

"I'm sure I can persuade her."

He turned on his stomach, his face so close that Luz could see the pores on his nose and a wild gray hair in his eyebrow. His thin lips were close to her ear, and his breath fell on her cheek. Desire flowed through her, stronger than ever.

"I want you to know that I am not an easy man. I still have episodes of depression, during which you would not recognize me. I also know we've just met, but I would like us to keep in touch when you're back in Seattle."

"Yes, I want that too." She raised herself on her elbows. "I have a lot of stuff to figure out, and I don't know what I'll do." She sat cross-legged and looked at him. "After last night, I'm eager to explore new ways of healing, not only with sacred medicine but in community settings."

"I can't wait to see what you are going to do."

A month later, Luz took her time hiking the trail up Mount Si or what she called Mount Snoqualmie, its original name. Strenuous switchbacks climbed over the hard-packed stony ground where she picked up a wrapper caught in the brush and stuffed it in her backpack. This is sacred ground. Picking up the pace under a gray sky barely visible between the branches of the pines and maples.

A giant gold leaf floated softly to the ground in front of her. It was shortly after dawn, and few runners were on the empty trail. Luz compared herself now to when she'd made this same trip twenty years ago and shook her head; so much had changed, and so much was still the same. The campsite where her mother disappeared was empty except for a half-burned log in the middle of a pile of ashes and wrappers.

Luz knelt by the pit, scooped out the log, trash, and ashes into the bag. When it was clean, she took out two small logs from her backpack and placed them in the center, on top of the pyrite. She crumbled some newspaper and lit it. Soon flames danced on the logs. Sitting by the fire, Luz looked up to the sky and said, "Thank you, Mami, for what you did for us. I poured the ashes in El Real, where your parents are buried. I hope that was ok. I love you. You are my *Alma*, my soul."

Luz hiked back to her car. She had so much to do, having secured a sabbatical traveling through Mexico to study indigenous ways of healing. Feeling light, she looked ahead and smiled, hopeful.

# Still Waters

**EVERY AUTUMN AND SPRING** equinox, I sit at my window, keeping watch through the night: a bat, pepper spray, sharp kitchen knife, and my mother's rosary in easy reach. Chewing a serrano *chile* to stay awake, I press my forehead against the cold window, searching for his menacing figure.

The trouble started when my father was killed. That day, we walked to his VW parked on the street. Shedding red paint and rust, its front bumper dangling from a wire, my father lovingly called the VW his steed.

"See my little star?" he said, putting the key into the car's lock, "It's still here; no one wants to steal a—"

A van turned the corner. The vehicle accelerated toward us. Father's face drained of color.

"Get down!" he yelled, shoving me into spilled oil and dead leaves.

Bullets ripped through the VW. Glass shattered on me. In a time-bending flash, all was quiet, the profound silence suffocating all words, all thoughts, until my mother burst out of the house, shrieking. Yanking me up, she searched for bullet holes and blood. "Are you alright?" she repeated in a torrent, not hearing my strangled answer. Neighbors approached us, wary but wanting to help. "Jaciel!" Mami cried over and over until a neighbor lifted and pushed us into their home. I never saw Papi's body.

My father named me Citlali, morning star, a Nahuatl name anchoring me to my indigenous roots. "Remember everything comes from the stars," he would tell me. And I would point things, a bug, the sky, a car while he nodded at each one. He believed there was an invisible net connecting all living things. Mami said that's why she fell in love with him when they were young.

My father was a journalist. "The most dangerous job in Mexico," he'd said. He wrote about the logging of a monarch butterfly sanctuary, exposing an American soft drink company's deal with thugs to murder indigenous environmentalists' leaders. Mami said my father knew the dangers, but he chose butterflies over us because he was *Indio*. Papi said we are all interconnected; everything is part of the spirit. "Close your eyes and feel the spirit," he would say whenever we came to a waterfall, or cave, or impressive tree. I don't know if I felt a spirit, but I felt what he meant, there was no us and them; if butterflies and trees died, so would we.

After my father's murder, Mami and I flew to Los Angeles to live with her older brother Juan. His house was loud and crowded; Mami didn't get along with his wife, but I never felt alone. We overstayed our visa, and Mami became a receptionist at a motel where Alan worked maintenance. She thought him good-looking in a rugged, lumberjack-sort-of-way, and a year after my father's death, dated him. A large man, he ducked at every doorway. Stores didn't carry his shoe size. His dark, curly brown hair had a copper sheen, as did his mustache and beard. His brooding brown eyes looked right through me, as if I wasn't there.

When Alan's mother died and left him a house in Washington state, Mami said she was marrying Alan and we were leaving Los Angeles. I tried to talk to her about how deadly quiet Alan was, about how his silence didn't seem right to me. But my mother had a ready response.

"Still waters, deep thoughts, *hija*. You babble like a brook. Alan is serious."

Mami deserved happiness, I told myself, she had suffered so much! So I stopped complaining. I didn't contradict her when she continued to say that Alan was a man of "still waters and deep thoughts," even though in Spanish we'd been warned about—*agua estancada, agua envenenada*—still water, poisoned water.

Alan's house stood in a timber and farming community that crisscrossed the three forks of the Snoqualmie River, the ancestral home of the Snoqualmie Tribe. Thirty-two miles east of Seattle, the house lay in the shadow of Mount Si, a hulking piece of granite that loomed over the valley like a misshapen headstone.

On that first day, we parked in front of the one-story house built in the sixties; the peeling green paint faded to a sickly gray. Giant cedars, hawthorn, and overgrown rhododendrons guarded the home's secrets and diffused the roar of the unseen river. Mami zipped her jacket against the drizzling rain, staring at the decrepit rambler and the empty country road.

"How close is town?" she asked, biting her lower lip.

"Six miles more or less, seven miles to the falls."

"How will Cici get to school?" she asked, studying the empty road, bordered by an impenetrable barrier of thick ferns, overgrown blackberry, and thistles.

"The bus," replied Alan.

"But—"

"I did until I dropped out." He opened the front door and disappeared inside.

I walked over the spongy ground trailing a backpack and a pillowcase stuffed with my prized possessions. Cedars competed for sunlight with giant maples whose bare branches clawed the sky like arthritic fingers. I wrinkled my nose at the rotten egg smell oozing from beneath the house.

"Is that a gas leak?" I asked, looking at Alan, who was unlocking the moving van's door. He shook his head. Mami sniffed the air and stared at him, "Dead animal?"

He shrugged, "Stagnant water under the house."

My bedroom was at the end of a hallway. It'd been Alan's sister's and still contained her bed and faded homemade quilt. After five years of sharing a room with cousins, it was nice to have my own space, and I made plans to decorate it.

We unpacked the van and arranged our belongings. Mami made sandwiches while Alan chopped wood and built a fire. The power hadn't been connected so we ate by candlelight. That night not even a down comforter and wool blanket could keep the November chill from settling in my bones. I strained my ears, catching unfamiliar sounds, the rush of the river, voices whispering through the trees. Curling into a ball, the covers over my head, I prayed to Our Lady of Guadalupe until I remembered she'd never answered any of my prayers. As the wind rattled the roof and rain pelted the window, dread crawled into bed with me.

Two days after arriving, I jumped midstream into the freshman class at Snoqualmie High School. Three different groups of kids made up the school. The middle-class students came from The Ridge, a gated community whose golf course sprawled across the valley's rim. Another group was the descendants of the town founders who resisted the transformation into a Seattle suburb. Like Alan's, their parents were former or current loggers, farmers, and mill workers. Then there were the transients from the motels, the subsidized apartments, and trailer parks.

I didn't fit into any of those, which was fine with me. I looked for the other misfits to join. I'd inherited my father's body: short, bowlegged, round torso, dark skin, large head crowned by unruly, frizzy hair. To my mother, I complained about not inheriting her lighter skin and delicate beauty. "*La suerte de la fea, la bonita la desea*," she'd answered, "the luck of the ugly is desired by the beautiful." The proverb didn't help, especially since a week before she'd smiled at herself in the mirror saying, "Beauty is power; a smile is its sword." I understood I wasn't pretty, so I strived to be kind and cheerful. I thought of myself as a cool, babbling stream, so clear you could see the cobbles on its bed.

Amanda, Hailey, and I stood as the rest of the social studies class sat in small groups of friends. "You three leftovers!" called the teacher from his desk, "you're a team." We gathered in the back of the room, pushing desks together in a small circle to decide on our final project about the valley.

Amanda was everything I wasn't: slim, tall, hair tamed into tiny braids. Her smooth brown skin was unravished by angry red pimples, like mine. Her father worked at Microsoft and they lived on the ridge. Pretty girls like her were usually picked first, but she was the only black girl in our class, for the moment, as much an outsider as me.

Hailey recently moved into a trailer in Truck Town with her mother and younger siblings from Portland. While her father did time in prison, her mother worked as a hairdresser. Her blond hair was almost white; her eyes the palest blue I'd ever seen.

"What's our topic?" asked Amanda, who was instantly our leader.

"How about the TV show *Twin Peaks*? They filmed it here, you know," Hailey proposed.

"I bet everyone's doing that," dismissed Amanda.

I cleared my throat. "How about haunted Snoqualmie?"

Amanda frowned, "Isn't that the same as Twin Peaks?"

"No. We'll talk about Snoqualmie as a dumping ground for bodies."

Hailey took out her phone and started typing. Amanda looked at me, twirling a strand of hair around her finger.

I blushed. "Criminals from Seattle have always used Snoqualmie to dump bodies. The Green River Killer buried five in this area."

"They also found a dead baby in the forest, Baby Kimball. It's all true," added Hailey, holding up a photo on her phone. A wooden memorial overflowing with stuffed animals contrasted against the gloomy woods.

We researched the bizarre happenings in the valley, which started when white settlers invaded the Snoqualmie Tribe's ancestral lands. The mystical forest became infamous for murders, suicides, ghostly sightings. An outlandish website by the Snoqualmie Warden described magical creatures and shapeshifters that stormed through Snoqualmie's many trans-dimensional portals. Even the elk that grazed in the fields had a turbulent history, having been nearly exterminated twice. We picked a topic and became close because outsiders need to stick together, especially in a haunted place.

Fall surrendered to a brutal winter of endless rain. Streams that had trickled like tears down the mountain's face now froze above the low-hanging steel-colored clouds. The anemic sun couldn't pierce the deep shadows under the hundred-foot cedars where old-growth stumps transformed into menacing creatures. If this place had a spirit like Papi claimed, it was an ancient, dire one.

Every morning wrapped in my parka, I waited for the bus. While I waited, I vainly tried to silence my chattering teeth. Seven thirty in the morning was as dark and ominous as midnight. It didn't help my sense of fear that just a couple of miles away, a cougar had attacked some cyclists, devouring one of them. Bears were hibernating, but I knew cougars and wicked spirits thrived in winter.

I enjoyed school. The warm, bright building was a welcome respite from Mount Si's deep shadow. Hailey, Amanda, and I became inseparable, meeting for lunch to exchange gossip, visiting each other's homes after school. Amanda was the youngest of four, and an authority on the latest trends in pop culture gleaned from her older brothers that Hailey and I crushed on.

At Hailey's, we would play with her mom's makeup and do each other's hair. Our attempts to straighten my frizzy curls yielded only brittle, burnt strands. We'd make mac and cheese for dinner for her younger siblings and helped them with homework in their trailer.

Mami would cook something special when they came over, and I'd set the dining room table; Alan eating in silence while we chatted and laughed. For a while, I was a regular kid.

Mami worked six nights a week as a receptionist at the Salish Lodge. In her free time, she decorated the rambler, cleaned out closets, but the house still felt alien. The shadows in the corners shifted into ominous shapes, their gaze following me, making me skittish while I washed the dishes and emptied the trash after Mami left for work. Alan dozed in front of the TV, while I hid in my bedroom, reading about Snoqualmie's darker history until I drifted off into nightmares.

In spring, the days stretched and the river roared, engorged from the snowmelt. Roads flooded. Windstorms knocked out the power. Like a giant barreling through the forest, wind gusts hurled cedar branches at the house and ripped off roof tiles. Despite the sun's growing presence, the howling spring winds and driving rains dampened my mood.

Alan built a chicken coop and, when he could get them, did handyman jobs. But those were few and far between. Soon, watching television consumed his nights, leaving a pile of empty beer cans on the coffee table until Mami returned from work. He slept all day, rising for dinner, which he ate in brooding silence as he sank into his phone.

One night, after Mami left, Alan lingered at the table, drinking and staring at me while I washed dishes. He examined me like the dead rats he trapped in the garage before dumping them in the trash. I shuddered.

"You're different from your mother." I hesitated to answer because I wasn't used to him talking to me.

"I know. I look like my father."

"Shame," he said in a low voice.

"I'm going to my room."

I did homework until I fell asleep. Sometime later, I woke up, startled as the door to my room opened.

"Mami?" I asked hopefully. She always looked in on me, but it was too early for that. I sat up. Alan stood in the doorway.

"What?" I asked, my heart pounding.

"Shhhh," he said, swaying, drunk.

"Get out!" I said, fear grinding my voice into a coarse whisper.

He sat on my bed, his weight tilting it toward him, and pushed me down. His hands came down rough on my breasts. I shoved him away, squirming.

"Hold still, bitch!"

I scrambled off the bed, opened the door. "Get out!"

"Get back here!" He gripped my arm. Too strong. I couldn't fight him.

"Get on the bed now, or I'll have you and your mom deported."

Mami said that when she married Alan, we'd get our papers. She was saving to pay for a lawyer and fees, but we were still undocumented and could be deported. I laid down, closed my eyes, and tried not to feel anything as his hands roamed my body. My mind flew far away, to Mexico. My father and I sat by a waterfall and counted the monarch butterflies, one, two, until I got to a hundred and started again.

I was still listening to my father's calm voice count when Alan jerked himself off.

"You tell your mother, you're both gone," he warned.

Since that night, I tossed and flinched at every sound, waiting for the monster to return. The putrid smell from under the house penetrated, lingering in my room.

That spring, Alan invaded my room once a week before staggering away. He had forced me into his secret, vile world. I became more like him, uncommunicative and full of voiceless thoughts.

Mami fed me vitamin D and got me a sun lamp. My friends grew concerned, asking if I was alright. I was still water, poisoned water. I wanted to run, but I couldn't leave Mami. I crushed some allergy pills and blended them into Alan's mashed potatoes. But that didn't poison him. Nothing worked. Then on Memorial Day, he didn't just touch me. On that day, he forced me to give him a blow job.

My friends and I shared many intimate things: Hailey's father's incarceration; Amanda's brother's addiction; my father's murder. I was afraid to tell them I was undocumented, but not as much as I was ashamed to share Alan's abuse.

One Friday night, at a sleepover in Amanda's home, we huddled on our sleeping bags on the floor, dunking cookies in cold glasses of milk. "I need to make my stepfather disappear," I said solemnly.

The silence spread like the blanket of fog that hides the Snoqualmie Valley.

"What'd the asshole do?" Amanda asked, shattering the dam inside me. Burying my face in my arms, I cried long-wracking sobs until only whimpers sounded. They held me, patting my back and glancing at each other. I wiped my eyes and said, "He beats my mom."

They hugged me, and I swallowed the shameful truth, like hot, putrid vomit. Self-hatred welled up inside me.

"We'll go to the police with you," offered Amanda, sitting and wrapping her arms around her knees.

I shook my head. "My mother and I are illegal. Alan said he'd call ICE if I told my mom—I mean—if she went to the police."

"Asshole!" Hailey said, "I'll kill him!"

"Not kill him. Remember the Snoqualmie Warden?" I asked, diverting them from my slipup. They looked at me blankly. "The weird guy who said that Snoqualmie has portals to other worlds?"

"You don't believe that shit?" asked Amanda, glancing from Hailey to me.

"Haven't you wondered why so many people throw themselves off the falls?"

"Suicide," said Amanda.

"The Warden says it's because one of the portals is behind the mist."

Amanda rolled her eyes, picking cookie crumbs from the shag rug.

"What about all the bodies they never find? Where do they go?" I challenged her.

"The ocean?"

"Even in the summer when the river is so low you can wade across?" asked Hailey leaning toward me.

"You wanna throw Alan over the falls?" asked Amanda.

"Not the falls but through a different portal."

We spent the rest of the day planning.

Finally, one afternoon, we got Alan to bring us to the Blue Hole, off the Middle Fork of the Snoqualmie River. Amanda's string bikini was the most convincing voice. Alan retreated to a folding chair in the shade of a broad-leaf maple, his cooler in reach. In his field of view, the three of us lay on towels on the sandy bank below. We clustered in the sun, nervous, whispering encouragement.

I struggled to say something. There was something about this place. The sound of the river blended with the rustling of the leaves. Mount Si stretched its twin peaks into an expansive blue sky. On the bank, pink and lavender foxgloves dotted moss-covered tree stumps, ferns, and blackberry canes. It was beautiful and deadly. The Blue Hole was a deceptively perilous stretch of the Snoqualmie. Its surface appeared placid, but fast currents roiled below. Underwater trees, strainers, trapped and drowned unwary swimmers and kayakers every year. The Snoqualmie Warden claimed it was a portal into other dimensions. The county had put up a fence, but undeterred swimmers and kayakers still came; some still disappeared, some just died.

Time slowed down as we laid in the sun, waiting, watching people come and go. Unusually quiet, I wondered if Alan noticed. From my towel, I counted eight discarded beer cans.

"Cici!" hissed Hailey, "We're the only ones left on the beach."

"It's time," Amanda whispered.

"Be careful," I cautioned.

I glanced at Alan. His eyes bore into Amanda, not caring that we noticed.

"I will. Let's hope there really is a portal." Amanda walked to the river and jumped in.

"Get out of there!" yelled Alan. "No swimming."

"I'm just gonna rinse off," she answered.

Alan walked down to the bank, brow furrowed. Hands on hips, he stared at Amanda until she suddenly went under just as we had planned. She resurfaced. "Help!" she screamed and sank again.

Alan looked at the now empty banks. "Swim over here," he shouted. Amanda flailed her arms.

"She needs help!" cried Hailey as we glared at Alan.

He looked around again. "Fuck!" he shouted, taking off his boots.

Alan jumped into the river fully clothed, swimming toward Amanda, who drifted farther from him, toward the whirlpool at the center of the Blue Hole. Her head bobbed. Surfaced and disappeared again.

Amanda didn't resurface; Alan was still a few yards away.

Something cold and dark clutched my heart. "She's not pretending!"

Hailey and I jumped into the cold water. I pulled hard toward Amanda but couldn't see her. A current gripped me, forcing me underwater. Hailey screamed. The whirlpool had us, its powerful force dragging us down. Soon we would be caught in the strainers.

I stopped struggling. "I'm sorry, Mami," I intoned in my head, "forgive me." I surrendered and sank toward a tangle of waterlogged trees and roots where a vortex sucked fish and branches into its ravenous maw. A shadow creature, bear-like, guarded the entrance. I thought of Amanda and Hailey, how they'd stood by me, how I loved them. They would drown trying to help me. I prayed to the spirit of the river, "Please save my friends! Take me, I begged, but save them."

The membranous figure, now shaped like a beaver, slapped its paws together, causing a current that propelled Hailey and me toward Amanda. We slammed into her, the force springing us out of the whirlpool. Hailey and I held Amanda by the arms and kicked toward the bank, leaving Alan spinning in the vortex. I prayed again to the river, take him away. Its surface shimmered like a rainbow.

We reached the shallow water and crawled onto the bank of the Blue Hole. Hailey pounded Amanda's back until she vomited, while I watched Alan disappear below the surface. I looked up at the mountain, then at the river. Thank you, I said silently.

It's been six years since Alan disappeared. Mami cried for a while, but soon life called, and she answered. Hailey moved to Oregon and we lost touch. Amanda is studying bioengineering at Stanford; we keep connected through social media. We stayed in Snoqualmie because Mami owns the house. I'm a creative writing major at the University of Washington.

I don't know if Snoqualmie is haunted or a gateway to other worlds. Ecosystems, when altered, react negatively to keep the balance; it follows then that this beautiful place also retaliates for the evil it has undergone. So do I. Maybe I'm the haunted one. Keeping watch every equinox night, recording every acre clear-cut and species extinguished, I write the earth's obituary like my father once did. I worry that when the suburbs consume the forest and the river stops flowing, becoming still, poisoned water, there will be no spirits left to stop monsters when they return.

# The Cicada's Song

## Yquiza Tonatiuh - Sunrise

### 1

*"My boyfriend strangled me when I tried to leave him because he beat me. He used a telephone cord. The police will say I was a drug addict and a dropout. They will rule it a suicide."*

**IXCHEL TIPTOED DOWN THE STAIRS,** cringing every time the hardwood groaned; her feline eyes focused on the front door a few feet away. Holding her breath, she reached for the door when her phone blasted the song "In the Heights".

"Ixchel?"

"Shit!" she said, underneath her breath, shutting it off.

"I made you breakfast."

Ixchel sighed and walked into the kitchen where her aunt Jimena was busy at the stove scrambling eggs even though she'd explained she was vegan. Until her daughter's death, Jimena had been a middle-aged and divorced vibrant woman, still hit on by thirty-year-olds and usually the last one dancing at weddings and parties. Now, collapsing into her chest, she stooped over the stove like an infirm elder. Ixchel sat at the table and Jimena placed a plate of cubed papaya and black coffee in front of her.

Ixchel gripped the ceramic mug and sipped the bitter brew, savoring the faint cocoa taste of Mexican coffee. "Thank you, the fruit is enough."

"I forgot you don't eat eggs, can I make you a quesadilla? Or beans? Mariana loved my bean tacos." Jimena choked on the last words, as if saying her daughter's name reopened the wound.

"No, thanks," said Ixchel, eating papaya in silence while racking her brain for words to console her aunt. What can I tell her? Her twenty-year-old daughter, Mariana, had been dead for four months. The police found her beaten and stabbed in a downtown alley, her body full of drugs. They arrested a druggy who'd confessed to stabbing her during a mugging, and the case had been closed.

"Was that your mother on the phone?" asked Jimena.

Ixchel nodded, her mouth full of fruit.

Jimena sat down with a plate of scrambled eggs. "You need to talk to her."

"I will when I'm ready to go back to Seattle. I can't stand her telling me how dangerous it is in Mexico City."

"She's right to be worried. When are you going back?"

Ixchel shrugged. "A couple of more months."

"But you have a job interview next week."

Ixchel stood up and poured coffee into her travel mug. It was time to flee. She didn't want to argue again about trying to get justice for Mariana or why she shouldn't be writing on femicide. "I already canceled the interview."

Jimena pushed her intact plate aside and lit a cigarette. "You need to get back to your life."

"And you need to eat something!"

Jimena tapped her ashes in her cup. "I will. I need to buy some ashtrays. I quit when I was pregnant but now—"

Ixchel hugged her aunt with one arm. Jimena and her mother shared the same short, dark body type, while Ixchel had inherited her American father's green eyes and height. At five feet, ten inches, she towered over most Mexicans.

She let go and dashed to the car, hating not knowing what to say. On the hood of the silver sedan was Neno, her aunt's cat; a knife sticking through its skull. Ixchel's stomach rolled and she almost hurled the papaya and coffee. She peered around but this early the street was empty. She searched for a way to hide it, she couldn't let Jimena see it.

After wrapping the dead cat in a reusable shopping bag, she stuffed it at the bottom of the trashcan. Then, Ixchel sat in the locked car, gripping the steering wheel, counting as she slowed her breathing. Every time a panic attack seized her, she stopped and practiced counting and breathing, evenly and slowly inhaling and exhaling, and it helped. *Was the warning for Jimena or for me?*

Ixchel drove her cousin's little Kia toward Ecatepec de Morelos, Mexico City's second most populous suburb—and the most dangerous city in the entire country. Crowded and impoverished, it sprawled less than thirty minutes from Teotihuacan, where tourists and students climbed the Pyramids of the Sun and Moon. She sighed, wishing she was going to the pyramids instead of hell,

Soon Mexico City's modern streets, shining buildings, well-kept fountains, and monuments were replaced by dirty, dusty, busy avenues bursting with factories, slaughterhouses, and dairy processors. The buildings became shabbier and more menacing as she approached her destination. Ixchel bit the skin from the cuticle on her thumb. A weight settled in her chest and grew heavier with each mile.

## 2

*"My stepfather molested me when I was nine years old. I was eleven when he forced me to have intercourse once a week. One day I told him I was bleeding. He got very mad and beat me until I died. They will bury me and say I died falling down the stairs. In a few months, my stepfather will molest my little sister."*

When she reached Ecatepec, Ixchel sank into the densely populated slums of tin-roofed homes marching up the hills like haphazardly discarded boxes. Crosses marked where victims' bodies had been found. Stray dogs snuffled through heaps of trash looking for something to eat, while a pale, sickly sun fought to shine through the smog.

Near the canal, two men with bandanas covering their noses and mouths worked a dredger dragging the channel. Thirty miles long, it was Mexico City's sewer. Its brown, foul water flowed through the heart of Ecatepec, emptying the decaying waste of the city's residents—tires, mattresses, dead animals, discarded wives and girlfriends. Sparse, emaciated vegetation fought for survival amidst the plastic bottles, wrappers, bags, discarded shoes, and vomit that littered the banks of the canal.

Ixchel wrinkled her nose at the putrid, gassy smell emanating from the thick, greasy waters. She approached the men, hand outstretched, and yelled over the roar of the machine, "*Buenas días!*."

The men cast a quick, stony glance at her and continued working. She got closer and took out her recorder but stopped, frozen. A woman lay naked and bald, her breasts stained with tar. Ixchel gasped, then realized it was a mannequin.

With weak knees, she advanced. "*Hola.* I am a reporter. Would you mind if I asked you a few questions?" She flashed her biggest smile as she took slow deep breaths. I'm safe, she repeated mentally.

The men traded looks. She was taller than them, with long brown hair falling in unkempt waves over shoulders molded slightly forward from hunching over trying to look shorter than she was. Her smile was wide, innocent, and curious. The larger man, who was built like a linebacker, shrugged and walked away but the other said, "I was about to take my break. Buy me a soda and I'll talk with you." He jumped off the dredger and strode unhurriedly toward a small stand on a corner where a woman sold street tacos.

After introducing himself as Everardo, he launched into nonstop chatter with Ixchel, the taco vendor, and another customer who stood a short distance away, brazenly undressing Ixchel with his gaze. The customer wore a bandana reminding Ixchel of a pirate. His dull eyes weighed on her as she tried to ignore him and focus on Everardo. She bought the dredger a soda and three tacos of *suadero*, a sinuous, cheap cut of beef, and a soda for herself, distrusting the tacos' proximity to the canal. They sat on rickety, soiled plastic chairs as Everardo talked, shouting over the steady roar of the traffic.

"I was hired by a family. Their daughter went missing last week," he said, biting into a taco. He paused chewing and wiped grease and salsa from his chin with his sleeve. "We haven't found her yet. In 2015, a judge ordered the canal to be dragged and they found a lot of bodies. A lot of body parts too—hands, feet, even a head in a plastic bag." He continued eating casually, as if discussing the weather. "They also found a fourteen-year-old girl missing from the year before."

Ixchel shuddered. She had been unable to locate the family, but she had seen the photos from the coroner. She squeezed her eyes shut as the images of her poor tortured body came rushing back. No wonder her family was gone; sometimes the only thing left for them to do was to run from the horror and pain. Can they? She imagined her aunt, and all her family, running forever because such terrors were always snapping at your heels, ready to consume when you least expected it.

Ixchel burped into her hand. "Have you personally found any bodies?"

Everardo leaned back in his chair and looked up, squinting at the gray sky. "Only body parts and bones, but I am new at this. Families pay us, but we don't always find their loved ones or we find someone else's relative. They have to pay up front, so I still make my money."

"Advocacy groups argue the authorities don't report the real number of bodies. What do you think?"

"Ah, *guerita*, I think they're right. My friend *el piojo*," he tilted his head in the direction of his work partner, "has been doing this for so many years that he just stopped talking. They say he's seen too many dead girls to say anything anymore."

"What do you think?"

"The canal smells worse now because of the drought. When the waters come back, if they ever do, it won't smell as bad but this place will stay evil."

He stood up and returned his plastic plate to the stand. "People say the canal is the gateway to hell. I think *el diablo* lives there. You should be careful too, even *gringuitas* are not safe here." He walked back to the canal. Hopping back into the dredger's driver's seat, he turned the key, making the huge machine cough into life in an explosion of black diesel exhaust.

Recording some thoughts, Ixchel walked back to her car, the man with the bandana, the pirate, following her. He leaned on the driver's door.

Ixchel stepped back and searched for help, but there was only the old woman at the taco stand and Everardo busy with the machine. The dredger wouldn't hear a thing if this guy shot her with a machine gun.

Ixchel squared her shoulders, pulled out her keys, and glared at the man.

"I need to leave."

The man moved aside, his beady, red-rimmed eyes fixed on her breasts, chipped teeth flashing every time his lips smacked.

"I can tell you stories too, *guerita*. I've seen everything. Most of those girls were bad, you know? They liked to do bad things."

Ixchel unlocked the door, trying to keep her distance, but the man leaned over and whispered in her ear, "Do you like to do bad things? Do you want me to do—"

The man they called *el piojo* yanked the pirate from the collar and slammed him on the ground.

"Hey! Take it easy *pinche piojo*! I'm just helping the *señorita*."

Ixchel got in her car and turned to *el piojo*. "Thank you."

The large man barely nodded as he balled his hands into mallet-sized fists and glared down at the pirate who scurried away.

## Nepantla Tonatiuh - Noon

3

*"I was sixteen and would hang out with my two friends from childhood. They said I was one of the guys. One day we were getting high on cement and weed when one of them grabbed my breasts. I told him to stop but he didn't. My friends raped and stabbed me. I was still alive when they doused me with gasoline and lit me on fire. My crime was never investigated."*

Ixchel drove a few miles to the headquarters of a nonprofit created to advocate for the protection and safety of women in Ecatepec. The agency was on the second floor of a government building. Tile floors, fluorescent lights, metal file cabinets, and old, wooden desks in the reception area had long lost any pretense of comfort or efficiency. The receptionist led Ixchel to the lawyer and director of the center, Yolanda.

Curvy and tall, almost six feet in high heels, Yolanda wore her business suit tight and her skirt short, revealing long, shapely legs. Her dark hair was long and styled in rolling locks that must have taken at least an hour to set. Heavy makeup and bright red lipstick completed her look. Yolanda stared Ixchel in the eye, then looked at her jeans and a button-down sage-colored shirt. "I rarely meet women as tall as me!" she smiled.

They sat in two armchairs that flanked a small table upon which the receptionist placed a tray with two cups of steaming coffee. Several framed degrees and plaques lined the walls along with photos of assorted family members and miniature dogs. Ixchel thanked Yolanda for the meeting, turned on her recorder, set it on the table between them, and asked about the center.

"We are a small nonprofit funded by the state. We educate the community about femicide, help families through police procedures, and counsel families of murder victims," Yolanda said in a well-practiced monotone.

"Why do you do this? Isn't it dangerous?"

Yolanda sighed. "If not me, then who? Mexico is among the twenty-five countries with the highest rate of femicide. According to the UN, nine women are murdered every day in Mexico; some say it's much higher. From 2013 to 2017, 1,420 women were murdered right here in the state of Mexico."

Ixchel sipped some coffee. "Why do you think it's happening? What makes Mexico State so deadly for women?"

"The official reason is that the state of Mexico is the most populous in the country and we lack resources, services, and infrastructure."

"You said the official reason. What is the real reason?"

"Well, while I agree economic factors play a part, they aren't the only reason. It's not just in Ecatepec either. Remember Juarez? It's worse in poorer communities but upper-class women also get murdered."

"Why do you think gender violence is so bad here?"

"Misogyny. Half the women in Mexico experience gender-based violence from their husbands, partners, fathers."

"And boyfriends," said Ixchel.

Yolanda leaned back in the armchair and crossed her legs. "My turn. Why are you here? Your email said you moved from Seattle four months ago."

Ixchel turned off the recorder and put it in her purse. "I graduated from college last year and I'm writing a—"

"Ixchel Cumings is an unusual name, and easy to find on social media, your cousin was Mariana Villa."

Ixchel nodded even though it wasn't a question. "Mariana's mother, Jimena Gándara, is my mother's sister. My father is American so I was born in Seattle and came to help when Mariana happened. The report on femicide is a freelance project."

Yolanda crossed her legs. "Does your family believe the druggy killed her?"

"Do you?"

Yolanda uncrossed her legs and leaned in grasping Ixchel's arm. "I'm on your side."

Ixchel sighed. "We know he didn't! An independent autopsy reported Mariana died of strangulation, the stabbing wounds occurred after she was dead. A private investigator procured video from a security camera outside the club where Mariana's friends had last seen her. The video showed her ex-boyfriend putting a very intoxicated Mariana into his sports car, but the ex swore she leaped out of his car at a stoplight and ran away; he even produced witnesses."

"I'm so sorry. Does your family believe it was Dante who killed Mariana?"

"We know it was him! The first time Mariana broke up with him, he beat her up. He convinced her to keep it secret. My aunt blames herself because she told her to let it go."

Yolanda squeezed her hand. "And because Dante Vignau is a famous soccer player and nephew of Mexico State's prosecutor, he wasn't even considered a suspect."

Ixchel nodded and slumped in the chair. "I haven't told my aunt yet but the druggy that supposedly killed Mariana was murdered in jail yesterday. Then today, I found my aunt's cat on the hood of my car. Dead. A knife through its skull."

Yolanda gasped. "Those are serious threats!"

Ixchel shrugged.

Yolanda frowned. "Mothers seeking justice for their daughters are routinely murdered; a few years ago, they murdered one in front of the courthouse. Both you and your aunt are in danger!"

Ixchel stood up. "Neither of us is giving up."

"I'm sorry this happened to Mariana and your family." Yolanda reached for Ixchel's hand. "But you are out of your league. This isn't the United States; if you cross the wrong man, the police won't protect you. The police might even kidnap and kill you."

Ixchel reached for the door. "I appreciate your concern but I'm going to the prosecutor's press conference."

"Wait!" said Yolanda, scribbling on a legal pad, then tearing off the page and handing it to Ixchel. "Look for Amaya; she's an artist and educator helping victims heal and working on stopping femicide. And please be careful. Just last year, twenty-two reporters were murdered in Mexico. This country is dangerous for women and journalists."

## 9

*"I was twenty-one years old and cleaned the priest's house and took care of him. Some nights he would ask me to take a bath with him and then he would have sex with me. When I got pregnant and started showing, he asked me to go to the Sierra with him. After having sex with me on the ground, he strangled me. He will tell my parents that I ran away with my boyfriend. My bones will be scattered by animals, never to be found."*

A woman wearing an apron over a calf-length cotton dress and a gray wool cardigan waited for Ixchel by her car. Her graying braids framed a wide face and deep brown eyes, she had the look of a victim's mother as if something inside had been rubbed out leaving a permanent void.

"*Señorita*, can you help me? I heard you're an American reporter."

"I'm sorry, *señora*, but I need to be in Toluca."

"Please, *señorita*"— the woman followed—"my daughter's husband killed her and he is still free."

"I'm sorry, that's terrible. I wish I could help." Ixchel got to her car and unlocked it.

"Please," the woman insisted, showing her a wrinkled photo of a girl in a violet *quinceañera* dress. "The center can't help me. We went to the police after he beat her up. She had a black eye, a fat lip, bruises on her ribs and stomach and back ..."

Ixchel opened the door and sat in the driver's seat. The woman stood holding the car door open with her body.

"They said she couldn't file charges because her injuries would take less than fifteen days to heal. He killed her when she went to pick up her clothes. He—"

"I'm sorry, *señora*," said Ixchel tearfully, pulling on the door until the woman stepped away, then yanking it closed. She drove off wondering what she was doing.

## 5

*"I was a thirty-six-year-old doctor. The husband of a patient who had a miscarriage forced me into a car at gunpoint. He drove to a vacant lot and shot me in the head. Then he decapitated me, flayed the skin off my head, and threw my body in the canal."*

Thick woods stretched into the surrounding hills that flanked the road to Toluca. Pine resin and moist, rich earth scented the air. The woods reminded Ixchel of the Pacific Northwest. She stopped at a roadside tent for a *quesadilla* with squash blossoms, but it sat heavy in her stomach. She dialed her aunt leaving her a message. "Hi. You said Mariana fought with her best friend when she posted photos of her after Dante beat her up and the post has since disappeared. Could you check on her computer or iPad if she still has them? *Gracias*."

Ixchel closed her eyes. The girl in the violet dress, her mother's face, intruded on her thoughts. She blinked and shook her head, trying to dislodge them, but now body parts floating in water and trash clouded her mind. Her stomach rolled and clenched. Ixchel bolted out of the car, vomiting her lunch. Still retching, she got back in the car and gripped the steering wheel waiting for her hands to stop shaking. She took a couple of deep breaths and bit her index finger, something she hadn't done since she was twelve years old.

"Calm down!" she said, starting the car and continuing on the highway.

## 6

*"I was fourteen years old and loved One Direction and Justin Bieber. On my way to meet a friend, a man grabbed me and forced me into an abandoned business. He raped and strangled me, dismembered me, and threw my remains in the canal. Eighteen months from today, they will find my skull and feet in a plastic bag."*

Ixchel parked in a lot near a modern, sleek courthouse made of concrete and marble. The large plaza in front of the building was packed with protesters. "*Ser nena no es condena*," chanted the crowd. Mothers raised pink signs bearing photos of their dead or missing daughters as grandchildren clung to their skirts. A young woman with a shaved head spoke through a bullhorn.

"We are here to protest the lack of action by the governor, the prosecutor, and the police. Their apathy is part of the problem. No one is talking about this but we are! In the last year, we had almost as many women murdered here as Ciudad Juarez had in ten years combined!"

The crowd chanted, "*Ni una mas!*"

"As family members of those who have been slaughtered, we are here to make sure they are never forgotten!"

A young man wearing a purple T-shirt, with a drawing of an insect with a stout body and membranous wings, handed her a flyer. At least two dozen young people wore the same shirt. Pointing at it, she asked what it meant.

"It's a cicada, a symbol of resiliency and resurrection. Like them, we always rise up to live and fight for change," he said.

Ixchel weaved through the crowd until she spotted the sound system and the performance director. A heavyset woman in her mid-thirties, with fine-drawn features, hazel eyes, and fair skin, was monitoring a sound board.

"Amaya? I am Ixchel. Yolanda gave me your name."

The woman looked up in surprise, ignored Ixchel's outstretched hand, and kissed her on the cheek. "Hola! I'm a little busy at the moment; do you mind waiting here until the end of the performance?"

A conch trumpeted through the square, its hauntingly ancient basso note silencing the crowd. Holding the conch was a trans woman, dressed in a scarlet *huipil* embroidered with branches, leaves, and flowers in green and gold. Her headdress was almost three times the size of her head and shaped like a tree, an image of a bird interwoven among the feathered branches. From the branches, butterflies, spiders, and streaming ribbons simulating water fanned out and flowed with each of her rhythmic steps. Multicolored beads hung heavily on her chest; large, feathered earrings obscured her earlobes; a pendant from which three menacing fangs dangled elongated her nose. Children in bright clothes followed her, carrying baskets brimming with fruit and corn. She danced slowly, proudly playing the conch and keeping time with her feet until she had made her way to the center of the plaza. The children placed the baskets around her and danced away.

Two performers dressed in heavily embroidered leather loincloths beat out rhythms on large drums made from animal hides. They were joined by the tsch-tschush, tsch-tschush, tsch-tschush of rattles wrapped around the wrists and ankles of six female dancers. One of the female dancers said in a loud voice, "Thank you, Great Goddess, for your gifts. Thank you for allowing us to live in peace and harmony with nature and one another."

Without warning, the deep resonant drumming thundered again through the plaza. The dancers spun and twirled in intricate patterns around the goddess, matching the drums' cadence with their ankle rattles.

Just as suddenly, the drumming turned chaotic. The dancers flung themselves to the earth as two loincloth-clad males, brandishing obsidian daggers, leaped into their midst. They thrust menacingly, flying acrobatically, back and forth. Pointing their daggers at the goddess, they simulated stabs and slashes into her body until she lay crumpled on the ground.

One of the male dancers unfurled a long banner and held it high in the place where the goddess had been. A fanged, horned toad dominated the banner, its thick-lipped mouth spread widely to reveal opposing rows of pointed bloodstained teeth. A different male herded the female dancers into a line before the toad and ritualized a blood offering to it from each woman. The female dancers staggered to one side, standing shoulder to shoulder, except for the last woman. As a woman got on her hands and knees, one of the warriors took the sixth and final woman and laid her over the human altar. Handling his dagger, he mimicked extracting the woman's heart, holding it high above his head in the direction of the sun before offering it to the toad. Once the sacrifice was completed, the warrior brusquely kicked the woman off the altar onto the ground.

A martial cadence thundered from the drums across the plaza. Two conquistadores approached in lock step, aimed their blunderbusses, and shot the two male dancers. To the relentless beat of the drums, the conquistadores pantomimed the rape of the female dancers and the destruction of imagined columns and temples.

Ixchel looked around at the swelling crowd. Men and women stood transfixed; parents hoisted children onto their shoulders. A man in a suit stared at them from across the plaza, out of place in a crowd of families and women.

She pointed him out to Amaya. "He's not here for the performance."

Amaya sighed. "They're always watching, and they want us to know."

Ixchel shuddered and forced herself to focus on the performance.

Cassocked in black and wearing horrific masks, three new male dancers entered the plaza, gyrating and gesticulating lewdly, punctuating their lascivious moves with exaggerated signs of the cross. They were devils; their features angular and sharp, blood dripping from their jowls, hands painted crimson. Surrounding the female dancers, they performed a dance of rape and death. With four strident beats, the drums fell silent, and the devils froze. Female dancers lay strewn on the ground, limbs askew at impossible angles, a portrait of slaughter and dismemberment.

From somewhere amidst the crowd, another conch sounded a higher pitch note. A woman of around sixty years of age, dressed in a long pink dress with a photo of a young woman pinned to her chest, walked into the circle leading eight other women similarly attired. They cradled *veladoras* in small, roughened brown hands and slowly encircled the goddess' body. Low, slow thrumming came from the drums, accompanying the women as they danced in an ever-tightening spiral around the goddess. As they drew closer to the center, they lifted the masks from the devils and cast them down. The men behind the masks stood for a few drumbeats, downcast, repentant, before joining the dance. Slowly, the slain female dancers gathered themselves and pulled children and men from the audience. Dancers passed the baskets of fruit and sweets among the crowd. Spectators, actors, and dancers shared the food and chatted, as if at a party.

Amaya stretched her arms above her head, allowing the gaping sleeves of her traditional Mexican blouse to reveal her unshaved armpits. Lowering her arms in a graceful way, she said, "What do you think?"

Ixchel swallowed, blinking. "Dramatic."

Amaya raised her eyebrows. "It's a way to stand up for the victims, to bear witness to their life and murder and make sure they are remembered. This is one way we hold the powerful accountable for the social constructs behind femicide."

The woman with the shaved head ran over to them. She kissed Amaya on the mouth and, without speaking, rolled cable around her elbow.

"Valeria, this is Ixchel."

Valeria glanced in her direction, nodded, and continued packing.

Amaya pulled out a bin from under the console table. "Our performance mixes trained actors and dancers with members of the community.

Together they can express their internal and communal struggles through myths and metaphors. In this case, to address the killing of women."

Blushing, her heart pounding in her ears, Ixchel said, "Isn't this just a Band-Aid? A little magical thinking. The victims' families sing Kumbaya and go home to the graves, while the murderers kill again. "

Amaya opened her mouth but Ixchel raised her hand. "I've got a press conference to catch."

As she dashed away, Amaya's voice rang in her ears. "The only way to stop femicide is by creating a new cosmology."

## Onaqui Tonatiuh - Sunset

### 7

*"I was sixteen years old and took a public van after school to get home. One day I was the only passenger. The driver took me to an empty lot. He raped and tortured me, biting off my nipples and toes. After he broke my neck, he left me covered in trash. I was taken to the morgue, but they could not identify me and buried me in a common grave. My mother will look for me every day for a year and never find me."*

Ixchel hustled into a seat in the front row. The presentation started with the typical formalities and a long-winded speech by the state prosecutor. He exaggerated his accomplishments and blathered on about the changes made. When her phone buzzed, she glanced at it, recoiling. The room around her shifted and swirled, time slowed down. Mariana's photo appeared on her phone. Eyes downcast, she held a towel covering her breasts. Purple and violet bruises covered the right side of her face;

her left eye swollen shut. But it was the bite mark above her left breast that made her stand up.

Maybe because she was young and pretty, the prosecutor looked at her. "*Señorita,*" he said politely, nodding, waiting for her question.

Ixchel took the wireless microphone from an aide. "Mr. Prosecutor, how can you sleep at night after covering up the murder of Mariana Villa by your nephew, Dante Vignau?" Ixchel held up her phone. "Look! This is what your nephew did to her a month before he killed her! You had it removed from social media."

The court official who had given her the microphone tried to wrest it away from her, but Ixchel held on as people stared. Heart pounding in her ears, she stood on the chair. The prosecutor recoiled, his face beet red.

"Your nephew murdered Mariana Villa, not only did you cover for him your thugs threatened us!"

The prosecutor glared at Ixchel. "I'm sorry about your cousin, but if she hadn't been so drunk that she jumped out of Dante's car, she'd be alive today." He turned taway.

An officer seized Ixchel by the waist and another yanked the microphone out of her hand. "Do something! *Ni una mas!* Women are not disposable!"

A few hundred people stared as the police dragged her from the auditorium and pushed her down the long corridor toward the exit. Ixchel struggled. I'm going to die and it's going to hurt. Her legs buckled and the officers yanked her up, one on each side.

"Please! Where are you taking me? I'm an American citizen."

They dragged her toward a patrol car. One of them whispered in her ear, his breath hot. "We're going to take you for a ride."

This can't be happening! Ixchel racked her brain for a way out as the men's fingers dug into her arms.

The transgender woman, still dressed in full regalia, stepped in front of the patrol car and charged them, screaming, "Help! Help! I'm being kidnapped!" She crashed into the three of them slamming them on the floor.

"Help her!" someone yelled, and two dozen masked protesters, many wearing the purple cicada T-shirt, tackled the officers.

A woman yanked Ixchel up by the arm. "Run!"

Ixchel bolted through the crowd, holding her bag underneath her arm like a football, until the other end of the plaza. In the parking lot, an officer was leaning on her car.

"Fuck!"

She crossed the street when Amaya drove up in an old '69 VW Beetle with the bumper tied to the chassis by a length of wire, "Get in!"

Ixchel flung herself into the back where a blanket hid the torn seat. Valeria, the bald-headed woman from before, sat in the passenger seat, scowling.

"You're kidding me!" said Valeria. "She isn't coming!"

Yoali stepped on the gas. "We have no choice. The police are after her. She will be safe with us."

Valeria glared at Ixchel. "You're lucky they didn't take you! What do you think you're doing? You can get killed for something like this here. You're not in the US!"

"I'm sorry I just lost it. Why are you so angry?"

"Because we live here! We don't have the luxury of losing it, then running back to the safety of the United States. You're putting us all in danger. There is a lot more at stake than avenging your rich cousin."

Ixchel kept silent, not knowing what to say. She used her jacket to cover the wet stain on her jeans; she'd peed herself when the police were dragging her away. Amaya maneuvered through the traffic, weaving from lane to lane and in between cars. Valeria watching their rear.

Valeria's eyes bulged. "Someone is following us!"

Amaya glanced at the mirror. "Are you sure?"

"Yeah. You can't miss the tinted windows."

"Hang on!" Amaya stepped on the gas and they lurched forward, as again she threaded through the traffic but now at much higher speed.

Without a seat belt, Ixchel slid from one side of the car to the other, grateful her stomach was empty. Amaya broke suddenly, sending Ixchel crashing into the back of the front seat. Blood sputtered from her nose.

"Sorry!" Amaya yelled as she jerked the car in a sharp angle and sped off down another road. She turned into a narrow street and waited with the motor running.

Ixchel pulled tissue out of her bag and held it against her nose.

"Are you alright?" asked Amaya as she put the car in neutral and studied the road.

"It's just a bloody nose." A metallic taste filled Ixchel's mouth.

They waited in silence. Ixchel jammed her hands under her armpits to keep them from shaking, the scent of their fear permeated the car.

After ten minutes that felt more like an hour, Amaya exhaled. "We lost them."

Ixchel blushed. "I'm sorry to cause you problems. Thank you."

Valeria turned in her seat. "You could've gotten us killed."

Amaya drove down the street, the three of them watching the cars around them, until she found the highway. A few miles later, they left it for a bumpy, country road heading west into the mountains. Unbroken stretches of pine trees flanked the fractured asphalt road. As they climbed into the foothills, the temperature dropped.

"Where are we going?" asked Valeria, turning to Amaya.

Amaya stared at the road. Lips pursed.

Valeria's eyes grew wide. "Fuck! You can't bring her to Teonantli; she's a gringa!"

"I'm not a gringa! I'm a Chicana," said Ixchel crouching in the back. "Where are we going?"

"We're going to see a friend that can help."

"Where?"

"I can't tell you," Amaya said.

Valeria kept up an uninterrupted monologue during the drive on colonialism and paternalism. Ixchel rode in silence, recognizing that Valeria's discourse was meant for her. She swallowed. I'm an idiot. I made things worse for nothing!

They left the highway and took a road that twisted up a forested hill for miles until turning onto a narrow dirt road. Long past twilight, they pulled up in front of a corrugated gate that bridged large stone walls topped with barbed wire and broken glass and obscured the property beyond. No signs or numbers identified the address. Amaya honked the VW's horn three times. The gates swung open noiselessly, allowing access into the compound as a man stepped out of the shadows to close the gates behind them.

On a narrow, unpaved, rutted path they crept forward in the dark until they came to a large house. The car's flickering headlights illuminated a *temazcal* in the center of a clearing, which opened up to the side of the main house. Ixchel texted her aunt that she would not be out until tomorrow before turning her phone off.

## 8

*"I was forty-two years old and very close to my children. Their father strangled me because a divorce would have been bad for his political career. He had lovers but wanted a new wife. His influential friends said I was depressed and hung myself. There will be no investigation and no autopsy. My daughters will always resent me for taking my life."*

The wooden door swung open, and a thin, middle-aged woman dashed out to greet them, hugging each one of them. "Martina called about what happened. You're safe now. I'm glad you are here."

She ushered them into a cabin of wood and rock. The living room's vaulted ceiling had rustic beams and panoramic windows that invited the forest into the house. A fire crackled in a stone fireplace at the front of the living room. Floor-to-ceiling paintings in bold reds, blues, oranges, and purples hung on the white walls. Ixchel recognized the Great Goddess from the performance painted against a lava-spewing volcano. Then her eyes landed on a woman with the lower body of an ahuehuete, a Mexican cypress. Gasping, she regarded the magical creatures, the vibrant colors, and the illusion of movement. "I'm in Yvette Krauss's home!"

"You must be Ixchel. Please come have something to eat," said Yvette, trying to tame her cascade of black curls with a scrunchie. She smiled, and little wrinkles spread from the corner of her brown eyes. Ixchel found it hard to believe she was in her early sixties; she moved with grace and ease, with a youthful flair.

Ixchel blushed. "I hate to bother you, but I had a little accident," she looked down at her jeans, "I peed myself when the police dragged me away; I didn't even realize it at the moment."

Yvette took her by the arm. "Come with me." She led Ixchel up the stairs to her bedroom, the unmade bed reminding her of their intrusion. The alarm clock flashed ten thirty. Looking Ixchel up and down, Yvette pulled yoga pants from a drawer, some black panties, and handed them to her. "You can shower in my bathroom."

After a shower and a change of clothes, Ixchel walked into the living room where Yvette and a couple of women she recognized from the performance were huddled.

"How many?" asked Yvette.

"There are two pickups; they may have been waiting for more," said the transgender woman from the protest, "they glared at me when I passed them."

Yvette turned to Ixchel. "Ixchel, Martina, I think you've met. We don't have time for niceties. The two men that were following you are hiding nearby, probably waiting for reinforcements."

"Have you called the police?" asked Ixchel, her heart sinking as the alarm started up again.

Yolanda walked in, holding her phone. "*Cariño*, these men are state police; the prosecutor sent them."

Ixchel's heart pounded in her chest. "I've put you all in danger; I should leave." But her feet felt cemented to the floor.

Yvette turned to the man who'd opened the gate. He rubbed his face and glanced out the window. "Teofilo, take your family in my car and drive the backway to Toluca. Go to my house and stay there until I call you."

"With all due respect *Señora* Yvette, I'm staying. My place is here with you and Teonantli."

Yvette smiled. "*Gracias,* Teofilo, I appreciate your loyalty, but you know Teonantli's mission and our parts in it. You and your daughter must continue in case we fail. Go now before they arrive!"

"Your husband would never forgive me if I left you—"

"He'd never forgive you if our mission fails. He too understands Teonantli's work is more important than our individual lives."

Teofilo looked around at the women and sighed. "I'll say goodbye to Teonantli." He hugged Yvette, then dashed out of the room.

A cold weight settled in Ixchel's stomach; her lungs constricted forcing a dry hack out of her mouth. She wished she were back home in Seattle, drinking coffee with her mother as they watched the rain, catching up on gossip. I should've called her! She swallowed, imaging her aunt when she found out she'd also been murdered. Taking a step forward, her locks dripping water down her back, she said in a shaky voice. "Let me go to them; I'm the one who fucked up. I shouldn't put you in danger."

Yvette grasped her hand. "No! *Ni una más!* You have a choice; you can leave with Teófilo and his family, or you can stay and help us."

Ixchel looked around the kitchen; Valeria and Amaya were leaning against the wall, their arms around each other. Martina, Yolanda, and two other women in their thirties, dressed in the purple T-shirts from the march, and a woman in her fifties with short curly hair stood in a cluster around them. How could they stop the killers? There was no way these women could resist corrupt armed police officers. But there was no way out. At least I'll stand up to these murderers! "I'm staying."

"It's time!" said the oldest and tiniest woman Ixchel had ever seen. Teófilo guided her slowly, grasping her arm. Her wispy white braids laced with colorful red and gold ribbons fell on her red *huipil.*

Yvette knelt in front of the ancient woman. "Teonantli, we don't have time to purify in the *temazcal*, should we begin?"

Teonantli nodded. She whispered something in a strange and musical language.

Yvette nodded. "Martina, please get some bread from the pantry."

Martina yanked open the cupboards and pulled out a brown bag which she emptied on a platter piling it with *bolillos*.

Yvette took a black clay bowl filled with gray cones and lit them. Sweet copal incense drifted through the kitchen. "Take this to the living room," she said, "I'll prepare the sacred tea."

The short-haired woman led the way holding the smoking bowl.

Martina brought the bread while Valeria and Amaya lit candles and placed them around the room; another woman led Teonantli to the couch.

Ixchel was cutting the bread when Valeria touched her arm. "I'm sorry I was rude in the car; I thought you were a spoiled American with a savior complex."

Ixchel nodded, placing slices of bread on a ceramic plate.

Valeria stared at the wall ahead. "My sister was murdered."

"I'm sorry."

"Her name was Irene. I wanted to bring her justice, but I learned the movement is more than her, or me, or Mariana."

"I get it. Who is the older woman?" she asked, glancing at the elder.

"Teonantli is a *curandera* who practices a medicine older than the Aztecs and Teotihuacanos," Valeria said as she washed clay mugs in the sink. "The patriarchy brought us science and civilization but also pollution, war, inequity, and misery and it's destroying us. Yvette and Teonantli have taught us those old medicine ways which we have to share with the world before it's too late. Tonight, we're going to birth a new cosmology, a different way of viewing ourselves and our relationship with the world and others."

Ixchel kept silent, not wanting to antagonize Valeria after she'd just apologized. This talk was magical thinking, a way to avoid thinking about what would happen to them in a few hours. She was terrified but the company of the women somehow soothed and strengthened her.

The women sat on the floor around Teonantli, who had positioned herself, cross-legged facing east. Yvette turned out the lights and cast them into flickering candlelight as shadows danced on the walls and paintings. She sat next to Teonantli and passed the plate with bread. Holding a piece of flaky bread to her mouth, she said, "Take a piece, hold it in your hand, and tell it all your sins." She murmured into it.

Ixchel looked around at the women whispering to their piece of bread and did the same.

Yvette put her piece back on the plate and passed it to the woman next to her. "This is the tradition of the filth eater. Reflect on the bad things you have done and send them to the *pastry*, then give it to Teonantli to eat."

Ixchel thought about all the things she hated about herself, her regrets, and the times she had hurt others. She watched Teonantli shove the pieces in her gap-toothed mouth. Yvette gave the old woman tea to help her swallow the bread.

Martina blew the conch.

"It's time," said Yvette.

## Yohualnepantla - Midnight

Yolanda and a woman from the protest brought trays with mugs of steaming tea and passed them around. At Yvette's signal, they drank. The taste of earth and honey washed across Ixchel's palate and down her throat. Wrapping her hands around the warm mug, she cleared her throat, fixing her eyes on Yvette. "If the men are coming, shouldn't we arm ourselves? At least we'll go down fighting, maybe kill one or two."

Yvette smiled. "You're trying to stop femicide using the patriarchy's tools. Tonight, you'll experience a new way that embraces the feminine, that targets evildoers, and that doesn't subjugate but lifts everyone."

Ixchel was about to ask what she meant, but Martina placed a drum between her legs and beat out a heartbeat while Teonantli sang in a high, reedy voice in a language beyond time.

Ghostly shadows flitted across the walls and the bodies and faces of the women who sat in the firelight. A dull ache spread from the base of Ixchel's skull. Sipping tea, she willed the queasiness away. The flames in the fireplace, the dancing candlelight mesmerized her as drumming filled the room. Colors vibrated, pulsing with each drumbeat as she stared transfixed by the weave of the wool rug. The room stretched beyond her vision.

"What was in the tea?" she asked, expecting Valeria to be seated next to her. Instead, an older woman, her face as brown and wrinkled as Teonantli's, met her eyes. Indigenous women replaced the women in the circle. Ixchel's smooth hands were now deep brown with prominent, pulsing veins tracing the outlines of her bones; her fingers were gnarled and twisted. They'd transformed into their ancestors. Ixchel inhabited the body of the first women on earth, experiencing a different way of knowing which she could never put into words.

"What did you give me?" Ixchel asked, unsure she'd uttered a sound. Cemented in place, her body swayed with the drum's relentless cadence, pulsing from deep within, from the stones of the fireplace, the heart of the earth.

Flesh melted from the women's faces, exposing their skeletons, transforming them into *catrinas* from the Day of the Dead.

Thunder roared, hammering her ears, and the walls disappeared. Pines surrounded them on three sides. Ixchel blinked. I must be dreaming, but light rain fell on her head, rolling down her face. Where the circle opened, and from beyond where the fireplace had been crackling just a few minutes before, the majestic volcano, Popocatepetl, dark and menacing, its peak covered in snow, beckoned.

Teonantli stood facing the volcano, arms raised, chanting. As one, the women repeated the unfamiliar but beautifully fluid mantra. The air thickened with energy. A low rumble from deep in the earth rose in a crescendo of waves. Drumbeats kept time as the chanting matched the earth's moans and groans, louder and faster.

Pines, oaks, and *oyamels* creaked as they swayed back and forth. The volcano appeared to inhale before roaring to life in a frenzy of lava and ash. Black smoke spewed from the mountain's maw, forming a gigantic tarantula, its legs black, hairy, striped with red rings. A low hissing sound came from its fang covered jaws. The black arachnid advanced on the circle, molting. As it shed its skin, a woman's skeleton, wrapped in a red and black rebozo, emerged from the discarded shell. Standing in front of them, the volcano behind her, she raised her hands and sang in a high voice, each syllable vibrating in Ixchel's core.

"For centuries men ruled, imprisoning the Earth Mother in the bowels of the earth. Humans forgot where they came from and where they will return.

Men fooled themselves into believing they were masters of the earth.

Your ways are greed, war, destruction. The farther from your mother, the more violent you've become.

You have called me back, releasing me from prison.

The Earth Mother summons all mothers, sisters, and daughters.

The Earth Mother calls all fathers, brothers, and sons.

The Earth Mother demands no sacrifices.

I give myself freely.

The Earth Mother loves all her children, but those who hurt or oppress others will cease or pay.

The Earth Mother will cool the fire, pacify the rage, and restore balance.

The Earth Mother reminds humans that they are part of nature, not above it, not apart from it.

The Earth Mother together with you gives birth to a new era."

Popocatepetl erupted with a deafening blast, igniting the forest sky in a blood red, ethereal light. The house shook, as if someone was trying to rip it off its foundations, flinging the women to the floor that rippled underneath them. A low, basso grumble from deep in the earth assaulted their ears together with the crashing of glass and thumping of objects. The house creaked as white dust fell like snow from the ceiling. Ixchel yelled, "Why won't it stop?" but a fine ash filled her mouth, drying her throat.

After the longest eight minutes, the shaking ceased. The women sat up slowly, looking around, dusting the white ash off their clothes and hair. The shards of window glass littered the floor, allowing the cool night air to fill the room, making Ixchel shiver. Ixchel peeked into the kitchen and gasped. Mounds of shattered dishes, smashed jars, baskets, and dented cans from the cupboards and shelves covered the floor. Fissures and cracks decorated the once smooth white walls. The tarantula woman was gone.

"Does anyone have a cell phone?" asked Yvette looking at her phone, "I don't have any signal."

Ixchel pulled hers out; there were no bars. Amaya turned on the light switch, but the power was out.

Valeria helped Teonantli up from the floor and guided her back to the couch. Ixchel and Amaya headed to the kitchen to clean up when the front door burst open. Two state police officers stood pointing automatic rifles at them. The women froze except for Yvette, who bolted to shield Teonantli.

"Don't move, or I'll shoot! We're going to wait here until the vans come for you," said the man with a mustache, glaring at them.

Yolanda said, "Please, there's no need to—"

"Now, we can do it the easy way," the man growled, shooting at the ceiling, making plaster rain on their heads, "or the hard way. Either way, we get paid."

Teonantli's voice blasted, strong and firm. "They are all dead. The mountain buried them in the landslide. Part of the road is gone."

The younger officer scoffed and spat on the floor.

Yvette took a step forward. "It's over. No one can get here, and you can't leave. There is no other way off this mountain."

The older officer with the mustache took out his radio and tried several times to get through to his comandante. Finally, giving up, he glared at Yvette. "Then I'll just kill you all now."

"Please, you don't have to spill any more blood; it's over," said Yvette.

The officer raised and aimed his rifle at Yvette's chest. A hissing sound came from a plate-sized tarantula on the ceiling. The man glanced at it, then back at the woman. "It isn't over until the prosecutor orders it so." As he fired, the spider slammed into him as it grew to its original size now five times the man. Amaya shoved Yvette to the floor. The spider straddled the officer sinking her bat-sized fangs into his neck; blood spurted from his mouth smothering his screams. The other man fired into the spider's back, but the bullets bounced off, ricocheting around the room. The wake of a bullet caressed Ixchel's left cheekbone as she ducked under the couch. The spider ripped out the man's neck, almost decapitating him, letting his body crash on the floor, then advanced on the other officer, who dropped his gun and turned to flee. But the spider slammed him into the earth, holding him down with her back legs. Weaving long filaments of tensile silk from her front legs around the thrashing man, until only his muffled cries emanated from the brown cocoon he had become, the spider picked him up with her fangs. She carried him out the open gap that was once sliding glass doors, disappearing into the early morning dark.

# 9

*"I was in my home in Ecatepec, and my husband was beating me because he was in a bad mood. This time, I was afraid he would kill me. The house shook, there was a roar, and suddenly everything was dark. When I woke up, my husband was on his back, trapped under debris up to his neck. He whispered, 'Hurry up, puta, and get me some help.' I crawled out and away when two rescue workers ran to me. They asked if there was anyone else trapped in the house—I said no."*

Ixchel blinked rapidly and looked around the room. Was she hallucinating? Amaya and Valeria stared at the gap where the spider had disappeared. They saw it too! Was this a collective illusion? A soft moan interrupted her thoughts.

Teonantli was on the floor, Yvette kneeling by her. "Teonantli's been shot!" she cried, pressing her hands against the tiny woman's right ribs, a dark brown stain spreading over her red *huipil*.

The women rushed to her. Teonantli blinked rapidly, and her mouth moved. Yvette leaned over, placing her ear close to Teonantli's mouth, and listened. They whispered in Nahuatl.

Martina leaned over, taking Teonantli's pulse. "If we don't get her to the hospital now, she won't make it."

Amaya grabbed her purse and pulled out her keys. "We can't call an ambulance, but I can drive her."

Yvette shook her head, grasping Teonantli's hand.

"If we don't take her, she'll die!" said Amaya, glancing at the other women's faces in signs of support.

"The road was destroyed by a landslide that buried the vans. There's a secret way out, but it's over dirt roads and would take at least two hours to get to the nearest hospital."

Amaya jingled the keys. "Are you sure there was a landslide?"

"You know there was." Yvette wiped a tear from her eye. "Teonantli says it's her time to leave. She wants to die here, with us. Help me carry her to her room."

Amaya threw her purse on the floor. "Fuck!"

Yolanda rushed out, saying, "I'll check for damage in her room."

While Amaya and Valeria taped cardboard to the shattered window, Ixchel and Martina carried Teonantli to her room. She was light as a pillow. They laid her gently on the bed as the women gathered round. Yvette sat holding Teonantli's right hand in both of hers. "Teonantli says to give her messages to take to the other side."

The women took turns whispering messages of love to Teonantli. She sang softly in a language Ixchel did not recognize, the sibilants cascading out in between shuddering intakes of breath.

When it was Ixchel's turn, she leaned over and murmured in her ear: "Please tell Mariana I'm sorry I didn't stay in touch. She didn't deserve what happened to her, and I promise I'll never stop fighting against violence. Tell her I'll watch over her mom as my own. I love her."

Ixchel took her place around the bed. Martina put her arm around her. They watched Yvette speak softly in Teonantli's ear.

"What language is that?" Ixchel asked.

"Nahuatl," said Martina, "Teonantli was Yvette's nanny; she taught her the old ways."

Teonantli's breathing became imperceptible. Even with the cardboard over the window, dawn's pink and golden light snuck into the bedroom as birds called to each other from their nests. Valeria sang in a high and clear voice about a cicada rising from the earth to sing to the sun. The lyrics by Chilean singer Mercedes Sosa pierced her soul. A song for the disappeared, the silenced, the erased, the invisible, the raped, the dispossessed, the forgotten, the conquered, the colonized, the abandoned, the solitary, the tortured, the murdered. The pain engulfed her, unbearable; she feared it would break her until Martina squeezed her shoulder as Valeria sang, "During the shipwreck and darkness, someone will rescue you." She wasn't alone, together they could bear the world's pain and their own.

Teonantli died. There was no flash of light, no sonic boom; she simply stopped breathing. The women stood side by side, arms wrapped around each other. Valeria sang "Gracias a la Vida" with most women joining in.

Ixchel swallowed, flooded by images of her mother and aunt Jimena singing it during Thanksgiving in Seattle. She closed her eyes, watching her father complain about the turkey having mole instead of gravy as Ixchel and her brother Jose Luis cleared the table. Mariana, laughing with delight, dashing to the window to greet a rare snowstorm that stranded them for two days.

Ixchel returned to the present when Yvette closed Teonantli's eyes, muttering a prayer in Nahuatl. The women scattered, some to prepare the body, and Ixchel, Amaya, and Valeria to pick up the debris and check on the power.

At six thirty in the morning, Martina called them to the kitchen. "The power is back!" The women huddled around the small television in the kitchen. Images of destroyed buildings filled the screen as a scroll on the bottom read: "9.2 earthquake strikes central Mexico at midnight for eight minutes. Epicenter under the Popocatepetl."

A female anchor spoke to the audience, and Martina raised the volume.

"The president has called this earthquake miraculous because the damage was less than would be expected during an earthquake of this magnitude and duration. Still there are many victims and our hearts go out to their families. The state police headquarters was destroyed while the prosecutor was conducting an emergency meeting with top officials. Although the search for survivors has begun, no one is expected to survive." Video over the journalist's right shoulder played scenes that resembled a bombed-out Palestine after weeks of missile strikes. A pile of rubble was all that remained after a hotel, closed to tourists to host the leaders of Mexico and Colombia's drug cartels, collapsed leaving no survivors. The club in the basement of the hotel, where a party was underway, had ignited and exploded, burning the drug lords and their minions to death. Hope stirred in Ixchel's chest. Was this the start of the new way? The earth purging itself of the evil to usher in change. Her phone buzzed. "There's cell phone signal again," she said, stepping out into the clear morning as everyone scrambled for their phones.

"Hello, hello."

"Gracias a Dios!" her aunt Jimena said, "I have your mother on the line."

"Are you alright?" asked her mother, fear and anxiety distorting her voice.

Ixchel stood in front of the scorched gap in the vegetation the size of the spider. "I'm in the safest place, out in the country. How was it at your house, Jimena?" Ixchel asked.

"Terrible! It felt like a giant was shaking my bed! All my dishes shattered; the kitchen is a mess."

"I'm sorry, I'll help you clean up," Ixchel said, looking into the kitchen through shards of glass and scraps of the officer's uniform. She shivered in the cool, pine-scented breeze.

"I don't mind at all. Thanks to the earthquake, Dante is dead so he'll never abuse and murder another woman again!" said Jimena.

"What happened?" asked Ixchel.

Jimena answered excitedly. "It's on the news! Dante was driving under a freeway's overpass when it collapsed, burying him in his car. It will take at least a month to remove the concrete."

Ixchel heard a smile in her aunt's voice.

"My Neno is missing; I'm going to look for him."

"Don't," said Ixchel. She wanted to wait and tell her aunt in person about the cat. "I'll help you search as soon as I'm back."

"Ixchel," asked her mother, "When are you coming back to Seattle? Jimena, you should come too."

"It would be nice to get away," said Jimena.

Ixchel's mother asked, "Ixchel? Don't you think it's time to find a job and focus on your future?"

Ixchel stared into the kitchen at the women on their phones checking on loved ones. Together, they'd unleashed something very powerful she didn't understand but which filled her with hope.

"I agree, Mami; I applied for a job in the Coalition Against Violence and Sexual Assault."

"Where?" her mother and aunt asked at the same time.

Ixchel smiled, her eyes fixed on Yvette. "In Seattle. I'm inviting a Mexican artist to come share the ways she's combating femicide, to teach us and build a coalition that will change the world."

# Iris

How old Iris, how old?
When childhood dreams withered
like un-watered vines,
neglected cuttings sucked dry
by the needs of others who soon too
would awaken to the crushing weight of hunger-filled,
Love-drained days.
How old Iris, how old?
When you nurtured those that orbited you
protected them, lifted them when life's blows
laid them low.
You loved them as you learned to
love yourself in the slurry of privation.
How old when the fences appeared
Their barbs both subtle and overtly cruel
marring the open landscapes of your

promise and potential.
How old when those unyielding, immutable
spikes raked across your breast when you crawled,
under and over and through
those savage, taut strands to escape
only to have the tether between you and the
mother you adored snap you back
And so tethered, nobody would have blamed you
had you surrendered and settled
into a life that would never have been
of your own choosing.
But Iris you, like your namesake,
emerged,
pushing through snow-encrusted humus and
flowered
Your example, an indigo star guiding me
into grace.
Vito de la Cruz

# Acknowledgements

**WHEN SEARCHING FOR A** title for this collection, I remembered driving to Pachuca from Mexico City with my children Jose Bernardo and Pia, listening to Sylvio Rodriguez's "Mujeres". My son, then eight years old, turned to me and said, "You and Pia are women of fire." My stories are inspired by the women of fire and snow I've had the privilege to know. Their examples of love, sacrifice, drive, creativity, resilience, and hope encourage me to write and work for change.

Thank you to all the readers who gave up their precious time to read my drafts and gave me advice and encouragement: Jose "Bernie" Molina, Pia Molina, Gigi Sefchick del Paso, Sophia Sefchick del Paso, Jose Luis Olivares, Kyle Johnstone, Konstantin Sefchick del Paso, Miguel Acuña, Max Godoy, Mary Beth Canty, Ireri Rivas, Diane Tomhave, Tricia Smith and Renata Cummings.

A heartfelt thank you to artist Raphaella Godoy Sefchick who created a cover that reflects the stories with artistry and beauty. Special thanks to Regina Olivares, Jill Twist, Marcela Landres, and Ned Hayes for their valuable edits and comments.

I am eternally grateful to Vito de la Cruz, without whom there would be no stories. My first editor, sounding board, coach, critic, investor, and relentless encourager. He takes over my chores to give me time to write. Vito inspires me with his life, work, art, compassion, social justice advocacy, and love. And he keeps me from writing soft porn. I love you forever.

# Nati del Paso

Nati del Paso is a writer, counselor, and student of Indigenous Psychology. Raised in Mexico by a Mexican mother and an American father, she is a lead counselor in the Office of Minority Affairs and Diversity at the University of Washington in Seattle.

Del Paso weaves psychology, mysticism, and magic realism into suspenseful tales surrounding the immigrant experience, women, environmental and social justice issues. She recently finished her first novel and lives in Snoqualmie, Washington with her husband.